MINK EYES

MINK EYES

DAN FLANIGAN

For information about this title or to order other books and/or electronic media, contact the publisher:
Arjuna Books
600 3rd Avenue, 42nd Floor
New York, New York 10016

ISBN: 978-1-7336103-0-8 (paperback)
ISBN: 979-8-9855614-0-1 (hardcover)
ISBN: 978-1-7336103-1-5 (eBook)

Publisher's Cataloging-In-Publication Data
(Prepared by The Donohue Group, Inc.)

Names: Flanigan, Daniel J., 1947- author.
Title: Mink Eyes / Dan Flanigan.
Description: New York, New York : Arjuna Books, [2019]
Identifiers: ISBN 9781733610308 (print) | ISBN 9781733610315 (ebook)
Subjects: LCSH: Vietnam War, 1961-1975--Veterans--United States--Fiction. | Private investigators--United States--Fiction. | Mink farming--Ozark Mountains--Fiction. | Organized crime--Ozark Mountains--Fiction. | LCGFT: Thrillers (Fiction)
Classification: LCC PS3606.L3587 M56 2019 (print) | LCC PS3606.L3587 (ebook) | DDC 813/.6--dc23

Printed in the United States of America

*This book is a revised edition originally published under the pseudonym of Max McBride.

"Sir," said Sir Ector, "meseemeth your quest is done, and mine is not done."

"Well," said Sir Gawain, "I shall seek no farther."

Le Morte D'Arthur

AS HE ALWAYS did when he wasn't hungover, O'Keefe forced himself into his gym shorts, T-shirt, socks, and tennis shoes and moved through the dark apartment toward his exercise room, believing that this was yet another decision, however small and seemingly insignificant, in favor of life and against death, like the times in Vietnam when he had fought off sleep on guard duty. The little men in the black pajamas, the little men who never slept, were just waiting for you to doze off so they could creep into your hole and quietly, and ever so gently, cut your throat.

The apartment occupied the entire bottom floor of an old Victorian house in a re-gentrifying neighborhood. He could sense, though he could not see, Kelly sleeping on the fold-out couch in the living room. She was spending the weekend with him—she under his care, he under hers. *The child will save you*, he thought.

The digital dial of the clock sitting on the fireplace mantel read 5:12 AM, 10-4-86. He passed through the living room and into the spare bedroom that he had converted into an exercise room and small home office. He flipped on the light and turned on the TV. The all-news channel headlined a statement from President Reagan concerning the shooting down of a plane over Nicaragua loaded with supplies for the rebel Contras. The Nicaraguan government claimed that the CIA had sponsored the plane. The U.S.

ambassador and CIA denied the charge. In Palm Beach, Florida, the FBI had accomplished the largest drug bust in U.S. history, seizing 4,620 pounds of cocaine, worth $41 million.

His exercise program was simple and took exactly one hour. Stretching exercises, sit-ups, side straddle hops, jumping rope, thirty minutes on the exercise bike or treadmill, squat thrusts, leg lifts, push-ups. He had done these exercises almost every morning for many years now, but he still disliked every second of this wrenching hour. He had disliked the exercises ever since he had first done them at the age of ten under the mock-savage goading of his grade-school football coaches. He had liked them even less, again, many years later, in the Marine Corps, as he strained beneath the razor eyes of the little fascist thug in the "Smokey the Bear" hat who liked to scream at you and kick you in the side as you struggled to complete that last fingertip push-up.

After boot camp, he had vowed never again to do exercises. For years afterward, he had kept that vow, but those years had been lost years. However much he hated these exercises, however stupid and dull this hour proved always to be, he knew he needed it the same way he needed food or sleep, needed it to survive. This morning's exercise routine was a critical link in his slender lifeline to reality, like the cord that attached the astronaut walking in space to his ship. If that lifeline ever snapped again, as it had done in those lost, drug-fogged years, he might drift for the rest of his days, trapped in the void, squandering the only life he would ever be privileged to live.

Yet he still wanted sometimes to reach out and sever the line, cut the cord. That void, that limbo of mind and soul, still attracted him, pulled at him like the flame pulls at the moth.

He was doing his last few push-ups when Kelly came looking for him. She stood in the doorway, flinching as she watched him grunting in pain, arms quivering, chest heaving. The last one was too much for him. He could not quite complete it before he collapsed face down on the floor, panting and wanting to throw up.

"Why do you do that every day, Dad?"

"Denial of death," he grunted, hardly able to get the words out.

"What's that mean?"

He pushed himself into a sitting position on the floor.

"Nothing. I need to keep in shape for my work. So I can catch the bad guys."

"Do you really catch bad guys?"

"Not really. Mostly I just watch and follow."

"Watch?"

"And sometimes they're not all that bad. Sometimes I'm kind of the bad one."

"Dad! You're always joking."

He was so exhausted he could hardly bring himself to his feet. As he limped past her out of the room, he said, "Breakfast at the French bakery today."

She smiled and hurried to get her clothes on.

KELLY THOUGHT HE looked much better after he had showered and shaved and put on his jeans, long-sleeved, button-down shirt, suede sports jacket, and loafers. She stood at the kitchen door, watching the back of him as he smoked his cigarette, sipped his coffee, and stared out the window at the fallen leaves swirling along the sidewalk. The radio played. Cyndi Lauper's "True Colors," top song of the day. *Such a nice song,* she thought.

He was so tall, over six feet tall, and he still looked thin though he often said he was getting "fat like a pig." She liked the way he was wearing his hair now, brushed back up off his forehead, just covering his ears on the side, hanging a bit over his collar in the back. He looked a little shaggy but a little neat too, as if he could not decide which of these things he really wanted to be. His nose was very thin and his cheekbones high. There was a white scar, two inches long, on his right cheekbone, which he had gotten in Vietnam from a piece of rocketing, whizzing steel that he called "shrapnel." He said he loved that scar more than any of the others because that piece of steel had been trying to kill him, but it had missed. He said he felt very grateful for that scar.

She loved his stories about the scars carved all over his body, and through the years she had made him tell her those stories over and over again. He had been run down by cars and bicycles and fallen off fences and horses. When he was only five years old, he had run smack-dab into a cement birdbath and broken his nose, and he still had a lump on the side of his nose that marked the point of the fracture. By the time he was her age now, ten years old, doctors had sewn thirty-two stitches into his body. She herself had never had a stitch at all and did not plan to have any.

His hazel eyes changed from brown to green and sometimes almost to blue, depending on what he wore. She had no doubt he was handsome. Most of all he was mysterious. Things went on in his head that she knew she would never understand or even want to. He said the strangest things, things that surprised her and made her wonder. Even his anger broke strange, a bolt of hot lightning that struck and then disappeared as fast as it had come. He could reduce her to tears with a few words.

She stayed with him every other weekend, and sometimes he took her out on week nights too, but she feared that all of this might end suddenly, that he might move out of the city or just stop coming to pick her up, or get married again and have other kids. Maybe he would do to her what his father, the grandpa she had never seen, had done to him—left him when he was just a small boy and not bothered to see him since. It would be best if he would come back home, but he wouldn't. He wouldn't even talk about it anymore. Mom said she wouldn't let him come back even if he wanted to, but Kelly did not believe that.

He was often so gentle and kind, yet he had left her and her mother and would not come back no matter how much she implored him. But then, when he had lived with them, she loved him, of course, but she really had not been very fond of him. It seemed like he was hardly ever there. Night after night, she and her mom had eaten dinner without him, Kelly trying to make conversation, her mom hardly responding to her because she couldn't help thinking about him, where he might be (really be, that is), why he hadn't called, why he always broke his promises. After dinner, Kelly would go play in her room while her mom sat by the bay window downstairs, drinking coffee, smoking cigarettes, and waiting. Sometimes she used to wake up at night and hear them fighting, loud voices saying words whose meanings she did not know but whose feelings she knew too well. At those times, she had clutched her blanket to herself as tightly as she could and rolled up into a little ball.

He still had not noticed her watching him. He poured himself another cup of coffee, lit another cigarette, and stared again out the kitchen window at the yellow and red-orange leaves that had fallen from the trees and now rustled gently around the wheels of the cars parked on the street. He seemed so sad so much of the time. He was always looking off into space like right now. *What's he looking for out there?*

She squinched up her nose as the smoke from his cigarette drifted toward her. "Did you know Mom quit smoking?"

That old anger flashed through his eyes but quickly passed on, giving way to that sad, mocking smile of his.

"Are you ready?" was all he said.

IT WAS A few minutes after dawn when O'Keefe and Kelly left the apartment, that time just after first light when the temperature suddenly and inexplicably drops. They walked through a small park across the street from his apartment. She fell back, shuffling through the grass, letting the dew soak her shoes.

"Don't do that," he said. "You'll ruin your loafers."

She hurried and caught up to him. They held hands and strolled out of the park and across a wide boulevard empty of traffic and into an area of older commercial buildings that had been redeveloped as shops, restaurants, bars, and offices. All up and down the street were flowerpots and flower boxes full of mums, carnations, and azaleas that this year's first frost would soon kill. The old brick streets and trolley tracks had been restored. During business hours, two trolley cars carried people from one end of the district to the other. In a few hours the district would be jammed with Saturday strollers and shoppers, but now the tall, dark-haired man and the ten-year-old girl were the only people on the street.

"I wish it was early in the morning all the time," he said.

"Why?"

"Before all the people come out and complicate things."

They walked on in silence for a few steps as she wondered whether to speak her mind.

"Mom says you don't like people."

"Well, I suppose she's sort of right about that."

"She says you ought to be a hermit on a deserted island all by yourself like old Robinson Carusoe."

"Crusoe," he corrected her. "I'd probably like that a lot. But then I'd never be able to see you."

He looked down at her, that sad mocking smile on his face again. She wondered what the smile meant.

"Would you go live on that island with me?"

She thought it over for a few steps and then told him, no, she didn't think she could really handle that, since there just wouldn't be enough to do. "It would get awful boring," she said.

That made him laugh. "Well, I don't think I'll be leaving for that island any time soon," he said.

O'KEEFE TUCKED HIS chin against the cold, but he could tell that the sun would soon burn the chill out of the air, and it would turn into one of those glorious October days—bright sun, no wind, cool but not cold. On such days there would be a moment when he would suddenly be overwhelmed as hope and yearning welled up inexplicably from somewhere within him, a rush of feeling that would catch him unawares and thoroughly surprise him though it had happened to him time after time, year after year, on certain autumn and spring days.

The French bakery was the only shop open this early. The old French woman in charge greeted O'Keefe by name. He chose a *pain au lait* and coffee. Kelly chose *pain au chocolat* and cocoa. He stared at her while she ate. He could not help staring at her sometimes. She had extracted the best physical characteristics of her father and mother—her mother's long, lean legs and large, round eyes, her father's dark hair, thin nose, and high cheekbones. She was more than pretty or cute—she was beautiful. People often stared and commented to each other when she passed them on the street. She sat there now with dirty fingernails and chocolate smeared on the side of her mouth, and she had only recently stopped picking her nose, but all that would be over too soon. He dreaded her growing up. Not because he would lose her. He had already reconciled himself to that. How could you lose what was never really yours? But he feared for her. He knew from his own experience and that of his friends that what happened to you from age thirteen to age twenty-one could break you into pieces. Or it could enslave you, plant you so firmly in a mental, financial, or other kind of rut that you would never escape it. If you were not very careful, you could go to sleep and sleepwalk your life away.

And she was a woman. Everything in the culture had already conspired against her and would continue to conspire against her to make her powerless, at the mercy of men's fickle eyes. Her beauty would be as much a curse as a blessing. He hoped that she would be able to find her worth within herself, not in the admiring eyes of others, not in her ability to manipulate and control the foolish men who would try to worship, possess, and demean her. How could he teach her the things she needed so desperately to know, especially when he had so little esteem for his own self, especially when he had spent too much of his life just drifting along like a fluff of dandelion in the wind, without plan, purpose, or envisioned destination?

"What are you looking at?" she said.

Caught in the act, nonplussed, his mind grabbed for a quick and sure retort.

"That chocolate on your face," he said. "And those dirty fingernails."

She wiped her face with her napkin.

"As soon as we get to the office, I want you to go in the john and clean those fingernails."

She shrugged away his scolding. She could have cared less.

"I'm growing my hair long," she said.

"That'll be nice."

"Do you like long-haired girls?"

"They're my favorite."

"That's what Mom said."

She paused, as if hesitant to say what was really on her mind.

"Mom used to have long hair, didn't she?"

His face tightened, his guilt welling up within him, as he nodded in the affirmative.

Yes, her mom did once have long hair, he was thinking, but that had disappeared somewhere in the mid-1970s along with so much else from the 1960s. He thought of all the changes he had lived through in the twenty years since 1965 when he had met Kelly's mother. Big changes, small changes. In '65, he and his friends would not even say "damn" in front of a girl. By '69, they would say "fuck" without thinking, and so would many of the girls. In '65, girls wore brassieres and tried to protect their virginity. By '69, you could see their bare breasts through their tank tops all up and down the block, and people were fucking in the streets. In '65, he believed in God and all the other teachings of the Catholic Church. By '69, he believed in nothing. In '65, twelve thousand dollars a year put you in the upper middle class.

By '69, it put you in the lower middle class. By now, in 1986, it put you near the poverty line. Everything had exploded in the '60s, most of all the money supply, and in the '70s, everybody had started chasing all that money. You could buy goods and services in 1975 that you would never have dreamed of being able to buy in 1965, and you were not yet even thirty years old. All you had to do was play the game, help keep the chain letter going. You paid more than you could afford to and sold your life for the income to pay the debt.

CHAPTER ▶ 2

THEY LEFT THE bakery and window-shopped on their way to O'Keefe's office, which was in a not-quite-restored building at the edge of the restoration district. Kelly kicked a small pile of leaves that had gathered on the sidewalk.

"Do you carry a gun?"

"Why do you keep asking me that? I've told you a hundred times I don't carry a gun."

"All the private detectives on TV do."

"Well, I don't."

"You wouldn't ever lie to me, would you?"

"Scout's honor."

"What's that mean?"

"Boy Scout's honor."

"Were you a Boy Scout?"

"No."

"Come on!"

"Cross my heart."

"And hope to die?"

"No." No, he never wanted to die, to be nothing. He wondered if he would be brave when the time came for him to be nothing.

Kelly's brow furrowed, and she said, "Mom thinks you drink too much."

He said nothing, as if he had not heard her.

"Do you?" She looked up at him in great earnest.

"Probably," he said sadly, but then he smiled that mocking smile, and his eyebrows turned up like the Devil's. "But at least I don't take drugs anymore."

"That's not funny."

They arrived at O'Keefe's building. Kelly eagerly rushed to open the door that led from the sidewalk to an interior stairway. There were offices on the second floor above the street-level shops. They climbed the stairs, and she skipped ahead of him down the hallway to a set of walnut-paneled double doors. On the wall next to the doors a brass sign with black etching said, "Peter O'Keefe." The double doors opened onto a small reception room. An oriental carpet covered the parquet-wood floor. The walls were painted a darker gray. The furniture was modern but comfortable, upholstered in gray and black. Sara, already at work, typed intensely on the word processor.

"Sara!"

Kelly ran to Sara's desk.

"Hey, Kelly!"

"Seven-thirty on Saturday morning," he said. "You trying to make me look bad or what?"

"I promised you the workup on that fire case for Global Insurance by Monday, remember? And Jarvis's report on the drug-testing program is on your desk."

Kelly asked if she could play on the big computer.

"Fire it up," he said. She hustled through a door that led to a hallway off the reception room.

"Remember," he said as Kelly left the room, "if she asks, I never carry a gun."

Sara moved her fingers across her mouth as if zipping it up. Her nails were painted with clear polish. Her lips were soft and full. She was in her early thirties, but she wore no makeup and did not need to wear any. You would not call her beautiful, or maybe not even pretty, but you would be attracted to her all the same.

"Is everybody in place? Have you checked?"

She swiveled around to face the computer screen and clicked the buttons on the keyboard. A list appeared on the screen. The list itemized each assignment, the person assigned, the place, the time. The list was two pages long. Only a few months ago, it had been less than one page. *Success*, he thought, *visually presented.*

"Everybody's in place but Carter," she said. "He called in sick."

"Saturday morning. Hungover again. As predictable as death. What's he supposed to be doing?"

"He's supposed to relieve George on the Damon Preston watch at nine o'clock."

"We haven't got Preston yet?"

"No. And Harrigan's getting pissed about it too. He called about it yesterday."

"I don't blame him. We're supposed to be such hotshots, but we can't even deliver a little piece of paper to a big-time deadbeat. We're getting too big. Don't let me take any more business."

She smiled, because she had heard this many times before.

"I'm not kidding this time. No kidding. No new business for a month."

She gestured around the room. "How are you gonna pay for all this then?"

He grimaced. You had to keep the pipeline full all the time. You were afraid to turn anything down because if you turned anything down, the pipeline might not stay full, so you took more than you and your people had time to do, and then you hired more people and you leased more space and bought more equipment and furniture. The pipeline got bigger, and then you had to keep that big God-damned pipeline really full all the time. So you were afraid to turn anything down . . . and on and on . . .

"Can George stay with Preston?"

"George has had a weekend at the lake scheduled for a month. He says if you screw this one up for him, you can find yourself another gumshoe."

"If George had a dollar for every time he's threatened to quit, he could have retired by now."

"How about letting me do it?

"I'll do it."

"Don't you think I can handle it?"

She was deadly serious. He knew what she was thinking: *"Why won't you let me do it? It's because I'm a woman, isn't it?"* This was a very dangerous moment indeed, for both of them.

"I thought you were working on that fire case," he said. This worked. This satisfied her. At least it appeared that way. He had slipped out of the net.

"George gets off at nine?"

"Nine."

"One more time for Carter. One more time, he's done. Make a note. Remind me I said that."

He turned abruptly and marched into his office with that quickened pace and those long strides that meant he was angry. She knew he would not do anything about Carter until he had worked himself slowly up into a rage, then he would lose his temper, and Carter would be gone. He was a lousy boss when it came to personnel relations. He avoided confrontations with his employees. He tried to lead by example rather than instruction, which just did not work for most people. His employees either met his expectations according to their own devices or they were gone one day all of a sudden, with a craw full of bile and no severance pay. But for people like Sara, he was a prize of a boss. He let her do whatever she was capable of doing—within certain bounds. He had not let her go out on the street yet. That was some sort of residual protective paternalism or whatever it was that still trapped even men of goodwill like him in what they called "male chauvinism." He told her once that he would not be able to forgive himself if something terrible happened to her.

O'KEEFE'S OFFICE WAS carpeted in a deep dark gray. A black parson's table with a high-gloss finish served as his desk. His desk chair was upholstered in black leather and trimmed with mahogany. The chair perched on a thin slab of parquet. A comfortable-looking black couch sat in front of a big picture window that let the sunlight in and afforded him an excellent view of the street. More than once Sara had come to work in the morning and found him sprawled out on that couch because he had worked too long or been too drunk the night before to stagger home from the bar downstairs.

His desk was fairly clean. To his surprise he had become more neat and orderly as he had grown older. Behind his regular desk was a stand-up desk littered with fire-investigation reports. Over the years he had become an expert in fire cases, but the work no longer interested him, and he was slowly turning it over to Sara, who was picking it up very well. A rueful thought—he was becoming an executive, moving from the doing of work to the supervising of it, from the real to the abstract.

A built-in mahogany bookcase covered one wall. The books on the shelf included many of the classics, ancient and modern.

People who did not know him well refused to believe that he had actually read any of these books. He poured a cup of coffee from the pot that Sara had made and placed it on a warming plate on the credenza. He rummaged through a pile of laser discs, chose one, and inserted it into his disc player. The precise, cool opening of Bach's Brandenburg Concerto No. 6 filled the room. The sound system had cost him too much but was worth it.

He sat down at his desk and read Joe Jarvis's memo on the proposed drug-testing program. Jarvis's tone was urgent. The country perceived itself to be in crisis. Nancy Reagan's "Just Say No" campaign wasn't cutting it. As always, the crisis would soon pass, making way for a new one. If they failed to move now, it would soon be too late. Jarvis had understated the projected expenses and overstated the projected revenues, but even so, the program would be a money-maker. Employee drug testing would be lucrative and would have the added benefit of giving the firm entree into the big corporations that might hire them for other work as well. There was every reason to do it, but O'Keefe had kept holding back. The word "totalitarian" kept intruding itself into his mind though he knew he was overdramatizing. Another assault on the right to privacy. He didn't like being part of that. But then, wasn't he just kidding himself? His success was composed of a series of successful assaults on people's privacy.

Yet this drug testing seemed different somehow. Urine samples, chemistry, technology. There was nothing in it of the kind of work O'Keefe liked, the lone searcher in solitary quest, using his craft and art to expose the shabby secrets of white-collar cheaters. This Jarvis thing was just chemistry versus the workingman's piss.

He wondered whether Jarvis would quit if he failed to approve the drug-testing program. Such a threat lurked between the lines of Jarvis's memo. Jarvis had been a frustrated plain-clothes cop when O'Keefe had found him, a bright, energetic, and thoroughly ruthless man chafing at the restraints that the law and the bureaucracy imposed upon him. O'Keefe had swallowed hard and paid Jarvis the money he asked for, but Jarvis had been an excellent buy. Suddenly O'Keefe had a communication link with the higher echelons of the police force. Jarvis conferred on O'Keefe's whole operation a new aura of legitimacy. Before Jarvis, O'Keefe was thought of as, at best, a lucky amateur. After Jarvis, the agency was considered highly professional, and a steady stream of referrals began to flow from the police department itself.

It would not be very long before Jarvis figured out that he could take his show on the road and start his own agency. To keep him, O'Keefe would have to give him a piece of the action. Harrigan would draw up a generous contract. The first few paragraphs of the contract would graciously bestow on Jarvis more money, more power, but, toward the end of the document, there would be a clause preventing Jarvis from competing against O'Keefe for a period of three years after leaving O'Keefe's employment. Jarvis might negotiate a bit, but it would end up no less than a two-year noncompete. The carrot—pay the man so much money that it would be a serious gamble for him to go out on his own and risk his lifestyle. The stick—if he goes out on his own, he's on ice for two years. If he tries to compete with you during that two-year period, the massed power of the state will intervene at your beck and call to restrain him, enjoin him, and seize every nickel he makes.

Another thought full of rue. There he was, drinking his coffee and listening to Bach while he devised ways to manacle Jarvis in economic chains. Little lines, external manifestations of his inner shame, formed under and around his eyes. But business was business. Meanwhile, he would have to keep Jarvis, tinhorn dictator that he was, smug little know-it-all that he was, from running off the rest of the employees. George was already fed up with Jarvis, and Sara was not far behind George.

So it was a problem to keep Jarvis and a problem to let him go. But you had to keep the pipeline full. O'Keefe wrote "Go for it" on Jarvis's memo and called Sara to tell her to schedule an appointment with the banker on Monday. He would have to borrow more to get the drug-testing program going.

Kelly came in and turned up her nose at the music.

"How about Madonna?" she said.

"We listened to that all night last night."

Bored, she plopped onto the couch and slumped down in it, her whole body a pout.

"Sara says you might be taking me home early?"

"Yeah, I have to. I'm sorry. Somebody didn't show up today, and I have to take his place."

"Will it be dangerous?"

"Not a bit."

"Why can't I go with you?"

"Because you'd be bored worse even than you are right now just sitting in the van all day waiting for a man to come out of a hotel."

"We were supposed to go to the movies tonight."

"I don't know if I'll be finished in time. If I am, I'll come and pick you up."

She did not cry. She hardly ever cried anymore. She just got up from the couch and said, "I'm gonna go talk to Sara," and left him alone with his guilt.

He picked up the telephone and dialed his former wife's number.

"Somebody didn't show up, and I'm the only one who can fill in. I'll have to bring her home."

"What's new? Nothing ever changes with you. What if I have something to do?"

"Do you?"

"No, but what if I did?"

"If I get done early enough, I'll come by and take her out tonight."

"No. I don't want her mooning around all day waiting for you and then have you not show up."

Years of disappointment and perceived betrayal envenomed her voice.

"I'm on my way," he said and abruptly hung up the phone.

They hardly talked in the van on the way home, her disappointment in him too much for both of them. If it had been a year ago, this would have been time for her to beg him to come back home to live. Now she just sat there in a sullen stupor, looking out the window. He wanted to be angry, but his pity for her overcame his anger. Tears welled up behind his eyes.

"I love you," he said.

She hesitated for a moment and then said, "I love you too, Dad," and kept looking out the window at nothing in particular.

CHAPTER 3

GEORGE NOVAK SAT reading a detective novel in a coffee shop across the street from the *Excelsior Hotel*. This reading on duty was a bad habit he had picked up from his boss, Peter O'Keefe. O'Keefe seemed to be able to read his damn book and still be able to sense everything that was going on around him. George had a harder time. Once or twice he had become so absorbed in the novel he was reading that the subject had flown the coop, walked out of the building right in front of George, who had not even noticed. Just now O'Keefe had pulled up in his van, gotten out, and started walking toward the coffee shop before George had even seen him. Shit, maybe Preston had checked out, hailed a taxi, and blithely rolled away while George was slavering over the scene where the detective finally got to hit the sack with his beautiful client.

"You ought to read poetry," O'Keefe had told him. "Not that hard-on stuff you read. Read something that won't absorb your limited mind so much."

"Poetry! Poetry, my ass!" he had replied.

This reading was an addiction, he thought, like drinking coffee or smoking cigarettes. He vowed once again never to read on duty.

George had not seen O'Keefe for many days. A rush of bubbling, warm affection surged up from his heart to his shoulders and through his neck to his head. They had known each other since kindergarten. They had been altar boys together, solemn and efficient as they glided about the altar in their starched white surplices and shiny black cassocks, performing the ancient ritual of Holy Mass. George was grateful to O'Keefe for rescuing him from that eternally cruising patrol car and the boneheaded partner and the belligerent, puking drunks and the domestic brawls, to say nothing of the spit-and-polish military bullshit that uniformed officers had to endure. But he was less and less grateful as time went on. It had been great working with O'Keefe until O'Keefe had started buying computers, until he had hired that insufferable little prick Jarvis.

Surely—George was quite sure of it—all of that made the O'Keefe George had known nearly all his life pretty miserable as well. Although O'Keefe was his boss, George envied nothing O'Keefe had except his van and his good looks. O'Keefe and their old grade-school pal Harrigan (and Harrigan was even worse than O'Keefe) had always suffered from the same disease—too much brain power for their own good. Just too damn serious. Christ, as kids they had wanted to be priests. Every month they had changed their minds about what priestly order they intended to join. One week it would be some outfit doing missionary work with the heathen Chinese; the next week it would be that monastery down South where those dumb sonuvabitches spent their whole lives scrubbing floors and not talking to each other. And then that deal of theirs about being modern knights in search of the Holy Grail, whatever that was.

George scrambled to hide the detective novel only after O'Keefe had already come into the coffee shop and was looking straight at him. As was usual with O'Keefe, there were no niceties. He got right down to business.

"Why can't we get this guy, George?"

"Well, 'Hello' to you too, and shit if I know. It's like the sonuvabitch was blessed or something. I was one step behind him all last night. For a while he was at a bar down the street here. *Gigi's.* You know *Gigi's,* don't you?" he asked, winking as he did.

"Yeah," George continued. "Where all the slightly higher-class hookers go who haven't scored by midnight. For what it's worth, Preston liked the lady bartender's action. Fabulous tits."

"I get the picture, George."

"In short, Pete, this Preston is a tit man all the way. Smooth old fucker too. But the lady bartender told me she took a rain check on his ball game, and he went away. I got here just after he'd gone inside the hotel here. And guess what he went in with? A hooker on each arm, according to the night bellman. I repeat, Peter—each arm. You understand French? A may-nage for Christ's sake. You ever done a may-nage? Ever been the meat in the sandwich, boy? Indescribably delicious."

George pointed to the dirty pavement outside the coffee shop. "So, while I'm standing out there all night feeding quarters to the winos and waiting for this pissant coffee shop to open up, he's up there sandwiched between those two hookers. Who says crime don't pay?"

"Who're you taking to the lake?"

"Guess."

O'Keefe shook his head "no."

"Some kind of detective you are, O'Keefe. Why, the lady bartender, of course. So save your breath, Boss. Nothing can deter me from that, not even the fun of following this old goat-fucker around."

George hesitated for a moment before he continued. Sometimes you had to watch what you said to O'Keefe.

"You're about due for some time on the street anyway. You can forget what it's all about back there in the office, playing executive with that dipshit Jarvis."

"Somebody's got to sign your paychecks, George."

George snorted his contempt through his nose.

"You ought to come see us sometime, George. People think you don't work there anymore. What's this that I have to mail you your paycheck? You won't even come in for your paycheck now?"

"Sorry, Boss, but that computer and me and that little fascist fuckhead Jarvis and me can't live together. And that's sad because I don't get to see Sara much anymore. You taken a run at her yet?"

"And to think that you are the product of a Catholic education. Is nothing sacred to you?"

"Can't say that there is. Not since Father Murphy stroked my ass that day in grade school."

"Good luck at the lake," O'Keefe said.

"I already got lucky. I ain't nothin' but lucky."

WALKING OUT OF the coffee shop, O'Keefe heard George say, "Fabulous, Boss. They're fabulous" loud enough so that everyone in the coffee shop could hear it. It was George who had long ago been the one to reveal to his gaping-mouthed friend Peter O'Keefe the "facts of life," satanically initiating the astonished and appalled ten-year-old O'Keefe into the dismal world of sluts and hard-ons, sperm and cunts, rubbers, and the dreaded "clap." O'Keefe still remembered it vividly. He thought maybe it had been the first thing in the world to break his heart. George had concluded his filthy narrative with a flourish: "So, you thought that little dick of yours was just to piss with, huh, Pete?"

George was still trying hard never to grow up, and O'Keefe wished him well. He mildly envied George his easygoing attitude toward life and its pains and pleasures, his way of taking life as it came, his way of not making a big deal about anything.

Since it was Saturday, O'Keefe was able to park the van directly in front of the hotel. He sat in the back of the van in a swivel seat and watched the front of the building through a custom-designed, one-way window that he had specially installed in the side of the van. The van also contained sophisticated, audio-visual snooping equipment, a portable toilet for emergencies only, a very narrow, built-in couch-bed, a hot plate, and a small refrigerator. An electronically-controlled panel in an interior wall concealed the guns he had lied to Kelly about. Out of the corner of his eye, he saw his mobile phone light up. He picked it up before it rang.

"O'Keefe," he answered.

"Having fun?" It was Sara.

"I was about to slash my wrists. I forgot how boring this really is."

"Harrigan wants you to call him right away."

"Is he pissed?"

"He's always pissed. Or acts like it anyway. He's got some new business for you."

"What did I tell you just a couple of hours ago?"

"No new business for a month."

"Right. But it's Harrigan. Never say no to Harrigan."

"Why?"

"Later. Got to move on." O'Keefe clicked the phone off and then on again and dialed Harrigan's number, still watching the front of the hotel. Julia, the receptionist, answered on the second ring. If she let it ring more than twice, Harrigan would not be pleased.

"Harrigan, Fremont, and Love."

"May I speak to the King of Spades in the Department of Frauds?"

"Hi, Pete." There would be a smile on her face at the other end of the line. "He's waiting to take your call."

Shit, here we go, he said to himself as she transferred the call to Harrigan's office. Harrigan would be sitting at his huge desk and looking out at the far horizon beyond the city thrusting up below him. He had the best corner office in the tallest building in town, one of those glass boxes that were so ugly on the outside but so satisfying for the guy on the inside looking out. The floor-to-ceiling windows sustained you with sunlight and gave you a dangerous illusion of command over the city beneath you. Harrigan would be sitting in there like the King of the Hill his very self. His mind would be working furiously as always, clawing and chewing at the raw information, breaking it down, sorting it, spitting out the irrelevant, putting the seemingly inexplicable things aside, back into the nether reaches of his consciousness, only to let them come forward later on when they would make more sense. Harrigan called it "puzzling." According to Harrigan, a good lawyer was just a puzzle solver. And a great lawyer? Well, he was the guy who invented the puzzles for the good lawyers to try to solve.

Julia's voice on the intercom told Harrigan that O'Keefe was returning his call. Harrigan hit a button, engaging the speakerphone on the left-hand corner of his desk.

"Harrigan," he answered.

"King of Spades, this is the Ace of Trump, and I'm after your ass."

But Harrigan was all business today. "Can you get down here right now?"

"I'm sitting in front of the Excelsior Hotel waiting for our boy Preston to come out."

"I can't believe you haven't nabbed him yet. This weekend. It's got to be this weekend. Because, on Monday, he gets on his big bird and flies away. And then who knows when or if we'll get another chance? But right now I need you here."

"I'm trying to figure out how I'm gonna be two places at once."

"Where's all those deadbeats on your payroll? Where's George?"

"I'd say that right now George has his hands full. Literally."

"Old George. Why didn't we turn out like him? He's got the world by the balls, and he's smart enough not to squeeze. I can still see him in the class spelling bees. He never once got past the first word they asked him. Remember when he missed the word 'apple'?"

Harrigan and O'Keefe both started laughing.

"He goes 'A P P' . . . and then he stops and thinks his ass off for a minute . . . and then he spits it out: 'E L'! Dumbest fuck in Sister Bridget's whole fourth-grade class. But life-wise, Pete, he's got us beat all to hell."

"He's Polish. We're Irish. What else can I say?"

"Send Sara down there to watch for Preston."

"Come on! She doesn't need this stuff."

"What are you, a male chauvinist? Give her a chance. She might like it. Since your boys can't seem to get the job done, maybe we ought to give the girl a chance."

Harrigan's voice ebbed and flowed, dimmed and then grew louder. O'Keefe knew what Harrigan was doing because he had seen him do it so often. He was pacing around his office, drinking coffee, smoking a cigarette, looking out the window into the distance as he listened, turning back to shout at the speaker box when it was his turn to say something. The sound of his voice rose and fell depending on whether he moved closer to or farther from the speaker phone. The speaker caused an echo effect, so it sounded like Harrigan was walking around talking in a box.

"Thirty minutes," he said. "There are two gentlemen in my conference room, waiting only for you. You'll like this one. It's different."

"What is it?"

"You ever heard of a mink farm? Or maybe it's a mink ranch? No, this is a tacky little deal, so we'll call it a farm."

"'Mink farm?"

"Thirty minutes. And the role you play today is the 'United States Marine.' 'A Few Good Men,' 'Semper Fi, Do Or Die,' 'Death Before Dishonor' and all that stuff. These gentlemen are patriots, and good Christians to boot. And whatever you do, keep a straight face."

CHAPTER ▶ 4

ON HIS WAY to Harrigan's office O'Keefe worried about Sara. If Preston came out of the hotel, she would have no idea what to do. He had told her to call him at Harrigan's office if Preston appeared and that he would give her instructions then. Well, he would eventually need to placate her with some street work, and now was as good a time as any to start, especially since she was chafing to do it. She wouldn't to be happy much longer just being his Girl Friday.

He would have to train her. That would bring them more intimately together as they sat in the van on stakeouts. That could get complicated. If he let it. If she let it. Of course, there would be no complications at all if he could just continue to mentally muscle through those times when she stood next to him and leaned down beside him, her left arm across the back of his chair as she reached down to point out something on the building plans that lay on the desk in front of them. Or if he would just look away when she crossed her legs. Or if he would avert his eyes instead of watch her as she studied something in front of her, her dark hair falling against the soft skin of her cheek.

SOMETHING IN HIS stomach wanted to snap as the rocketing elevator stopped abruptly and deposited him on the top floor of the tallest office building in the city in the middle of Mike Harrigan's waiting room. Harrigan leased the entire floor. He did not yet need all that space, but he did not mind if people thought he did. Besides, he would need all the space quite soon anyway, and the space on the floor below as well, on which he had taken an option exercisable in five years.

"You act big, and you'll be big," Harrigan had told him. "You act like the best, and people will perceive you as the best. You say you're an expert, and you will be an expert, so you can live up to what you say you are. The kind of clients I want aren't gonna hire some guy who works out of a scruffy, little shithole because he's trying to go easy on the expenses. It's dumber than shit maybe, but that's the way the world is."

There were enough light colors in the waiting room to keep it from depressing you, but it was the dark colors, the mahogany paneling, and deep blue-black carpet that gave the room its power. Power was what the room and Harrigan's whole setup was all about. Philosophizing as always, Harrigan had put it this way in one of their many late-night drunken talks: "The purpose of all this elegance is to induce awe in the beholder. The purpose is to intimidate. To intimidate my lawyer opponent who comes here to take a deposition. To intimidate my clients too for that matter. Most people think too superficially to figure it out. They think we just do all this shit to show off how much money we make. But that's not it at all. It's not money talking here. Except to the extent money means power. The nation-state in its infinite wisdom has given us lawyers the keys to the kingdom, the kingdom being the awesome, massed, crushing power of the state. All we have to do is file a piece of paper to unleash all the might and majesty of the law, with its tribunals and its penalties, its decrees and its dungeons. Listen to the language of the law, even the civil law. Summons, executions, replevins, garnishments, sequestrations, subpoenas.

Subpoena means 'under pain.' Under pain. The language of the law is the language of force, the language of power. We make the rules, and if you don't follow them, whatever they are, you're just fucked, that's what you are. We will break you into pieces just as easily as I can take that five-hundred-dollar vase over there and smash it on the floor."

O'Keefe paced slowly around the waiting room while Julia, who looked like she had been designed to go with the room, finished taking telephone instructions from one of the lawyers. Here the supplicants before the throne of justice waited to be ushered into the inner sanctum. One of the walls of the waiting room was a window wall. O'Keefe stood there looking down on the city. From up here the city seemed empty of people, a dead object, for contemplation only. From up here you could not see the winos and the bag ladies, you could not smell the exhaust fumes that belched out of the back ends of the buses, you did not almost wheeze and break out in a clammy film of sweat as you walked through the fetid air in the humid summertime. Up here in the wintertime you did not get knocked damn near backward by the biting wind that whooshed down the canyon-like streets and razored right through you.

He heard Julia flirting with the lawyer on the telephone. Was he sleeping with her? How many of them were sleeping with her? Certainly most of them wanted to. His heart, always ready to offer itself in silent pity, went out to her. She was like so many of the girls in the offices all over the city, hoping one of these hotshots she worked for would dump his wife and marry her, hoping to trade one kind of bondage for another, more opulent one. Her heart had probably been broken too often. But then, she wouldn't care a bit about some wife who had been betrayed because of her. He did not really know whether to dislike her, pity her, or try to take her to bed himself. She hung up the phone, smiled, and told him to go on back to the conference room.

The conference room was another of Harrigan's shrines to power. Harrigan sat with two men at an eighteen-foot-long conference table. The table was black and glossy. You could see your reflection in it. Harrigan and the two men sat in walnut chairs upholstered in a soothing, gray fabric, silently waiting, staring out the window. Harrigan stood up when he saw O'Keefe, and his guests followed his lead.

"Gentlemen, this is Peter O'Keefe. Mr. O'Keefe, this is Mr. Anderson, and this is Mr. Lufkin."

Anderson and Lufkin, each in his fifties, looked like church elders. Each wore an inexpensive, light-colored suit, a white shirt, and a tie that blended so thoroughly with the suit and shirt you could hardly tell it was there. Each had a small U.S. flag pinned to the lapel of his suit coat. Anderson, small and stolid looking, resembled someone O'Keefe knew or had seen before—Henry Kissinger, O'Keefe would realize later, with less forehead and less nose. Lufkin was jowly, a substantial piece of beef well marbled with fat. He had a full head of coarse, dark hair. He looked like a cross between a football linebacker and a small black bear.

The two men examined O'Keefe as if he were an amoeba under a microscope. It seemed like no one was going to say anything. The excruciatingly awkward pause was presided over, it seemed to O'Keefe, by Mr. Anderson. But Harrigan, as usual, got quickly down to business. He poured cups of coffee for everyone and sat down. The others sat down when he did.

"Gentlemen," he said to Anderson and Lufkin, "since Mr. O'Keefe's time and my own are expensive, and I know you're concerned about that, let me try to save as much of that expensive time as possible by summarizing the situation."

The two men nodded gravely. Harrigan had hit them where they lived, in their wallets, and they were appreciative. Today was a blue day for Harrigan—navy-blue suitcoat, pants, and socks, navy-blue Italian-made loafers, a creamy, light-blue, custom-made, French-cuffed shirt, cufflinks of dark-blue lapis trimmed with gold, and a tie made of blue silk with a touch of crimson in the pattern that caused the tie to stand out distinctively from all the rest of the blue. Even his watch had a blue lapis face. The only thing not blue was his wedding ring, a simple band of brushed gold. He was a man of only average height, but his clothes always made him look taller and thinner than he was. He had light brown hair, thick but straight, longer than a lawyer's hair was supposed to be. It covered the tops of his ears and touched the top of his shirt collar in back—a hint of rebellion, a genuflection back to the '60s. His nose was a bit too sharp. He had a hard face and soft eyes.

"Mr. O'Keefe," said Harrigan, "these gentlemen are members of the board of directors of Prosperity Farms, Inc., which is in the business of operating a mink farm down in the lakes area. They breed minks. Investors put up their money and buy a pair of minks. Sometimes they buy lots of pairs of minks. How much is it that you gentlemen personally have invested in this operation?"

"One hundred forty thousand dollars," Anderson mumbled, as if ashamed.

"One hundred thousand dollars," said Lufkin sadly.

"Now these two gentlemen," Harrigan continued, "have a lot more money in this deal than most of the other investors, but there's probably two hundred more out there with anything from five hundred to twenty-five thousand bucks in this thing. And the idea is exquisitely simple. You just put these minks into cages together and let them do what minks do best."

Harrigan smiled at Anderson and Lufkin, who force-smiled back at him without amusement.

"And pretty soon," Harrigan continued, "you've got little minks running all over the place. And when they grow up, you take some of those minks and skin them."

"Pelt them," interrupted Anderson. "Pelting is what it's called."

"You pelt some of them," Harrigan went on, with a sardonic glance at O'Keefe, "and you sell the fur. So you've already got some of your money back, and, yet, you've still got minks, more minks than you started out with, and they just keep on doing what minks do best. And, of course, the company generously permits you to reinvest your earnings from the pelting to buy more minks for your account."

Harrigan stopped to light a cigarette. Anderson and Lufkin looked at him as if he had just made a lewd proposition to their daughters. Harrigan blew some smoke their way and went on with the story. To Harrigan the clients were not really there anymore. They had told him their stories, and now he had their stories down cold. They had become their stories. That was Harrigan's way. People were just stories to Harrigan.

"And although these gentlemen are directors of the company, they don't really know much about what goes on, because this whole show is actually run by one guy, a Mr. Lenny Parker. Well, everything goes along just fine for a couple of years. Everybody's getting paid these fabulous returns on their investments, when, all of a sudden, the checks stop coming. When they call down there to the farm, Mr. Parker is always out, and his secretary doesn't know beans from mink droppings. And then, all of a sudden, yesterday, the secretary calls Mr. Lufkin here and says she hasn't seen Mr. Lenny Parker for almost a month. Mr. Lenny Parker seems to have just taken off or something. And the hell of it is they're running out of mink food, and there's no money in the bank to buy any more."

"They'll starve to death in no time at all," said Anderson.

"And, of course, that's a disaster," said Harrigan. "Because then the minks can't do what minks do best, and all those people's money is gone forever. So these gentlemen have retained me to do whatever I can for them legally. But the real problem is more up your alley, Mr. O'Keefe, and that problem is this. Where's the money? And, of course, there's the very related question of where is Mr. Lenny Parker? I explained to these gentlemen that you're quite expensive but that you're the best in the business, at least here locally, and even more important, you're the fastest in the business, so you'll get maximum results for the money these gentlemen invest in you. And accordingly, these gentlemen may wish to employ you, Mr. O'Keefe."

The story was over. Harrigan stubbed out his cigarette, got up, and started pacing up and down the room. It was someone else's turn to talk now, and he did not seem to care who. They endured another long pause. Lufkin sat there like a cow lazily chewing its cud. Anderson had the manner of a solemn deity who badly wanted to fart.

Finally, Anderson cleared his throat and said, "Mr. Harrigan tells me that you're a veteran."

"Yes, sir. I am."

"Vietnam?"

"Yes, sir. United States Marine Corps."

"Combat?"

"Door gunner."

"Tough duty," Lufkin chimed in.

"Yes, sir."

"Mr. O'Keefe," Anderson gravely intoned, "it's men like you that make me still proud to be an American."

"Thank you, sir."

"Call me Ernest," said Mr. Anderson.

"And you understand, Mr. O'Keefe," said Lufkin, "that we're not wealthy men. We don't have much money to spend."

He could play this one as well as Harrigan could.

"If I can get access to the books and the secretary, I can have a report on the financial situation after two days' work."

"Twelve hundred dollars," said Harrigan ominously from the far end of the room, his back toward them as he looked out the window wall and off somewhere into the far blue yonder.

"How about finding that little crook Lenny?" Lufkin asked.

"I can probably find out a lot while I'm down there looking at the books. Let's say another day spent on Mr. Parker, and we'll decide then the next step we should take."

"Eighteen hundred dollars," said Harrigan, still with his back to them.

Anderson turned to talk to Harrigan's back. "That's within the budget we discussed, isn't it, Mr. Harrigan?"

"I'd say so, Mr. Anderson."

"Well then," said Anderson, "we'll be looking forward to working with you, Mr. O'Keefe. May I call you Peter?"

"Please call me Pete."

"Good. We'll be going then," said Anderson as he got up from his chair.

"Just get that little weasel Lenny," said Lufkin. "I want him in the slammer if nothing else. Let's see how well he can sell to his new roommates."

Harrigan and O'Keefe walked to the door of the conference room with the two older men. Hands were piously shaken all around. Harrigan let them find their own way back down the hall to the waiting room. As they shuffled away, their humped backs seemed to carry an invisible but quite heavy burden of defeat, a defeat they had not been prepared to suffer at this stage of their lives.

After the two men had moved out of earshot, Harrigan turned to O'Keefe and said solemnly, "You make me proud to be an American, Mr. O'Keefe."

O'Keefe's smile was bitter, but he had done his duty and, despite everything, was pretty sure he would do it again if he had to.

"Just think, those are the kind of sonuvabitches that sent you over there. And they'll send you right back again if you give them half a chance."

Harrigan started abruptly down the hall toward his office.

"You want a drink?" he asked.

O'Keefe looked at his watch. It wasn't quite noon. Then Harrigan said what O'Keefe was thinking.

"What the hell. It's Saturday."

Julia rolled in a tea cart that carried a silver ice bucket with silver tongs, crystal glassware, a quart of Wild Turkey, a pitcher of water, and a large bottle of club soda. They each took a little soda and a little water with their bourbon.

"Now, what do you think about that?" Harrigan said, gesturing toward the tea cart.

"I think about the kid whose family didn't have a set of plates that matched, the kid that had moth holes in every one of his sweaters, the kid that had exactly five pairs of underwear. His name was Michael Harrigan."

"We gotta take a trip or something," said Harrigan. "We're losing touch. You're all I've got left of the old days."

Harrigan raised his glass in tribute. "To Mike and Pete. Blood brothers. Knights of the Grail."

O'Keefe raised his glass in response. "To Friday-night mixers and long-haired girls."

"To Bob Dylan," said Harrigan. "To poetry and wet dreams."

"To all our dreams," said O'Keefe. "To the boys we were and the men we thought we could be."

A darkness engulfed Harrigan then. O'Keefe could see it in his face. Harrigan's soul was plummeting, right down to the ground, for he hated what he had become. If it had been twenty years ago, Harrigan would have wept, but he was a different person now. He did not weep. Instead, he covered his despair with a brutal cynicism. Harrigan raised his glass again. "To frauds and scams. To bad faith and breach of promise. To embezzlement and defalcation. To mink farms. To suckers. Where would our bank accounts be without them?"

"How's the scam work?"

"Old, old trick. A Ponzi scheme. There's a mink farm down there all right, with about three hundred mink when there's supposed to be three thousand. And Lenny pays the first batch of suckers with the money from the next batch of suckers. And on and on until he runs out of suckers. Then he splits with the dough if he hasn't already pissed it all away on cars and boats and diamond rings for his honey girl."

"You know though, when you hear it for the first time, it seems to make sense."

"Well, I bet they'll sell you a couple of minks while you're down there. The problem is the little fuckers eat more food than their little pelts will ever be worth. It's a low-margin business even if you know what you're doing, and I guarantee you that Lenny Parker doesn't know diddly except how to give mighty powerful sermons to all those suckers looking to make five hundred dollars turn into fifty thousand."

"Hell, I'd have given him five hundred on that deal."

"And there you are, Pete—one born every minute."

Harrigan drained his drink and poured another one. He didn't bother with the water or the soda this time.

"Do a quick-and-dirty on this one. These guys can't afford much, and we've got to do whatever we can for the least money in the shortest time. Remember, the little fuckers'll be starving in a few days."

"I'll drive down this afternoon and be at the farm first thing tomorrow morning."

"Monday's soon enough. Get Preston first."

"Preston," said O'Keefe, shaking his head, disappointed in himself.

"We've been trying to get that guy for a month, Pete, and it costs Preston forty thousand bucks a month just to keep himself in whores and houses and yachts. Since he's living on our banker client's money, that means we've let him spend forty thousand of our client's money this month. And we didn't get where we are today by fucking around like this. Results. That's all they want from us. So get him today, okay? I want to shoot him down. It'll be a service to the country and give me enormous pleasure besides. And pleasure doesn't come easy these days. Not for me at least."

Harrigan had now drained his second drink. The muscles in his face were taut as bowstrings. O'Keefe noticed how black and deep were the circles below his friend's eyes. Something was ravaging him from the inside out. When O'Keefe finished his drink and got up to leave, Harrigan was looking out the window, far off somewhere.

"You know, Pete," he said, still looking out the window, "when we were kids in high school, we thought life was gonna be some wonderful quest. But it turns out to be just a fucking trench war."

After O'Keefe had gone, Harrigan sat for a long time, sipping his third drink and thinking about his old friend. O'Keefe made him feel that special warmth the heart reserves for the few friends of childhood you are lucky enough to still know in adult life and still care about. He needed O'Keefe around to provide evidence that his heart had not turned, irrevocably, to stone. He had to do some paperwork, some contracts and correspondence, but the only time he could stand to do paperwork anymore was when he started at it very early in the morning, the light in his office the only one on in the entire downtown area of the city. That's what he would do—get in here at five o'clock on Monday morning and start grinding away.

Once he had written poetry. Now he wrote pleadings and contracts. From the language of the heart to the language of the money vault. What a descent! Why did he get the blues like this every Saturday afternoon? The sky outside had darkened, the now-gloomy city hunched forlornly outside his window wall. He did not want to go home to the wife and kids. All he wanted was something worth hoping for. Failing that, he wanted to go to a bar and wrap some oblivion around him. And he did not want to be alone. He dialed Julia's extension. She would be getting off work soon. He would ask her to go have a drink. He knew she would say "Yes."

CHAPTER 5

AT HARVEY'S, THE bar downstairs from O'Keefe's office, Sara, bubbling with delighted self-satisfaction, recounted to the appalled O'Keefe her adventure of the day.

"I just couldn't stand the suspense anymore," she said.

"You're crazy!"

"Yeah. I kept thinking, 'What if he doesn't come out all day? What if he goes out the back or a side door? What if he's got a car in the garage? What if he's got a car pulling up to get him and is out the door and in the car before I can say 'Jack Robinson?'"

"Jack Robinson," scoffed O'Keefe.

"Just too much could go wrong. So I called up to his room."

"Tell me you didn't!"

"I sure did. And he answers! Mr. Whiskey and Cigarette Voice. And I said, 'Damon?' "And he says, 'Yeah, who's this?' And I say, hoping my voice isn't quavering too much, 'I hope you'll remember me. Last night. At *Gigi's*. The bartender.'"

"Oh shit, the bartender," O'Keefe said. "George told you all that?"

"I had to do my homework, didn't I? Not just sit there like a bump."

"So," she resumed, "Preston sounding pleased but suspicious, says, 'How'd you know where to find me?'"

She jiggled her ice in her near-empty glass as she went on. "Well, that one was a hard one, you can bet."

"No kidding."

"I said, 'You told me where you were staying. Don't you remember?' And he doesn't say a word to that. Which made me very nervous. And I thought, 'Oh shit, O'Keefe's going to kill me if I blow this.' So I say, 'I called because I didn't want you to think I was just brushing you off or something. I had a date I just couldn't get out of. I hope I'll see you again.'"

"And he jumps right on that. 'How about tonight?' he says. 'I'll take you to dinner. What's your favorite place?' Another big moment, that one. But I come up with 'I have to work tonight. How about lunch? I'm in your neighborhood.'"

"This better have a happy ending," O'Keefe said, with no hint of humor.

"And then he says, 'I'll call up room service. Champagne is on the way. How long will it take you to get here?'"

"You didn't," O'Keefe said.

"I sure did. I grab the subpoena and I'm thinking on the way up to the room, 'I can't believe this horny old goat. He was up there all night with two hookers and he's ready to go again.' And I get up there and knock on the door, thinking he is going to be a gentleman and come to the door and open it for me. But instead, I knock and hear from inside, 'Come in.'"

O'Keefe just groaned.

"Yes, Mr. O'Keefe, I fear that chivalry really is dead. But I say to myself, 'OK, I have to go in there. He will see right away that I'm not the bartender, but what could possibly happen to me in there, really? So I turn the knob, and I'm thinking, because I don't know, I've never done this, 'Can I just throw the thing at him and run, or do I have to get right up close and put it in his hand?'"

"Jesus!" said O'Keefe, shaking his head.

"But, of course, there was not exactly time enough to call you or Harrigan for an interpretation of the law. So I go on in, and there he is, and I say to myself, not kidding here, 'Well, this one's a dandy all right.' Because he's there on the couch, half sitting, half reclining, in a fancy robe, no hotel job, had to be his own, silk I really think, smiling big as the moon, tan brown legs crossed quite leisurely, liver spots all over his legs he's so damn old, but the most beautiful head of wavy, silver-gray hair you've ever seen. There's a champagne bucket standing next to the couch. But here it is, here's the cake that got took, Mr. O'Keefe."

"I don't want to know."

"I march right over to where he's perched himself and can't help noticing that the robe just below his waist is standing up like a little pup tent!"

"Not amusing," said O'Keefe.

"And as I'm marching over there, his face is changing fast, but before he can really register what's happening, I drop the subpoena right on his little pup tent and say, 'Compliments of Mr. Harrigan,' and I turn around and walk right out of the room, and once I'm in the hall, I hit the stairs—I sure wasn't going to wait for the elevator—down and out and in the van and back to the office. Mission accomplished."

She held up her glass in joyful triumph, inviting him to click her glass in a toast, which he did, feigning delight, trying to disguise his disquiet.

"That was great," he said, "unbelievable work, but you have to promise me you won't ever do something like that again."

"Well, I'll consider that," she said, "as long as there's an 'again.' Promise me there really will be an 'again.'"

"That's a deal," he said. "A solemn covenant."

They sealed the covenant with another toast. She felt guilty because she had lied to him, by omission if not commission. It was the "walk right out of the room" that was the lie. Yes, she had turned to walk swiftly out of the room, but as she did that, she could not see the sudden rage in Preston's face. She could not see or hear him leap up from the couch. But she did hear him say "You fuckin' bitch," and felt him coming after her. She had started to run just before he knocked her down.

"You cunt," he said. One of his fists bounced off the side of her head. She tried to fold herself into a fetal position, but the blow had stunned her, and it seemed like she now moved in slow motion. Then he suddenly stopped beating on her. Instead, he had forced her dress up to her waist and was ripping at her underpants. Struggling to free herself, she somehow instinctively perceived the futility of that in view of his superior strength and, instead, suddenly relaxed, went entirely limp, which caused Preston himself to unthinkingly relax in response, which gave her a precious moment or two to raise both of her knees and shove her feet hard into his gut, and she quickly wriggled free as he groaned and feebly grabbed for her. She came to her knees and then to her feet and dashed toward the door, taking a quick look backward as she grabbed and turned the knob, and saw that he had only managed to struggle to his knees ("age catching up with you" flashed through her mind) as she quickly opened the door, ducked out, slammed it shut, and ran fast toward the exit sign leading to the stairway and safety.

Yes, she felt guilty but with only a little regret for the lie because she knew that if she told him the truth, her chance of ever getting out from behind that secretary's desk would disappear.

Oblivious, O'Keefe kept his eyes on her as long as he dared. Her neck was soft and white. Her dark brown eyes seemed to bid welcome. *Oh, Sara, be careful, or I'll fall into your eyes.*

Their eyes met and quickly looked away.

O'KEEFE WAS ONE of the "characters" that Harvey liked to have hang around his bar. Harvey took special pride in O'Keefe, whose presence imparted a sense of adventure and even some danger to the place, which had become, regrettably, according to Harvey's 1960s way of thinking, just another after-work watering hole and meat market for the yuppie crowd. Harvey would look around the place at Happy Hour, shake his head, and say to O'Keefe, "Fuckin' yuppies. What did I do to deserve to live in a world full of yuppies?" But then Harvey would not hesitate to shamelessly use the exotic O'Keefe, the ex-hippie, ex-Vietnam "baby-killer" private detective as a drawing card to keep these same yuppies coming back to his place. "See that guy over there at the bar?" he would say to them. "That's Peter O'Keefe. He's a private dick, and he carries a gun all the time." And the type of yuppies who frequented a place like *Harvey's*, ex-romantics most of them, would look at O'Keefe and envy him for the life they thought he led. They would keep hanging around *Harvey's*, just hoping some of whatever O'Keefe had would rub off on them. Little did they know that his life was really not much different from theirs, that he was sort of a yuppie himself.

Harvey's was almost empty now, at 3:30 on a Saturday afternoon, except for a couple of lone, middle-aged men sitting a couple of stools away from each other at the bar, drinking resolutely and watching a college football game on the big-screen television that Harvey had reluctantly installed.

"Now I'm runnin' a fuckin' sports bar, for Christ's sake," he had grumbled. Harvey was waiting in vain for the return of the beatnik coffeehouse, the return of the good old days when life had really meant something. O'Keefe was glad not to have to tell the story of the day to a gaggle of half-envious, half-contemptuous bankers, accountants, and lawyers. They were at home today, raking leaves or standing on the sidelines watching their kids play soccer, urging them to do better, always to do better. He winced inwardly as he recalled that he had missed so many of Kelly's soccer games this year. He vowed to make a much better showing in the upcoming basketball season.

Sara ordered a big meal and delicately wolfed it down as O'Keefe drank his *Moosehead* and stared at her in amazement at the large size of her appetite versus the relatively smaller size of her.

She noticed him staring at her and looked embarrassed.

"Funny, huh? That made me hungry as hell," she said.

"When I tell Harrigan about your adventure today, you'll enter his hall of fame."

She shrugged and said, "Who cares?"

"You don't like him?"

"I keep looking for something to like."

"What's wrong with him?"

"Well, let's start with his rudeness. You can't even get a 'good morning' out of him. 'Slam bam, thank you ma'am' all the way. Then we'll move right along to his arrogance. Then . . ."

"Okay!" he interrupted. "I shouldn't have asked."

He took a long thoughtful drink from his *Moosehead*.

"It's funny though," he said. "That's not him. Or at least, it didn't used to be him. When he was a kid, even in high school, he was the most sensitive of us all. He'd cry at the drop of a hat. He worried about everybody, tried to take care of everybody.

He was our class poet. But then, when he got into the law business, he adopted this pose. Maybe he did it to disguise his fear. Nothing in his childhood got him ready for what he was trying to be. So he got tough to overcome the fear. And then, at some point, the man became the pose."

"How come when he snaps, you jump?"

"For old, old time's sake. We weren't just friends. We were blood brothers. The real thing. Slit our fingers when we were eight years old and pressed them together. Harrigan and O'Keefe. Knights of the Grail."

"Knights of the Grail?" she said, with a questioning, skeptical smile.

He finished his Moosehead and waved at the waitress to bring him another. "A legend. King Arthur's knights set out in search of the Holy Grail. I forget what it really was. Some kind of vessel. Our Lord's chalice or something. Harrigan and I thought it meant truth, the meaning of life, perfect love, the ultimate, the best of everything."

"I never heard of it."

"Read *Le Morte D'Arthur*," he said, pronouncing the French awkwardly. "It's all in there."

She had a funny look on her face, a puzzled half-smile. He noticed and asked her what she was thinking.

"That fits so well, that 'quest for the Grail' stuff. I wonder if either one of you ever really grew up."

O'Keefe shrugged, thinking how puerile it all must seem, but then, there it was: it hadn't gone away, nothing to be done about it.

"Apparently we did," he said.

He fell into a brief reverie, having lost his train of thought.

"Go on," she said. "You were blood brothers, Knights of the Grail . . ."

"Yeah, we were inseparable. Until college. We started out there together too. We were both English majors. But then I started drifting away. Into booze and drugs and just not caring about anything. And all of a sudden I was drafted. Not just drafted. Drafted into the damned, Jarhead United States Marine Corps if you can believe it. They were so desperate back then, even the Marines were drafting people. But I showed up and did my duty, horrible as it was. 'The Universal Soldier,' you know. And meanwhile, Harrigan scores a ridiculously high draft lottery number and just goes on and sails along out of college and into law school like he really knew what he was doing. And when I came back from Vietnam, I got into rage and drugs and just screwing my life up any way I could, and Harrigan sort of picked me up off the street, and so I drifted along with him until it started sticking to me, and here I am. Harrigan's the one who got me started in this business. I didn't know my ass from third base. Neither did he really. He was just a semi-poor young hustler then, a blue-collar Irish kid trying to make good. He hardly knew a corporation from a cow patty back then. And we kind of grew up in the business together. From the divorces and the car wrecks to the banks and the conglomerates. We've always been sort of a team. And we became the best at what we did—getting the result, grabbing the assets. I guess I don't even need his business now, but he'll always be first priority with me. Without him I'd just be a splash of dried puke on the street right now."

"And so who are you now? Harrigan's monster? You don't seem to enjoy your work very much."

"That's because I don't."

"Why don't you?"

"Look at who I hang around with all the time. Guys like Preston. Actually a few of the guys I work for are just like him.

If your environment stinks, you start to smell too. Look what's happened to Harrigan."

"Then you ought to do something else. You talk like you don't have a choice. There's no cage in this world a guy like you can't walk right out of. At least if you're willing to face what's outside."

Abruptly he changed the subject. "Make a note, will you? I have to buy two bicycles before next Saturday. Can you believe it? My kid doesn't even have a bike. Can't even ride a bike. She's got some great parents."

"She's turning out just fine."

"I don't know. She's getting more like her mother every day. Wanting to control everything. And that makes me sad because it's gonna cause her nothing but pain."

She felt him hesitating, debating whether he should tell her the next thing he had in mind to say.

"You know," he said, apparently having decided to say it, "I've thought seriously maybe a dozen times about going back and trying it again. But I don't have the heart for it, even for Kelly. Is that lousy or what?"

"They say self-condemnation is just another way of refusing to change."

Nothing he could say to that. She was not going to help him talk himself off of the hook he was wriggling on. But maybe there really was no hook. "There's no cage in this world you can't walk right out of," she had said. Nice thought. He would have to remember that.

She finished her glass of wine. He signaled to the waitress to bring them two more.

"No more for me, Pete. One more, and I'm in trouble, and who knows what happens?"

He smiled. *Why didn't she think that was a good idea?*

"Let's take a walk," he said.

They walked to the small park near O'Keefe's apartment. They waded through the fallen leaves. The sky was growing even darker, a warning of rain coming soon. O'Keefe was suffering from the same affliction that had stricken Harrigan earlier in the day, the Saturday-afternoon blues. It was going to be a long time before morning. He hung back and let her walk a step or two in front of him, her hands in the pockets of her windbreaker. A tiny scarlet leaf clung to the dark-brown hair at the back of her head. She was neither thin nor fat, just ample, a promise of softness. He wanted very badly to take this ample woman home with him, wanted her to play with him, very gently, in the dark. But he was afraid, for many reasons, to make any move in that direction.

They sat on the swing set, side by side, not really swinging, just pushing back and forth with their feet.

"So" he said, "what's your wish upon a star?"

"You mean why am I thirty-something and still alone?"

"Not necessarily that."

"Heading for spinsterhood?"

"Probably too choosy."

"Not really. Not at all. I would just be looking for a place inside someone's heart. Not even a big space. But a safe one. And I haven't found that yet."

It was her turn to abruptly change the subject. She quickly pushed herself up from the swing.

"I have to get going. Are you going down to the lakes tomorrow?"

He nodded his head.

"Be careful" she said.

"Always."

"Never."

He watched her walk away. When she was halfway across the little park, she turned around and looked at him. He thought for a moment she was coming back. But then she just smiled, waved, turned around, and walked on out of the park. He sat on the swing for a while and kept looking at the spot where she had stood and smiled and waved.

He considered going back to *Harvey's* for the evening. There would be yellow light and brown whiskey there, and cool jazz, and maybe even a long-haired girl. But it didn't seem worth the effort. Besides, he wanted to rise early, clearheaded, welcoming the new day and the promise of a new adventure down at the lakes, at the mink "farm." Only the promise of such adventures kept him trudging through the dullness of all the unremarkable days of his life.

The sky drizzled on him as he trod heavily, like a man carrying a load, across the park, back to his apartment. The telephone was ringing when he let himself in the front door. He did not hurry to answer it, didn't care if it stopped before he got to it, but it kept ringing.

"O'Keefe," he answered.

"Pete, this is Ernest Anderson. I'm sorry to bother you at home."

"No problem."

"I just wanted to tell you that Jane, Lenny's secretary, said that she would be glad to meet with you tomorrow if you wanted to do it then instead of Monday."

"That would be great. Tell her I'll be there late morning or early afternoon."

"I will."

Anderson hesitated. There was something he was having a hard time trying to say.

"There's something else."

"What would that be, sir?"

"I couldn't be completely forthright with Mr. Lufkin there today. As you heard, he's very down on Lenny right now. He's very irrational about it. But I know Lenny well, believe me, and the Lenny I know would not do what he seems to have done. Something terrible must have happened."

"What makes you think you know him so well, Mr. Anderson?"

"He's my son-in-law. My daughter's husband."

O'Keefe squinted as he tried to evaluate this disclosure.

"Have you asked her what's wrong with him?"

"I'm afraid my daughter and I don't communicate very well."

"You don't talk?"

"Sadly, not very much."

Something serious must have gone down between those two, O'Keefe thought.

"I don't even know," Anderson went on, "whether or not she went off with Lenny. And I hope you'll check on her when you're down there. Make sure she's coping with all this somehow. She's an incredible girl. Extraordinary in every way."

"I'll look in on her if she's there. And if she'll see me." But he hoped she would not be the one or do the other, because he could not believe that the daughter of this man could be "extraordinary in every way," or in any way at all.

Anderson seemed to be stifling a sob. "Please give her my love." His voice almost broke, but he recovered himself. "But really," he continued, " I just wanted to tell you that the Lenny

Parker I know would not do these things, would not even dream of doing these things. Something terrible must have happened."

After he hung up on Anderson, O'Keefe tossed a salad, baked a potato, and barbecued chicken on the grill on his patio. He sat at the patio table in the darkness, his windbreaker hood up to protect him from the drizzling mist, hoping it would not rain any harder, at least until the chicken was done. After dinner, he sipped *Wild Turkey* on the rocks while he took a hot shower. He put an old Ravi Shankar album on the stereo, got into bed, turned the lights off, and continued to wonder until he fell off to sleep how any daughter of a man like Ernest Anderson could be an "incredible girl, extraordinary in every way."

CHAPTER 6

IT WAS STILL drizzling early the next morning as O'Keefe's van sliced through the almost empty streets of the fog-drenched city. He felt like the lone survivor of some deadly sickness that had seeped into the town and sucked away its life. He drove through miles of suburbs that seemed to grow daily of their own accord and out of control, gobbling up the countryside.

The mink farm was in the lake and hill country, a five- or six-hour drive to the south and east. He had visited the area many times from boyhood on. City dwellers rushed there on summer weekends, pulling their motorboats behind them. The city side of the lakes area was built-up and crowded. The mink farm was on the far side of the lakes, where the resort culture had not yet triumphed completely.

By seven o'clock O'Keefe had left the city and its grasping suburbs behind him. He steered with one hand and poured a cup of coffee from his thermos with the other. Bach played on the tape deck, C.P.E. Bach this time, his *Magnificat*. It seemed like the van itself could soar aloft, lifted by the perfection of the music. A moment of wholeness, all too fleeting. And, indeed, that moment soon did flee; that brief respite of utter serenity soon gave way to the other, stronger emotions that stirred within him now, the queasy excitement of a new adventure.

A couple of hours away from the city, the ground began to rise, and the cleared fields gave way to forests of hickory, oak, and short-leaf pine. These were mountains he was ascending, but the locals called them "hills," perhaps in deference to the big mountains out west, the real mountains, the ones you could ski on. He drove along a ridgeline, above him towering bare bluffs, below him canyons and valleys full of trees shedding their leaves, spreading before him a palette of exquisite colors. His human words could not describe these colors. Red, yellow, yellow-gold, orange, burnt-orange, russet, scarlet, crimson—words wholly inadequate to describe the scene. These colors below him were of some other spectrum. The word "ineffable" came to mind. New words needed to be invented to describe the true colors of these leaves. But it was not the words alone that were inadequate, he thought; his mind, his understanding itself was faulty, always seeming to miss the mark. Here, below him, was another process, another essence entirely, one he could never grasp but could only behold in alienated wonder.

And it came to him that it was death itself, the death he had seen so much of in the back of the helicopters, the death he had feared then and feared now, that spread so magnificently before him. "We're dying," the leaves seemed to be saying. "We must pass on, make way for others. Only the tree goes on." He watched, and he meditated, but he suspected he would never really understand any of it, not even the slightest thing.

He had brought his hiking boots, sleeping bag, and camping equipment, and he would try to make time on this trip for a hike in the deep woods, among the streams and meadows, the glades and springs, crushing the fallen leaves as he trudged along. If it did not rain, he would spend a night in his sleeping bag. Just before crawling into the bag for the night, he would douse his campfire and stand watching a sky full of stars.

He had found a route that would take him to the mink farm without passing through the resort side of the lakes. That side of the lakes always wilted his spirit. But the small rural towns were depressing in their way too. Few things could darken the soul more than a certain kind of small town, where form so perfectly follows function, where everything is marginal, bare, cheap.

This was the Bible Belt, churches everywhere. The people would stand outside, being neighborly after the service, big men in eyeglasses and inexpensive suits, string ties, and cowboy boots, the women almost as big as the men, looking weary and drained out in their knee-length dresses and cloth coats. Assembly of God, Church of Christ, Pentecostal, Free Will Baptist, First Baptist, all proclaiming the certainty of salvation and immortality. Yet the churches themselves (often they were only tiny houses made into churches) and the towns they ministered to seemed like nothing if not monuments to the futility of hope.

A few miles outside of one of these towns, on an obscure and bumpy country road, he passed a sign that said, "Prosperity Farms. One Mile Ahead." Another sign directed him off the road onto an asphalt driveway with huge oak trees on both sides that shrouded the driveway in perpetual dimness. The farm was tucked into a small valley of its own, a few acres of flat ground surrounded by hills. Far to his left, as he drove out of the trees and into a small parking area, stood a grand old barn, huge holes in its roof, its wooden frame weather-bleached almost white.

The farmhouse loomed up to his right, smaller and more modern than he had expected it to be—white with a bright-red trim freshly painted not very long ago. Despite the hopeful colors, the house cowered under a huge oak tree that shadowed it in gloom. Something about it made him feel queasy.

The driveway extended past the parking area along the side of the house, turned a corner at the back, and disappeared from view. He could see behind the house a path that meandered into a stand of trees that hid whatever lay beyond it. *They keep the minks back there.* In the parking area there was an old Ford Mustang and an ancient, battered pickup truck that looked undrivable. The truck sported a brand-new bumper sticker that said, "When Guns Are Outlawed, Only Outlaws Will Have Guns."

Someone had painted in red directly onto the front door "COME IN!" but, when he tried the door, he found it was locked. There was no doorbell and no answer to his knocking. He walked around the side of the house along the driveway. At the back of the house, the driveway plunged steeply down into a basement garage.

A high, concrete, stoop-like stairway led up to a back door to the house. He climbed the stairway and knocked on the back door. He looked inside the back-door window at a large kitchen. No sign of life and again no answer to his knocking. He descended the stairs and stood in the backyard wondering what to do. The secretary was supposed to be expecting him. The two vehicles in the parking lot indicated that someone was there. Maybe she—or they—were wherever the minks were, perhaps down beyond the stand of trees. He walked back to the driveway and looked down at the basement garage. The doors to the garage were the old-fashioned wooden kind that had to be swung or dragged back and forth when opened and closed. One of the doors stood slightly ajar, beyond that only darkness.

The garage door scraped harshly across the concrete floor when he pushed it open, and he thought of a fingernail scratching across a blackboard. He stood in the garage, letting his eyes become accustomed to the darkness, listening for human sounds within. The garage was empty except for a few soggy-looking cardboard boxes and miscellaneous junk—paintbrushes, a dented hubcap, a tire iron, rusty old chains. An archway at the other end of the garage appeared to lead into some other part of the basement.

As he neared the archway, he noticed drops of dried liquid on the floor. *Maybe it's the red paint that they used for the trim on the house.* He passed through the archway into a narrow hallway. The basement walls were crumbling. Chunks of the plaster littered the floor. He decided to follow the drops of paint. *Maybe it's not red paint,* he thought, as he turned a corner in the hallway.

The man—huge, ugly, and fierce—stood not more than five yards away, a couple of long strides away. His hands and arms and the front of his shirt were spotted with red liquid that was not paint.

O'Keefe almost choked on his fear. He wanted to run, but he was frozen like a rabbit freezes when panic seizes it and it is so scared it cannot think to run. He decided he would go for the giant's testicles. He would keep his hands high as if he were going to box with this monster, but he would kick out with his foot when the giant was a stride away from him. If his kick proved true, the giant would double over in pain, and then his knee would crush the giant's nose back against his skull. Then he would run. To the van. Where the weapons were. But if he missed the first kick, it would probably be all over for him. The giant's upper arms looked like the haunches of a steer.

"What is it, Roy?"

The female voice came from somewhere behind the monster.

"Roy?"

The giant said nothing.

The woman came into view. O'Keefe said nothing. He couldn't tell whether she was the secretary he was supposed to be meeting or the giant's accomplice in some unspeakable butchery. She had red hair, but there was no blood on her.

"Mr. O'Keefe?"

"Yes, ma'am," he said, trying to keep his voice from breaking. "I knocked, but nobody answered."

"I'm sorry. I didn't expect you this early. Come on in."

O'Keefe waited for the giant to move. He was not going to pass him, give the giant a chance to grab and crush him. The woman acted as if everything was just fine, but O'Keefe was not so sure. The blood . . .

"Roy is pelting, Mr. O'Keefe. Skinning. Mink."

O'Keefe acted like he knew that all along.

"Come in, and we'll show you how it's done. Come on, Roy."

Roy turned abruptly and lumbered into the room the woman had come from.

She smiled and held out a hand with five bright red fingernails for him to shake. "I'm Jane," she said.

"Is that Tarzan?"

Jane laughed, and he liked her as soon as she laughed. She was forty or close to it and rather pretty. She did not need as much makeup as she wore.

He followed her into a typical basement room that contained a typical basement workbench, except that blood was spattered all over it. On the floor O'Keefe saw three devastated piles: a pile of mink bodies with the fur still on; a pile of mink skins or furs, he didn't know what to call them; and a pile of skinned mink bodies, naked and desolate, exposed and violated.

"Show him how it's done, Roy."

Roy grabbed one of the still furry bodies and affixed it to a small machine on the worktable.

"That's a pelting machine," she said.

O'Keefe was not really paying attention. He hadn't come for this, and he wanted it to be over quickly. Roy operated a lever on the machine, and the machine neatly sliced and stripped the mink's fur from its body. Then Roy flung the fur onto its pile and the little naked bloody body onto its pile. It seemed to O'Keefe that a crime of some kind had just been committed.

"Interesting," he lied. "How much is that one worth?"

"Hardly anything," she said. "It's not a high-quality mink in the first place, and this isn't the pelting season. But it would just starve to death otherwise. We're running out of food. We're trying to keep the best ones alive as long as we can."

Roy grabbed another mink. O'Keefe turned away. The woman must have sensed his discomfort. She smiled, and it reminded him of a nurse's smile just before she pokes you with the hypodermic needle.

"Would you like to see the live ones?"

He nodded.

"Come on."

He followed her back through the hallway and the garage. The light blinded him for a moment when he walked out into the sun. He pushed the sleeves of his cotton sweater up to his elbows. It had turned into an Indian summer day. Roy had not accompanied them, which pleased O'Keefe immensely. He had started to tag along, but she had said, "Roy, why don't you go ahead and finish up the pelting and then clean up in here?" Roy complied, saying nothing, and O'Keefe wondered if the giant could talk. He followed her onto the dark path that led through the trees toward a hole of light, where the stand of trees ended. O'Keefe thought of Hansel and Gretel abandoned in the forest.

She stopped suddenly and turned around to face him, and he thought for a moment that she would start crying. "I'm afraid your investors aren't going to get much of their money back," she blurted. "Everything's mortgaged to the hilt. There's no money left, at least any that I know about."

"What happened to it?"

"I don't know. I really don't."

She turned around and started walking down the path again. They emerged from the grove of trees into a large field. The cages were built up off the ground and lined down the field in a series of long, parallel rows. There were more cages than he had expected, at least two hundred, he estimated, maybe more. He caught up to her and walked alongside her.

"About a year ago, Lenny started keeping the bank accounts to himself." She was still very troubled and seemed to be trying her best to give a complete answer to his question about the money. "I suppose it's the same old story. It just got frittered away. Houses, cars, jewelry, trips to exotic places. Lenny and Tag lived pretty high on the hog."

"Tag?"

"Lenny's wife. That's her name—'Tag.'"

"Funny name, huh?"

"If there was any money left, I guess Lenny took it with him. But I still can't believe he took off. It's not like him to do something like that."

"Maybe he didn't want to stay around to face the music."

"That's not it," she scoffed. "You don't know Lenny. That wouldn't have scared him a bit. He'd have explained it all away and probably sold the same people enough contracts to start another mink farm."

They were walking between two rows of cages that faced each other. More than half the cages were empty. From the occupied cages, small, dark creatures peered at them through the wire mesh that covered the doors. He peered back at them. The cages were quite large. A man could sleep in one of them if he tucked up his feet a little. The minks seemed to know what fate had in store for them—either starvation or Roy and his pelting machine. He had a strong urge to start opening the cage doors and set them free. *What the hell kind of people wanted to make their fortune off killing minks and skinning them?*

"The investors would travel down here. In their campers, mostly. The whole family. And he'd bring them down here to the cages. And he'd point to one of the cages and say, 'There, Mr. and Mrs. McGillicuddy, those are your minks, the very ones.' And then, a week later, he'd show Mr. and Mrs. Jones the same minks and tell them the same thing."

"So you knew what he was doing?"

"Is this for the record?"

He liked her and did not feel like lying to her. He lied to so many people. It went with the job.

"Maybe," he said.

"Who cares anyway? What can they get from me anyway?" She silently answered her own questions. The answers were "no one" and "nothing."

"I didn't really know the first couple of years what was going on," she continued. "The money just rolled right in here and rolled right back out again. For two years he paid them like clockwork. Incredible returns on their money. Double their money in a year sometimes. I know. I wrote the checks. Most of them were happy to reinvest it. Wouldn't you be?"

He said nothing, but yes, he would have been, and he remembered what Harrigan had said. "One born every minute. I bet they'll sell you a mink or two while you're down there."

"And who was I to figure anything out?" she asked herself. "Just a small-town girl not even smart enough to get out. The high school homecoming queen gone to plump. Do you believe that, Mr. O'Keefe? You're looking at the 1969 homecoming queen for Boondocks County Consolidated High School."

"Why shouldn't I believe it?"

She was growing too heavy and getting tired, but you could see in her face, in the large, round intelligent eyes, the pretty nose, the soft skin just above the freckles on her cheekbones, why they had crowned her their queen.

"Knocked up the night of the last football game. I never even graduated. Divorced now. Two kids. Stuck. Stuck in every way you can be stuck. So what did I know? But then I started understanding how damn little, really, the pelts brought when he sold them. I mean, these are real crappy minks, real inferior breeds. And the cost of feeding them is outrageous. And the way Lenny and Tag lived so high on the hog. Well, it became obvious, even to one such as me, that the place didn't even break even, let alone produce those incredible returns on investment."

"A Ponzi scheme."

"What's Ponzi?"

"Not a what, a who. It's the guy's name who invented the scheme. Back in the 1920s or something. You give your investors these fabulous profits. But it's not from the investment at all. It's from the money put in by new investors. But as you bring in more and more investors, you have to come up with more and more money to keep all those suckers happy. And there's only so many suckers out there, so it gets harder and harder to get new investors. And then, well, that's all she wrote."

"But what's funny is that Lenny really ran out of new investors a long time ago. A year ago or more. He just stopped selling.

I think he convinced himself he'd become a country gentleman or something. He fell in love with the farm and the lakes and the big house on the hill and the trips to Florida and Arizona. And he just stopped taking care of business."

"Florida and Arizona?"

"Yeah. Especially Arizona. Tucson or somewhere down that way. They loved it. Or at least Tag did. She's a horsewoman type."

"And no new investors in the last year?"

"Hardly any. Except for Mr. Canada."

"Who's that?"

"I don't know. I've never seen him, never talked to him, don't know his address, don't know his phone number. Lenny was real secretive about him. But he poured some bucks in here in the last year, I'll tell you that."

"Do you think Mrs. Parker knows who Mr. Canada is?"

"I doubt it. She always acted like she was too good for this Mickey Mouse farm and this Mickey Mouse town. As long as Lenny brought the money in, I don't think she cared where it came from."

O'Keefe stood in front of one of the cages, thinking about Mr. Canada and Lenny Parker and Lenny Parker's wife, the woman with the strange name. He looked at the half-starved mink inside the cage. It was afraid but did not cower. It paced back and forth at the rear of the cage, head to the front even as it turned to pace back the other way, muscles taut, always watching O'Keefe's and Jane's hands. It knew that it was the hands that killed. Its body seemed brave, even insolent. Only in its eyes could you see the fear. The eyes knew it was trapped, and doomed.

"Imagine that," he said. "All your life in a cage. Your destiny—screw your brains out until Roy comes after you with his pelting machine."

CHAPTER 7

ON THE WAY back to the house she kept talking, volunteering information. She appeared to be open and candid, withholding nothing, but she would be hiding something, and it would be O'Keefe's job to discover that hidden thing.

"I was here from the first," she said. "I helped remodel the house, build the cages, type the sales materials, everything. It was exciting. Most exciting thing this little burg had ever seen. Something special. Lenny and Tag just knocked the town off its feet. It was kind of like a fairy tale."

"Are any of the investors from around here?"

"I don't think so. He never tried to sell anything around here. He went out of his way not to."

Back in the basement Roy was busy pelting the last of the minks, and he did not bother to look up at them when they passed through the pelting area. His gut hung over his belt, but there was no fat on those arms.

O'Keefe followed her upstairs, and she showed him around. The kitchen had been redone in high-modern style. The front of the house had been transformed into office space. Lenny had a large office next to an even larger conference room.

"Do you have a picture of Lenny?" O'Keefe asked.

"I've got better than that. I've got a video of one of the investor seminars. You can see Lenny in action."

In the conference room she inserted a cassette into a VCR hooked up to a big-screen television. A man in his early thirties smiled at the camera and a room full of people. He stood next to a large American flag on a pole and a row of cardboard dollar signs as tall as the man himself. In front of the dollar signs was a stand holding flip charts. Like Anderson and Lufkin, the man had a small American flag pinned to the lapel of his suit. Lenny Parker was not handsome, he was pretty. His short hair looked like it never had to be combed. *He is more than clean cut*, O'Keefe thought, *he is razor cut*. The man on the TV smiled patronizingly at his audience. His smile told them that he understood, that he was harmless and loving, that he had only their best interests at heart, and above all, that he was sincere. "Such a nice young man," is what people would say about him.

"Is everybody here?" he asked sweetly.

O'Keefe's dislike of Lenny deepened considerably as soon as he heard his voice, which oozed a studied, cloying gentleness. It could have been a kindergarten Sunday school class. The voice soothed and coaxed. A close shot of Lenny. Soft, smooth skin, no flaw in his complexion. O'Keefe looked for the telltale flicker of a muscle in Lenny's face, but he could not find even a flicker, not even a hint of nervousness. O'Keefe tried to look into Lenny's eyes, but they revealed nothing. If the eyes are the windows to the soul, O'Keefe thought, Lenny Parker's soul was neither good nor evil, it was vacant. The only odd thing about the eyes was their brightness, brighter than they should have been—they proclaimed a triumph that had not been fairly won.

"You just can't know," Lenny said. "I can't find the words to express how much Tag and I appreciate you being here today. And you're not going to regret it either. Because a large number of the people in this room are going to embark today on the road to a new life of prosperity and freedom from financial cares. That's just a dream for most of the world. Most of the hard-working people of this country live a life of anxiety about their financial future . . ."

Jane hit the pause button on the remote control device.

"Do you want to hear the whole rigmarole or just the highlights?"

"Just the highlights."

She hit the "Fast-Forward" button and held it for a few seconds.

"How old is Lenny?"

"Lenny and Tag both turned thirty-three this year."

When she hit the "Play" button again, Lenny had folded his hands in front of him.

"The world's just turned its back on the simple things, the true things, the real things, the things that made this country great. What's happened to patriotism? To morality? To religion? To financial responsibility? And you know what I mean by that. I mean not spending more than you earn, whether you're a country or a family."

He had driven the last point home with his voice and a finger pointed at the audience. The applause was spontaneous, honest, loud.

"Look where people are investing their money today. The stock market, for example. Why, you might as well just go on out to Las Vegas and throw your money down on the craps table. Who knows what's going on in that stock market? Nobody. Not really. One day it's up, the next day it's down. Some guys come on TV in five-hundred-dollar suits and act like they know what's going on. But just ask them to predict what's going to happen the next day, let alone the next year. It's an open fraud, that's what it is. "What about Social Security? I don't even need to say anything about that, do I? The biggest con scheme ever foisted off on the American public."

The applause was louder than before, and a few people whistled and stomped their feet.

"How about company pension plans? Look what happened to the railroad workers. Look what's happening all over. They're going broke. They can't pay the benefits. These companies are making promises to the hard-working people of this country that they can't keep. And a promise you can't keep is a lie."

Heads in the audience nodded vigorously in agreement. One woman wept.

"How about your IRA? How about the money you've got in the bank? Well, those bankers are giving your money to every hustler that walks in off the street. They've given it to foreign countries. Billions of it. So we'll have to fight wars to ever collect it. Then you say, 'But Lenny, my deposits are insured by the full faith and credit of the United States government.' And I say, 'What faith? What credit?'"

Jane hit the "Fast-Forward" button again. The speeded-up film gave Lenny's presentation the flavor of one of those old silent-movie slapstick comedies. *This is how Lenny's pitch ought to be shown*, O'Keefe thought. The fast-forward dissolved the phony sincerity of Lenny's performance into farce.

Lenny had not yet told a lie, only a series of small truths that he manipulated to serve a larger, unspoken falsehood. The falsehood would be the next item on the agenda. Lenny brandished a pointer at various charts and graphs. He wore a Rolex wristwatch and a gold pinky ring with a big diamond embedded in it.

"You know, it's the simple things, the real things, the true things, the things we've turned our back on that are going to save us from the terrible predicament we've gotten ourselves into."

There had been sin and repentance. Soon the collection basket would be passed.

"That's why a mink contract is the best investment there is right now. That's why a mink contract is going to be the best investment ten years or twenty or thirty years from now too."

"All you've got going for you is . . ." Lenny paused to heighten the drama. "Nature! Imagine that. Nature itself on your side. The instinct of the mink is to breed, and breed, and breed some more. So you start out with just two minks. And those two aren't going to waste any time producing another six or eight. And what did it cost you to have ten minks all of a sudden? The price of some food and a few cages. And then those ten pair off. There are five pairs there, each producing six or eight more minks. And on and on. Geometric progression."

O'Keefe remembered that it was the fur trappers and traders who had first thrust into the virgin womb of the American West, standard-bearers of a new empire of insatiable growth and unlimited consumption, hacking their way through the helpless forests, slaughtering the wild, doomed creatures that sheltered there. It had been a miserable enterprise all in all, but there had been adventure in it. Their souls must have quivered in delight at the awesome spectacle presented continuously before them. Here were their descendants, there on the big-screen TV. They bred minks in cages and devoured them with pelting machines.

"And you don't have to wait for your money. Not like real estate or pension plans or Social Security or IRAs. You take some of those minks right away and sell the fur. And all of a sudden you've got your money back. And you've still got all these minks going on doing what Nature tells them to do."

Jane engaged the "Fast-Forward" button again. O'Keefe looked away. He did not want to watch this Keystone Cop anymore.

"Here's the big finale," she said.

The room was hushed. Lenny bowed his head. He seemed about to cry.

"My family . . ." Again, a long pause for effect. "We were so poor. And that was all right. For me, at least. Thank God for this country, where a poor boy still can be anything he wants to be. At least they haven't taken that away from us yet."

More applause. More bobbing heads, nodding in vigorous and wholehearted partnership with their deceiver. More women crying, wounded to the soul. Ah, the shameless perfidy of the system we live in!

"But my parents . . .well, it was different for them. They died in a welfare home. I was still too young and poor myself to be able to do anything for them. I was barely out of high school. I visited them every week though. And it was a terrible place. A filthy place. They never complained. But I could see it in their eyes. They died in want, and in despair."

Real tears glistened on his face. "They had worked so hard all their lives," he said, building to an anguished, raging climax. And then he shouted: "AND THAT WAS THEIR REWARD! TO DIE IN WANT AND IN DESPAIR!"

The tears stopped, and his voice became quiet and gentle again. "And I vowed right then and there to dedicate my life to helping the hard-working people of this country escape that terrible trap that my parents fell into in their dear old age."

"I've seen enough," O'Keefe said, trying to conceal his disgust.

"One more thing."

She fast-forwarded the tape for several seconds. Lenny still stood there talking. O'Keefe never wanted to hear Lenny speak again, unless in a courtroom with Harrigan mocking and savaging him on cross-examination.

"So those of you who are ready now to begin a new life of solid, real prosperity, you're welcome to come up here and sign right now. But first, remember, I told you I'd have a surprise for you. Remember, I told you to keep your ticket stubs?"

"Did the investors pay to go to those seminars?" O'Keefe asked in amazement. Jane nodded.

"Well," Lenny continued, "we're going to have a raffle, and guess what the prize is?"

He extended his left arm in presentation of something off camera. She walked into the picture wearing a full-length mink coat. The women in the audience sighed collectively in praise of the coat. O'Keefe nearly sighed himself, but not in praise of the coat. She smiled at the audience, but her eyes bore a message of cool disdain. She pirouetted like a fashion model. She was tall like a model but not so thin. Her long, lush hair made the coat look shabby by comparison. Completing her pirouette, she faced the audience again. She seemed to know what a tawdry exhibition this was, but she was a thing apart, and she knew that too. "You can't touch me, not really," she seemed to be saying. It may have been arrogance, or it may have been an admirable natural dignity, O'Keefe couldn't tell which. And he thought he detected another, more tender thing that seemed something like sadness. Her beauty lanced at his longing like a scalpel slitting open a vein. Watching her, he thought his heart might break. He tried to look into her eyes. Clear aqua pools, infinitely deep. There was something in the eyes he had seen before but could not identify now. Then she walked out of the picture without even saying goodbye.

CHAPTER 8

"THAT'S TAG," SAID Jane.

"You're kidding." That's what Lenny had called her on the video, but it seemed beyond impossible to O'Keefe.

Jane's laugh had a bitter edge. "She has that effect on everybody." She sighed and switched off the VCR.

"Extraordinary in every way," Anderson had said.

"Tell me about Mrs. Parker." He tried to make his curiosity sound professional in nature. Jane laughed that quick, bitter snort of a laugh again. "Maybe I should say 'no comment.' It will probably sound like sour grapes, but I don't like her."

"Why not?"

"I'm not really sure. It's not because she's haughty and stuck up, which she is. It's not because she's unfriendly, which she is. It's because . . . it's like there's no feeling there. She's ice. Dry ice. And she didn't love Lenny . . ."

Well, Tag, you can't be all bad then, O'Keefe thought.

"And he knew it too. The last conversation we had he started to cry and said, 'Jane, I've lost her. I've lost her.' And I wanted to tell him he was wrong. He didn't lose her. He never had her in the first place. You just can't have someone like Tag. She's self-sufficient. Like an island."

"Did she take off too?"

"No, she's still here. Selling everything as fast as she can." There was a moment of silence as they both thought about Tag. "Do you want to see the books and records now?"

"Yeah, but tell me about Lenny first."

"Well, I thought he was a sweet guy. I mean, he lied a lot, but he was still a sweet guy. Sort of helpless really. You just saw him do the only thing he could do. Me and Roy did the rest. But the last year or so he changed. You couldn't tell from one day to the next, sometimes from one hour to the next, what he was going to do or feel like. He was like . . . like Dr. Jekyll and Mr. Hyde."

He thought she might cry. Her secret had been easy to detect. She loved Lenny, and he had broken her heart. He guessed that she knew where Lenny had gone or that she had some way to contact him. If he could not coax that information from her over the next couple of days, he would tell Harrigan to take her deposition. She was the kind of person who would have difficulty lying under oath.

"How about those books and records?" he said.

"What do you want to see first?"

"The general ledger. Cancelled checks. Deposit slips. Do you have records of the investments and the investors?"

"I think so. Lenny handled all that at the end, and he may have taken some of it with him, but I'll show you what's still here."

After she brought the items he wanted, she stood beside him, hesitantly, as if she did not want to leave.

"If I have any questions, I'll take notes and ask you later," he said.

"Okay. I'll just go into the kitchen and have some coffee. Or maybe I'll go downstairs and talk to Roy."

"You mean the Incredible Hulk can talk?"

"He's not as bad as he looks."

"That's not saying much."

She smiled and walked away. *A good person*, O'Keefe thought. Lenny and his mink farm had given her a purpose in life, now both of them gone. Her future stretched out in front of her, empty and bleak. A part of her soul was dying.

The entries in the general ledger were cryptic and unrevealing. The larger deposits were labeled "investment" and sometimes "pelt sales." Sales of pelts had brought in far more money than O'Keefe would have predicted. He made a note to ask Jane about that. Were there receipts from the sales? If mink pelts brought in that kind of money, then it was a much more lucrative business than Harrigan had thought. But Harrigan was almost never wrong about such things. As Jane had told him, investments had declined precipitously in the last year, but the investments that had been made, apparently by this "Mr. Canada," were large amounts deposited every few weeks. He found a demand notice from a local bank threatening a lawsuit if certain loans were not paid in full immediately and made a mental note to go see the banker in the morning. The larger expenditures were labeled "farm improvements" and "mink purchases." There were thousands of dollars of expense reimbursements and many more thousands of dollars of "loans" to Lenny Parker. On the back of one deposit slip someone had scribbled the word "Angie's." He wondered about that but saw no other references anywhere to that name.

The cancelled checks did not tell him much either. The loans and expense reimbursements to Lenny and the payments to the investors had been made by check. Yet no checks to Mr. Canada. His business was cash-and-carry all the way. And a little more than a year ago Lenny had started making large cash deposits and withdrawals. Many of these were not described in the general ledger. Lenny could have been stashing cash, but why then why had he so carefully documented the "loans"? *Probably to seem honest,* O'Keefe thought. *Just like his sales pitch. Small truths in the service of a big lie.*

A separate ledger book showed the amounts contributed by investors and the returns paid to them. Anderson had a sheet. Lufkin had a sheet. Both had invested more than they had admitted to at Harrigan's office. He looked for Mr. Canada's sheet. It should have been there between "Calkins" and "Carswell," but that page had been clumsily ripped out.

JANE WAS SITTING at the kitchen table, smoking a cigarette and drinking coffee, when one of the lines lit up on the telephone in the kitchen. She tiptoed to the telephone and carefully lifted the receiver, which would make a small clicking sound on the other end of the line. She wondered how good a detective he really was and what he would do if he caught her listening.

"Hello," a woman answered on the other end of the line. It was Mary, Harrigan's wife.

"Is Mike there?"

"Who's calling?"

"It's Pete."

"Well, can't you say, 'Hello'?"

"Sorry, Mary. Too preoccupied, I guess."

"Everybody's too preoccupied. That's the trouble with the whole damn world."

"Hello, Mary."

"Hello, Pete."

If Mary expected O'Keefe to say something else, he was unable to oblige her.

"I'll get him," she said.

Jane heard the woman raise her voice and say, "Mike, it's for you. It's Pete."

Harrigan came on the line. He even had a speakerphone in his study at home. "Well, how much have you invested so far?"

"I think you've got a disaster here, Mike. No money in the bank. Everything's mortgaged to the hilt. There's a secretary here named Jane and a creature named Roy who helps around the place. Neither of them has been paid in a couple of weeks. Lenny's flown the coop with any money that was left. His wife's still here, but she's selling everything they owned. I imagine she'll be gone next."

"Can you tell anything from the books and records?"

"Not much. It was sort of cash-and-carry around here this last year."

"You mean Lenny was carrying off the cash."

"Looks like it."

"All right—here's what we do. I'll have the company in bankruptcy right away. That'll hold the bank off for a while. Do they have a mortgage on the minks too?"

"They sure do."

"You know what I tell my clients—never take collateral that eats."

"Well, this collateral isn't eating very well."

"So the bank'll have to cough up the money for the mink food to protect its collateral."

"Okay."

"I don't know if the judge will give it to me, but I'll try to get a restraining order against the wife to keep her from taking the money anywhere or spending it. We'll ask the judge to make her give us an accounting. She'll have to show us the money didn't come out of the mink farm. I guess we can't do anything about Lenny right now. We don't have enough on him yet to get the authorities interested enough to chase him into whatever hole he's crawled into. We'll have to find him and pry that money back out of him ourselves."

"Did you know that Lenny's wife is Ernest Anderson's daughter?"

"No. He didn't tell me that, the old fart."

Harrigan pondered in silence for a few moments, then said "Well, tough shit. It's the investors as a group we have to protect, not Anderson personally or his daughter either. Have you talked to her yet?"

"No."

"See if you can talk to her. She may be the only link to any money in this deal. Watch her. In fact don't take your eyes off her. Try not to let her get out of town until after tomorrow. Tell her Daddy sent you or something. If I get lucky, I'll have a restraining order by Monday afternoon. But if she gets out of town before we can serve the order on her, say 'sayonara' to her and the money too."

"Is one of your clients a 'Mr. Canada'?"

"Never heard of him. Funny name."

"He's got a bunch of money in this deal. All within the last year or so."

"How much?"

"I can't tell. Are you ready for this? The ledger sheet on him has been ripped out of the book."

"Well, this is getting real interesting, isn't it? Not the usual old humdrum stuff here. Why don't you go see the wife right now? And I know I don't have to tell you, but keep your eye on the money."

"Always."

Jane hung up the receiver as softly as she could and moved quickly back to the kitchen table. She just had time to pick up her coffee cup before O'Keefe came through the kitchen door.

"Finished already?"

"Not quite. Do you have a copy machine?"

"They repo'd it last week."

"I have to go talk to Mrs. Parker if she'll talk to me. But I've got to come back and take some notes. Can you wait for me?"

"Sure. I could use the overtime."

O'Keefe laughed with her. *She was made for joy,* he thought, *but life has furnished her something else altogether.*

FROM THE FRONT window of the house Jane watched O'Keefe pull out of the parking lot and down the driveway into the trees. She certainly had not been expecting someone like him. She did not remember now exactly what she had expected. A hard-bitten type, a down-at-the-heels type, a suave type, anything but him. He looked like a college kid with his lavender sweater, blue jeans, and topsiders. He had called her "Ma'am" though he was probably older than her. He seemed like a boy who had prematurely aged. And what was a detective doing with a van like that, a real cockwagon? His interrogation of her had been superficial, like he wanted to avoid putting her on the spot. Some kind of detective! But why shouldn't it end like it had begun, as a kind of comedy of errors, with not one person from beginning to end, from Lenny to O'Keefe, having the slightest idea what he was doing?

She walked into the conference room and looked at the ledgers and bank records he had been examining. Had they told him anything? Was there really any mystery to solve? It had just been a bad idea, not even really a fraud. Lenny and Tag had just frittered the money away. All those "loans." Well, she knew one thing. Lenny had sure not spent any of the money on her. The best she had rated was a weekend at the Marriott in St. Louis. And that had been early on. At the end the best she had rated was a few minutes on that couch over there, Lenny bucking and grunting on top of her. And if Tag had not kicked him out of bed at home, there probably would not even have been the couch.

For the last year Lenny had been nutty as a fruitcake. From one day to the next, Jane had not known where or even who he would be. Poor Lenny. His life had turned into a nightmare. When he had called last night, he had been super-paranoid again. He had wanted to know about everyone who had called or come by.

"Why don't you just come on back?" she had asked him. "You'll have them eating out of your hand again in a month."

"You don't understand," he had whined. "It's too late for that now."

"Come off it, Lenny," she had said in disgust. She was tired of his dramatics, his grandiosity, his paranoia. He had hung up on her then. She had cried. Maybe she was missing something. Maybe Lenny had reasons to be afraid that she did not know about. She remembered that the change in Lenny had begun about the same time Mr. Canada had started putting money into the place.

She sat down on the couch, her and Lenny's love nest. It had never been much, Lenny and the mink farm, but it was the best thing that had happened to her since way back in high school when she had let Randy screw her that night, even though she had known it was the worst possible time. From cheerleader to mother in nine short months. She did not want to remember what her life was like before Lenny and his mink farm had come to town. Hanging around at the local saloons, picking up men and bringing them home for the night. One night she had been huffing and puffing away in bed with one of them, only to look up and see Anna, her six-year old, standing at the bedroom door watching. At least Lenny and the mink farm had rescued her from all that. But it was ending now in the same way everything else in her life had always ended. She was a few years older and had nothing to show for it except a broader behind. She brought her upturned palms to her eyes and tried to press back the welling tears with the tips of her fingers, but she broke down and bawled like a baby. She stretched out on the couch and grabbed hold of the cushions, as if her grip on them was the only thing that could keep her holding onto the world at all. Just when she thought she would never stop crying, she fell asleep.

ROY CAME UPSTAIRS and found her lying there. His fat face folded into a frown as he studied the tears drying on her cheeks. He wanted to bend down and kiss her, but he was afraid to. He had fallen in love with her and had no idea what to do about it. He ought to go home, but there was nothing to do there. He decided to go down and look at the minks. He had never watched anything starve to death before. He kept wanting to let all of the minks out of their cages and back to the forest where they belonged. But he guessed that would be wrong, and they might do something bad to him if he did that.

WHEN JANE WOKE up, two men in white shirts and suits and ties were standing over her. They did not seem to mean her any harm. She thought, *Now these guys look like detectives are supposed to look.*

CHAPTER 9

LENNY AND TAG Parker had found the choicest spot in the county on which to build their dream house, at the end of a newly developed lake road, on a hill above the lake. There was not a neighbor within sight. A name, he guessed it was "Parker," had been recently stripped from the mailbox. A "For Sale" sign stood next to the mailbox with a smaller "Sold" sign pasted on the front of it. The house was fifty yards off the road. Approaching the house, O'Keefe could barely see its outlines through an imposing line of trees that obscured his view.

He parked in the driveway. The house looked unoccupied and seemed to disapprove of him in some way. He approached the front door warily, for he had been shot at more than once by the occupants of houses as magnificent as this one. An architect must have been paid well for designing it. It was a Colorado-style house, a flashy collage of redwood, fieldstone, and tinted glass. To his right the house bordered on the forest. To his left a portion of the field had been cleared and sodded and made into a tennis court. The clearing extended farther to his left and down a steep hill for another fifty yards, ending at a boat dock that rocked gently in the water. The boat slips were empty. "Selling everything as fast as she can," Jane had said. He wondered how much of this little palace had been paid for by the investors. *Well, dummy, all of it, of course.*

No one answered the door. He turned the doorknob and pushed, but it was locked. The door could be easily jimmied, but he thought better of that and walked back to the driveway where his van was parked in front of a three-car garage. Through the garage windows he could see a white Jaguar parked inside. He wandered around the side of the house along the edge of the tennis courts. The house was two stories in the back. There was a kidney-shaped swimming pool in the backyard.

He stood beside the pool on the edge of the patio, looking up at a huge deck that extended from the top story of the house. The house towered over him, grand looking but bleak in the late afternoon shadows. He thought of the beautiful, long-haired lady in the mink coat. Was she in there, watching him from one of the massive slabs of black-tinted window? *Rapunzel, Rapunzel, let down your long hair.* Or was it just the house itself staring down at him, its occupants gone or otherwise engaged?

He walked across the patio, cupped his hands around his eyes, and peered through a sliding glass door into a country kitchen. The appliances were built-in and costly, the Parkers having spared no expense, but all the kitchen furniture was gone. A fireplace at one end of the kitchen contained unburned logs sitting on an iron grate.

It would be easy to break in through the sliding glass door, but someone might be in there waiting to do grievous harm to an intruder. Or, if he were reported to the cops, he would be guilty of breaking and entering, a felony if the cops wanted to stick him with it. He had not committed a crime since he had become a private detective, in or out of the line of duty. *Just walk away,* he told himself, but he kept seeing that face and that hair and those eyes.

The felony took only a few seconds to commit, and then he was inside the kitchen opening a cupboard, which was bare. The refrigerator also was empty, recently cleaned, and no longer plugged in. A broad archway led into a room that had probably been a dining room. There were indentations on the carpet where furniture had recently stood. The fireplace in the dining room occupied the middle of an outside wall between two picture windows that displayed the tennis courts and the lurking forest beyond. Stairs climbed from the dining room to the next floor.

There was a room toward the front part of the house to his left, probably a living room. He would have to make a blind left turn into the room. The house creaked occasionally. Metal things knocked a little. Electric things whirred a little. He considered going back to the van and getting one of his guns.

He darted his head around the wall of the dining room and quickly pulled it back again. No one could hit a target that was so small and moved so fast. But there was no one there anyway, just a couple pieces of furniture, an Eames chair, and an oriental panel, which made the room look even more forlorn than the empty rooms had looked. Little paper labels hung on both pieces of furniture that said, "Sold to Dean Doggett." *What a name to be stuck with*, he thought. *Dean's nickname would surely be "Hot."* There was another fireplace in this room. Lenny and Tag Parker had a thing about fireplaces.

He bounded up the stairs as fast as he could, prepared to dive right back down them if he had to. Upstairs he saw an open door that led into a master bedroom at the back of the house. The bedroom gave way onto a deck, which was above the tree line and had a view of the lake and the wooded hills beyond. He was not surprised to find another fireplace in the bedroom, but he was surprised to find a bed with several pieces of luggage on it including a large backpack and a strapless purple sundress laid out for someone to come and put on. Above, you would be able to see her bare shoulders, below would be her long, lean legs. She would look especially good in this dress and the luggage too. She was leaving soon or had been planning to anyway.

The bathroom off the master bedroom was larger than his bedroom at home. It had "His" and "Her" showers and a Jacuzzi on a raised platform. *The House That Mink Built*, he thought. Condensation dripped down one of the frosted shower doors. Someone had very recently taken a shower.

Back in the bedroom was a set of double doors that would lead, no doubt, into a large closet. He put his ear to the crack where the doors came together and listened, trying to open his mind and body to detect any presence within. He felt nothing. He grabbed the door handles and swung the door open as fast as he could.

Pain exploded in his left arm, but there was no noise, so he had not been shot. Someone had stabbed him in the arm and pushed him violently back into the room at the same time, and that someone, wearing nothing but a man's shirt that hung down to her thighs and armed with some small metal object, was coming after him, slashing at him with one hand and scratching at him with the other. When he fell backward, she leapt on top of him and tried to drive that small metal object through his left eye into his brain. He raised his arms in defense, and the small metal object gouged a small trough in his left arm. Exerting all his strength, he rolled her over and pinned her arms to the floor.

She kicked and squirmed furiously for a few moments, then abruptly stopped and lay still. He lay on top of her, between her spread-eagled legs, his forehead and nose buried in the carpet, his lips touching her neck. Later, he remembered how soft she was even as she struggled with him there on the floor. When he lifted his head to look at her face, her eyes danced and flickered like a flame in the wind.

"I'm not going to hurt you. Your father sent me."

She tossed her eyes and head, indicating his hands still pinning down her arms. "Do you mind?" she said.

O'Keefe let go of her, grabbing the scissors as he did. They stood up. He could not help but stare at the creature trembling in fear before him, eyelids rapidly blinking, a patina of sweat on her forehead and temples, the ends of her hair matting into the sweat, her bare feet gripping into the carpet, poised to spring at him if she had to, toenails and fingernails painted the palest shade of pink, crease of muscle at the side of her calf, tiny blue splotch of varicose vein beneath the skin on the inside of her thigh.

"Do you think Daddy would mind if I got dressed? Or did he tell you to watch?"

"Give me your car keys."

Her eyes told him to go straight to hell, but she was not ready to defy him yet. When she reached down to extract the keys from her purse on the bed, the shirt hitched up a little, and he tried to look away. She dug around in her purse for the keys. When she found them, she handed them over, grabbed the sundress, and headed for the bathroom.

"Wait for me out on the deck," she commanded, as if control of the situation had now suddenly shifted to her.

The deck was the only fully furnished part of the house, but there were labels on most of the items like those on the furniture downstairs. A powerful-looking telescope pointed at the sky.

An old-fashioned hot tub was situated such that its occupants would have a perfect view. A heavy, wooden lid leaned against the tub. He sat down in a white canvas director's chair and appreciated the scenery.

She came out barefoot in the sundress, sat down in the chair next to him, crossed her ankles, and propped them on the chair across from her as if it were a footstool. The purple sundress hung flouncy and loose except where it gathered under her breasts. She had brushed back her hair, which hung far down her bare back. Golden hoops hung gypsy-like from her ears. Her face reminded him of a white coral shell he had found once on a shoreline in Martinique, each line and feature sharply defined, no confusion anywhere in its delicate structure. He had to take his eyes away from her, out toward the lake, to keep from staring.

"This must be nice," he said.

"It is. It was. You can see every star in the sky out here."

"Are you an astronomer?"

"Sort of. A stargazer anyway." But she was quickly through with small talk. "What's my father want besides his money?"

"He sends his love."

"That's love all right. A man who breaks into my house."

"I'm a private investigator hired by some of the investors, including your father, to find out what's going on down here. To find out what's happened to their money."

The skin below her aqua eyes crinkled into little lines of pain. Her throat rippled as she swallowed hard. She locked her hands together and pressed them down on her stomach as if to hold herself down in the chair.

"You'll have to ask dear Lenny that question," she said.

"It looks like some of that money may be right here. This little palace. The Jag in the garage. All of the furniture gone. Did you have a little yard sale?"

"What's your name?"

"Peter O'Keefe. But . . ."

"'But I can call you Peter, right?"

"Actually, it's 'Pete.'"

"Well, Mr. O'Keefe, if you think those investors have a claim on me, I'll give you a hundred bucks right now, and you can take it and march right down to the courthouse and file a lawsuit. Otherwise, I suggest you vanish. Before I call the sheriff and have you arrested for burglary."

"Tough."

"I'm not tough at all, but nobody's gonna push me around anymore."

"Somehow I can't see anybody pushing you around."

"Well, you're wrong."

She tossed her head like she was trying to shake off a bad memory. "All my life I've just been a wisp, waiting for the wind to blow me somewhere, going along with whoever happened to be pushing or pulling me at the time. First your client, my father. Then Lenny. And look where I end up. Well, it's my life from here on. Whatever happens, it'll at least be mine. And nobody—not Lenny, not my father, not you, or your investors—is gonna take it away from me again."

"Do you know where Lenny is?"

She shook her head "No."

"Have you been out to the ranch?" she asked.

He shook his head "Yes."

"Was Jane there?"

He nodded again.

"Ask her where he is. He's been screwing her for two years now."

"She says he's madly in love with you."

"Well, if he is, the feeling's not mutual and hasn't been for a long time. I woke up one morning and realized I was living with a ferret. He's slept in a separate bedroom ever since."

"Who's 'Mr. Canada'?"

He was looking right into her eyes, and they changed, clouding with doom. Again he wondered where he had seen those eyes before.

She recovered quickly. "Lenny's mystery investor. I don't know anything about him."

"Did he ever come here?"

"Never. Lenny always went to see him."

"Where?"

"He never would say."

"Is 'Mr. Canada' his real name?"

"I always thought it was some kind of a code name, but like I told you, I don't know him or anything about him."

"Are you leaving soon?"

"How about tonight? I'm gonna get in that Jag and just drive. See the country."

He thought of the Bob Seger song.

"*Roll Me Away*," he said.

She understood him. "You've got it," she said and smiled. It was the first time he had seen her smile. Was she the tough bitch she sometimes talked like or the other person that the smile revealed? Probably both.

He remembered some of the lyrics of the song:

"Rolled across the high plains
Deep into the mountains
It felt so good to me
To finally feel free"

He wished she would take him with her.

She was looking out at the lake. "I loved this place," she said. "For a long time I really believed it was real. What a dope."

The wind kicked up, shaking the leaves on the trees and blowing some of her hair into her face. When she brushed her hair back, O'Keefe was staring at her again, his visage mournful.

"What's with you, Mr. O'Keefe?"

"I've seen it a hundred times. People think they can buy their dreams cheap and easy, and usually with somebody else's money."

"So you're a social critic as well as a burglar," she said. "Well, one thing I know is real is the sunset here. I'm gonna see it one last time. Tonight. Alone. And then I'm gone."

He remembered Harrigan's instructions not to take his eyes off her and decided to at least give it a try.

"Why don't you let me buy you dinner on your way out of town?"

"Now, why would you want to do that, Mr. O'Keefe?"

"I don't know. Because I like you. Because you're the best-looking lady in the county, I am very sure. Because I was always a sucker for a damsel in distress. Take your pick."

"Here's what I pick. You want to keep me under your watchful eye. So I won't get away with the money, money I don't have by the way."

"I have to go back to the ranch to take some notes on the books and records. Then I'm off duty. Then I owe nothing to anyone except you. At six o'clock I change into whatever you want me to be."

He didn't know whether he was lying to her or betraying Harrigan. He was thoroughly confused.

"Don't kid me. I have a feeling you're the type that's never off duty. I'm gonna pass on the dinner, Mr. O'Keefe. What I'm gonna do instead is put as much distance between me and this place and you and your investors as I possibly can."

He struggled to stay in the game, "How about telling me where you're heading? Maybe I can meet you somewhere along the way." *Lame, lame, lame,* he thought.

"You're too obvious, Mr. O'Keefe. I wouldn't tell you where I was going even if I knew."

"That's too bad."

"And much as I hate to break off such a promising relationship, it's time for you to go. Goodbye, Mr. O'Keefe."

She stood up and looked down on him tenderly, as if pitying him. When she extended her hand to shake his goodbye, he held it for a moment. A confident hand, smooth and surprisingly strong. And for a moment he thought he had won her, but she caught herself and pulled her hand from his grasp.

"Anything you want me to tell your dad?"

"Yeah. Tell him to get the hell out of my life and leave me alone. Tell him he's got no hold on me anymore."

"You know what's funny? I think I might have been telling you the truth about the dinner, about being what you want me to be after six o'clock. Too bad it didn't work out."

"Too bad," she said matter-of-factly.

He started to walk away.

"Haven't you forgotten something?"

He looked innocently back at her.

"My keys."

He smiled and pulled the keys out of his pocket. She stood with her hand out, indicating he should throw them across the deck to her, which he did. She caught them with a swift, supple move of her arm and watched him leave.

DRIVING BACK TO the mink farm, he kept thinking about the long-haired lady in the modern-day castle on the hill. He could do nothing to stop her from hitting the road in that Jag. Following her all over the country was out of the question. He had no evidence of any wrongdoing that would interest the police. She could disappear for a while, but he and Harrigan would be able to find her if they wanted to. Everybody left a trail. All you needed was the money and the time to track them down. He had the feeling he would see her again, wanted badly to see her again, but if he did see her again, he would certainly find her in a very bad spot, and he indulged in a moment of traitorous hope, for her sake, that she would make good her escape. Hell, if she had given him half the chance, he would have gotten in that Jag and rolled away with her. Yet he suspected her bid for freedom was doomed from the start. You just can't buy your freedom with other people's money.

As he passed the Prosperity Farms sign, he hardly noticed a dark car speed by with two men inside it.

"WHO DO YOU think that was?" asked the man sitting on the passenger side of the car.

The man driving was getting fed up with his short, fat companion who had body odor and was always asking stupid questions.

"How the fuck do I know?" he responded. "It's probably some kid and his chick heading out to hump all night in that van."

"It wasn't a local license plate. I'll bet whoever it is, is going to that farm. Should we go back?"

"Don't have time. We've got to pay the wife a visit and get the fuck outta here."

"Think she'll be home?"

Dumb questions. Nothing but dumb questions from Fat Boy. Yet the driver couldn't help himself but wonder whether maybe they ought to go on back to the farm and check out the guy in the van.

CHAPTER 10

HIS LEFT ARM hurt where Tag had stabbed him with the scissors. The instrument was too blunt to have done much damage, but it had gouged a nasty little hole in his upper arm and carved a painful gash across his lower arm. He had not bled much, but his sweater was ruined, and he worried about tetanus.

He tried the front door, which was locked, so he went around back again.

"Anybody home?" he yelled as he passed from the garage into the basement hallway.

"Jane? Roy?"

Roy had not obeyed Jane's instruction to clean up the pelting room. Little gobs of mink fur were embedded in the drying clots of blood on the floor and worktable. The pelts were gone, but the pile of skinned mink bodies still festered on the floor. He left the basement and garage and climbed the back stairway. The door to the kitchen was unlocked. There was a brown-spattered cup on the kitchen table and an ashtray with three cigarette butts in it. Jane's lipstick had impressed a thin red circle around the snow-white filter tips. He pushed open the swinging door that led from the kitchen into the front part of the house. He called to her, but it was obvious no one was in there. The vehicles were still out front, so she and Roy must be doing something down at the mink cages.

Someone had closed the double doors that opened onto the conference room. "Anybody there?" he said loudly as he knocked. He waited, listening; then he turned the doorknobs and pushed open the doors. The books and records were not on the table where he had left them. Everything else was in order. Except a smell that he remembered from somewhere. Vietnam. The men in the back of the helicopter. Blood. Then he saw Jane's foot dangling lazily off the lower end of the couch. The conference room table blocked his view of the upper end of the couch where her head would be.

"Jane?" he said as he walked slowly toward the couch. His conscious mind had not fully accepted it yet, but somewhere he knew she would not answer, could not answer. She lay there as if she had gone to sleep, but her jeans and underpants were pulled down to her shins. The turtleneck shell she wore was pushed up to her neck. Her heavy breasts sagged sideways in a kind of defeat. They were smeared with the blood that had gushed from her throat. The cut was so deep it had nearly severed her head.

The ultimate pornography, he would think later as he reflected in horror on this moment, worse than anything he had seen in the war. He tried not to look into the eyes that still bulged in terror, and he remembered the last thing he had thought about her before he had left for Tag's house. That she had been made for joy. And here she was, not just dead but hideously befouled. How horrible must have been those last moments of her life. The thought came to him that had come to him so many times. *It really isn't over 'til it's over. You're never safe until the very end.*

The dirty sonuvabitch, he thought. And he realized he had made a decision. He would gladly kill him if he had to. Roy. The beast with the pelting knife. Jane had been just another mink to him. He wheeled around. Where was the bastard hiding, gripping his bloody knife? O'Keefe ran for the front door of the house.

Roy was not outside. Both vehicles were still there. O'Keefe threw open the side door of the van, jumped in, and hit the button that gave entrance to the concealed panel where his weapons were hidden. He chose the M-16 because he wanted to shoot Roy while the hulking brute was still a long way from him. He rammed an ammunition cartridge into the bottom of the black plastic rifle, which looked and felt like a toy in his hands. The automatic weapon was illegal, but he wanted every edge he could get. It would pump a blizzard of steel at its target. He had not had to use this weapon since Vietnam, but he welcomed the opportunity to use it right now.

There was the barn on his left and the stand of trees in front of him. Roy would be with his other victims, the minks. O'Keefe loped toward the stand of trees and the cages beyond. As he got closer, he could hear the minks squealing and scratching at the sides of their cages. It sounded like terror. He did not take the path but headed into the undergrowth. The dry fallen leaves and desiccated twigs snapped beneath his feet. If anyone was waiting for him on the other side of the grove, they would hear him coming. A few yards from the tree line, he was able to see the field and the cages, but there was no visual evidence of disturbance. The only place anyone could hide was a small shed on the far side of the rows of cages where the mink food was kept.

He crashed out of the tree line, running as low to the ground as he could, and hit the deck at the first row of cages. When he hit the hard ground stomach first, it knocked some of the wind out of him. He could see underneath all of the cages. The only place Roy could be hiding was the shed.

He got up and walked down a row of cages toward the shed. He held the rifle in the ready position at chest level. One gentle squeeze of the trigger would propel five missiles of death toward the target. He was surprised that he had no fear. *Come on, Roy, you bastard, you sonuvabitch*, he kept saying to himself.

As he walked down the row of cages toward the shed, he could see in the periphery of his vision the minks scampering from side to side in their cages. The shed was only a few yards away now. It was padlocked. Roy could not have locked himself inside the shed. Fatal mistake? Roy must be behind him. He whirled and fired a burst that whistled down the row of cages and crashed harmlessly into the trees. Roy was not behind him. But O'Keefe had seen him when he had whirled around. And there Roy was, right next to him, in the cage, staring at him upside down, a bullet hole in the middle of his forehead. Someone had shot him and stuffed him inside one of the empty cages.

Confusion.

Roy had not raped and killed Jane. Someone had killed them both. He remembered the missing books and records. The mink in the cage next to Roy stood against the back wall, head down, back up, furious, snarling, trying to scare O'Keefe off. But it was merely a gesture. The mink knew it was trapped and at O'Keefe's mercy.

Tag Parker. Someone had killed Jane and Roy and taken the books and records. That someone might be after Tag Parker too.

He ran to the farmhouse. On the front desk there was a Rolodex. His hands shook as he flipped through the Ps, looking for "Parker." No card for the Parkers. He flipped to the Ls. The Parkers' number was typed on the card that said, "Lenny." He picked up the phone to dial the number. The farmhouse line was dead.

He ripped the index card out of the Rolodex and bolted for the van. He called her on the portable phone in the van. On the fifth ring his heart sank. Was she unwilling to answer the phone or unable to? He thought of Jane lying back there on the sofa. Was Tag lying that way too? He nearly sobbed in desperation, thinking of a sharp knife against that soft neck. Something awful had been let loose in the peaceful countryside. He let the phone ring on and on. He wouldn't hang up until he got there. It was a long way. He could call the cops, but he did not want to struggle with the police bureaucracy. He would get there before the cops could. He missed a curve. The wheels on the right side thudded onto the soft narrow shoulder, and the rear of the van swerved right toward a deep ditch at the side of the road. *I always turn the wrong way when this happens. Turn into the skid, however wrong that seems.* He got lucky this time and somehow wrestled the car back onto the road.

She picked up on the eleventh ring.

Before she said a word, he barked, "This is O'Keefe."

"You're interrupting my last sunset."

"I hope it's not your last. Jane and Roy are dead. Murdered."

"What?"

"Just now. Whoever did it might be calling on you next. Call the cops as soon as I hang up. Don't try to leave. They could be watching the house, waiting for you to come out. Find a place in there to hide. A better place than the closet. Do you have a gun in the house?"

"This is a crock, O'Keefe. I don't believe you."

"You'd better believe me."

She hung up on him. The sun had dipped below the hills on the far side of the lake. The lake was black and churlish, the darkening hills purple, the sky a pinkish blue. She did not believe him, but he was obviously headed her way, and she did not want to be around when he showed up. If he wasn't lying, there would be police, and she did not want to be around when they showed up either. She should have left earlier. It seemed like she always lingered too long.

SHE HAD JUST wrestled one of the big suitcases into the trunk of the Jag when she saw it through the trees. A dark car driving slowly by. It moved up the road out of sight. The road ended not far beyond the house. The car would turn around and come back. She waited for it to return. It didn't. She could jump in the Jag right now and get the hell out of there, but the other luggage was still upstairs. She could do without the hang-up bag and the bigger suitcase but not the backpack.

From the dining room she saw the men standing at the edge of the woods behind the tennis courts. She was exposed to their view, but she did not run for the stairs. She froze. Could they see her through the tinted windows? O'Keefe had not been lying. These men had come to harm her.

The men were looking right at her, but they could see only the dark tint on the windows.

"You think she's in there?" asked the little fat one, whose name was Otto.

"How the fuck do I know? You go around back. Find the phone line and cut it. Get in the back way. Kill her if she's there. I'll be around front if she comes out that way."

Karl, the driver and the taller of the men, moved off toward the front of the house and the little fat one toward the back.

They were not looking at her anymore, so she ran up the stairs. She had just finished dialing 9-1- when the phone died. She looked around. There was the bed, and there was the closet. Then she heard the little fat man down below, breaking into the house.

CHAPTER 11

FUCKIN' SWEAT, OTTO thought, as he stood at the top of the stairway trying to catch his breath. *Fuckin' sweat's pourin' outta me.* He pointed his pistol down the hallway at the partly shut bedroom door. *That's where she is.* She would be cowering in there, terrified. He would eliminate her as nonchalantly as he had dispatched the other one. This one was supposed to be a real sexy babe, and the idea of putting the meat to her excited him. It could be before he snuffed her, or after, it didn't really make any difference. He kicked the bedroom door open. Luggage on the bed. He looked under the bed. He looked in the closet. Nothing.

The glass shower doors in the bathroom were those frosted jobs that you couldn't see through. *That's where the little pussy is. Dumb bitch. She must not have seen* Psycho. *Well, I'll scare her so much she'll piss herself.* He leveled the pistol at the door and pressed the trigger. The bullet whooshed through the silencer attached to the front of the gun, the gun jerked upward in his hand, and the shower door exploded.

But she wasn't in there. He exploded the door to the other shower too, but she wasn't in there either.

The glass sliding door that led onto the deck was open. He looked. Nobody there. Some fancy-looking chairs. A thing that looked like a bazooka; no, it was a telescope. Across the deck one of those hot tubs things covered with a lid. *Nice setup.* He walked over to the hot tub. The top of it reached just above the level of his chest. You had to climb up little wooden steps to get into the thing. There were holes in the top of the lid to help you lift it up and off. His arms were so short he could barely reach the holes. He leaned forward against the tub and tried to plant his feet into the deck for leverage. The water sloshed back and forth against the sides of the tub when he leaned against it. He put the fingers of both hands into the holes and lifted. The lid came up a little but fell back again. He was out of breath. *And sweating again like a whore in church.* A sinew in his heart had seemed to pop when he had tried to lift the lid. *What the fuck am I doing? No broad could lift this lid, and the fuckin' thing's full of water anyway.*

KARL LOOKED PISSED when Otto opened the front door for him, but nothing new about that. He was always pissed. And he never sweated.

"I checked the whole house," Otto said. "Nobody home. Hardly a stick left. But there's luggage packed and ready to go upstairs."

"And a Jag in the garage," Karl said as he brushed by Otto and charged into the living room where he stopped and stood looking at the Eames chair and the oriental panel.

"So if she's going somewhere," he said more to himself than to Otto, "she'll be coming back for her stuff."

"Where could she go without a car?"

"How the fuck do I know? Maybe she's got another car. Maybe she's gone for a walk. Maybe she's hiding and you didn't find her."

"Ah, get off my ass for just a fuckin' minute, will ya?"

A rhetorical question thought Karl. "Make that Jag not work anymore. I'll be upstairs."

HOW STUPID TO hide in this damn thing, Tag was thinking. But there had been nowhere else. Certainly the closet hadn't worked so well with O'Keefe. She had been able to slide the heavy lid off the floor and up the side and partly over the top of the tub. Then she had lugged the backpack behind her up the narrow and steep wooden steps. There were steps inside the tub too. The tub was about half-full of water. She had managed to place the pack on the top step, then maneuver the lid across the top of the tub until it had dropped into place, leaving just enough room just enough room for her head once she bent it to the side a bit. Her sundress billowed outward and upward and floated just beneath the water's surface.

When the stubby chunk-ends of Otto's fingers had wriggled down at her through the holes in the top of the lid, she might have screamed, but her breath had abandoned her lungs, and she had only hoped he could not hear her gasping and gagging, choking on the fear. The plump fingers had hooked onto the underside of the lid above her. The water had sloshed from side to side when Otto had leaned against the tub. She had heard him grunt when he pulled up on the lid. Then the miracle. The fingers had gone away. Now she wanted out of that thing. It was like being buried alive in a well. Slowly, inch by inch, she pushed up the lid until she could see the glass sliding door. A movement. In the bedroom. She let the lid drop. It made a thudding sound. She waited for someone to come and open the lid.

KARL THOUGHT HE heard a noise on the deck. He walked to the sliding door and looked out. Nothing there. Squirrels, maybe. He turned back to the luggage. He opened the hang-up bag and big suitcase and rifled through them, strewing their contents about the room. None of the contents interested him, although he had the cynical thought that maybe he should save a pair of her panties for the little pervert downstairs. He checked for false bottoms and hidden compartments. Nothing.

He walked out onto the deck. Night would fall soon. The lake looked dark and choppy. He liked lakes. He wished he owned a boat, one of those hundred-thousand-dollar Scarabs that looked like fiberglass sharks. But that was out of the question. You couldn't show off your earnings from his line of work. He turned to watch Otto come out onto the deck, walk over to the hot tub, and sit on one of the lower steps. *Fat fuck. Fat, little, perverted fuck.* Karl had come back into the farmhouse after he had dealt with the big guy down at the mink cages and had found this fat little fuck standing over her, hurriedly pulling up his pants as she finished drowning in her own blood. *What a scumbag.* The Boss was really slipping, bringing in a guy like this for the job.

Now Fatso rubber-necked around, appraising the scene. "This must be nice," he said, gesturing around the deck and ending at the hot tub behind him. "You think that babe gets naked in this thing?"

"Did you look in there?"

"Sure did," Otto said, hoping his face was not revealing the lie. He hurried on: "No pussy in there, just water. What's next?"

"How the fuck do I know? Let's get outta here."

Karl was worrying about the guy in the van. If the guy in the van had really been going to the farm, and if he had found the bodies, the cops might be after them already. But to have found the bodies, the guy in the van would have had to break into the house to find the woman and gone nosing around the mink cages to find the big guy he had stuffed in the cage. Not likely. Parker's wife should be back any time. It would be best to move out of the house and over into the woods and watch the house from there so they would be close to the car if anything funny happened.

"Why don't we wait right here for her?" Otto inquired. "I could use a little dip in the tub here."

"You're a real jackoff, aren't ya?"

Fatso just smiled.

"Let's go," Karl said, and the little man scooted off after the big one.

As they crossed the big lawn in the back of the house, "Say, Chauncey, how 'bout a spot of tennis?" Otto joked.

Then they heard a car coming and hightailed it for the trees. Karl crouched down just inside the tree line and watched the front of the house. Otto stood behind him, looking over the taller man's shoulder.

"It's that van," Fatso said. "What the fuck is going on?"

"How the fuck do I know? Just watch."

The van was going so fast that its back wheels flew off the ground when it hit the little bump that separated the driveway from the road. O'Keefe hit the brakes, and the van screeched and skidded to the right, whipping into a spin. It would have turned completely around the other way except the rear end banged against the garage door, stopping the spin. He jumped out of the van and bounded into the house through the unlocked front door.

Otto's eyes bulged. Life was full of surprises. "Look at that God-damned rifle, will ya? Did ya see that God-damned thing? An M-16. Told ya we shoulda gone back to that farmhouse."

Karl buried his elbow in Otto's gut and told him to shut up. Karl was trying to think, and he couldn't think with that fat, little, perverted fuck firing questions and accusations at him. Life always dealt its wild cards, sometimes to you, sometimes to the other players, and the guy in the van was a wild card. *Was the guy some kind of local cop? No. Cops don't carry M-16s. Maybe I should take Fatso and sneak up to the house and blast the guy when he comes back out. But the guy's toting that God-damned M-16. And Fatso's about as useless as tits on a nun. Except for killing women, Fatso excels at that. Maybe we should just get the fuck out of here. No. Just sit tight and don't do anything stupid. Let events develop and take advantage of whatever opportunities come our way.*

O'KEEFE TOOK ONE careful step after another down the upstairs hallway toward the open bedroom door, the M-16 leading the way. Her luggage had been trashed and her things thrown around on the floor. She was nowhere to be found, but the Jag was still downstairs in the garage. Someone must have dragged her off, probably into the woods. Mortar rounds kept exploding in his head. He couldn't seem to see very well. He thought he might fall down. *There's a bed right there, sit down if you can.* He would not go looking for her. He had seen enough death for one day. Despite his line of work, he had not seen death like that since Vietnam. What a beautiful thing she had been. Gone. No telling what they had done to her. Grieving, that's what he was doing. He had fallen a little in love with her though he hadn't known her at all. He wanted to scream or at least yell, and he did. "God damn!" he kept yelling and pounding the bed. He wished he could cry, but the pain was too much, it stifled the tears. Whatever was on the loose out there, it was way bigger than he, the foolish pilgrim O'Keefe. He picked up the telephone to call the cops. Another dead phone line. He would go to the van and call them. Then he, the witness, would wait. But what was it he had witnessed? Like 'Nam—most of the action was over by the time O'Keefe and the helicopter arrived. Just the bodies to be policed up now. No explanations, no meanings, just casualties.

The call to the cops would make it official, bringing this misadventure to a very dead end. And suddenly he felt very weary. He didn't know whether he had the strength to make the short journey down the stairs, out of the house, and to the van. Maybe he would just sit here for a few minutes. Watch the sun finish setting, say a prayer for the dead. He wished there was a God somewhere for him to pray to. He wondered if people still paid the priests to say Masses for the deceased. If so, when he got back to the city, he would buy one for Tag, and Jane too, and even Roy, who couldn't help his looks after all, or the vicious vocation he had fallen into. He recalled how he had hated being an altar boy at funerals, even though the grieving relatives had always paid the boys a little something, even though the choir singing the *Dies Irae* had made him feel in his young soul all the power and majesty of even a common man's life and death.

Then O'Keefe witnessed a resurrection of sorts. The lid came up off the hot tub and Tag stood wobbling uncertainly in front of him. Her dress and hair were sopping wet. She seemed to be in some kind of pain, but he could not remember ever being happier. He stared at her.

"I need help," she said, barely more than a whisper.

He rushed to help her.

"I can hardly stand up," she said. "I don't know if I can climb out."

What's she doing with that damn pack inside that thing? She seemed reluctant to part with the pack for even a second, instinctively tugging back at it in resistance when he grabbed it from her to set it down on the deck. He put his hands under her arms and lifted her out of the tub, soaking his own clothes in the process.

She kept her grip on his shoulders when he set her down on the deck. "Hold onto me," she said. "My legs are asleep."

He would hold on as long as she wanted. Her face, only inches away from his lips, showed her emotions. Fear. And another thing. Cunning.

"There're two men," she said, "and I think they're still around here somewhere."

"Let's get outta here then. Are you okay? Can you walk now?"

"I think so," she said, taking a couple of faltering steps, reaching for the backpack.

"Forget the damn pack."

But she picked it up anyway

She followed him down the stairs and through the house. He could not see very much out of the small peephole built into the front door.

"I think they're in the woods," she whispered. "Across from the tennis courts."

He turned, and she looked up at him, waiting for instructions, like a child looks to its father for guidance and protection. Her life was in his hands, but he was probably as afraid as she was. The war all over again. He wanted to reach out and embrace her, hold her until the danger passed for both of them.

"I'll go out first," he said. "When I say 'go,' you run like hell for the van. Dive in and get into the back as fast as you can. . . . and leave the damn pack."

He jumped out the door, and pressed the trigger of the M-16, spraying rounds in an arc from left to right. When he completed the arc, he was facing the woods on the other side of the tennis courts.

"Go!" he barked, and she ran for the van, too slowly, weighed down by the pack. He emptied the bullets from the rifle into the woods, then turned and ran after her. She struggled to climb into the van. The pack had wedged against the steering wheel. He pushed her in, and the backpack went in behind her. Then he pushed her again and sent her sprawling into the back of the van.

THE MEN IN the trees had decided to eat some dirt when the bullets started crashing around them. They did not look up even when the rifle stopped firing, not until they heard the van door slam and the tires squeal as O'Keefe peeled out of the driveway.

"Let's go," said Karl.

Otto wanted to ask what they were going to do now but thought better of it.

O'KEEFE PRESSED THE accelerator to the floor and wished he was driving something that would move much faster and negotiate curves much better than this clumsy-ass van. He glanced back and saw her stripping off the sopping-wet sundress.

"Don't look," she said.

He thought of Jane. And Roy. Jane and Roy were dead, and she was back there blithely changing her clothes. He listened to her move around in the back, cloth sliding on and off of her.

"Are you done?" he asked through clenched teeth when she stopped moving around.

"I'm done."

He thought of Jane again. He intended to pry the truth out of this Mrs. Lenny Parker right now. Keeping one hand on the wheel, he reached back, grabbed her arm, and yanked her into the front seat. She cried out. Her head banged against the dashboard. She untangled herself, leaned back against the passenger-side window and held her shoulder, her jaws clenching, biting back the pain.

"You bastard," she said. "Who do you think you are? Don't ever handle me like that again."

"I come down here to investigate a pissant mink farm scam and all of a sudden I'm in the middle of a war. So you'd better come clean with me right now. What the fuck is going on?"

"I wish I knew," she said, looking intently into the side view mirror.

Darkness had fallen. He turned on the headlights. They sped on in silence for a minute or so, he ashamed about roughing her, she chastened by the roughing. She pushed down on the chrome switch and lowered her window. The wind whipped furiously at her damp-heavy hair. She had put on a one-piece white jumpsuit and had neglected to button one of the buttons. Her right breast was partly exposed, a small feast for the eyes.

"I think you forgot something, O'Keefe. Those men were trying to kill me too."

He thought about it for a few seconds. She had a point.

"I'm sorry," he said.

"Where now?" she said.

"The cops," he said, reaching for the mobile phone in the console between them, but she beat him to it, ripped it out of its connection and dumped it on the floor, then grabbed the wheel and almost pulled them off the road. He straight-armed her and knocked her away. The van lurched out of control, and he hit the brakes, trying to keep it out of a skid. He had to use both hands to keep the wheels straight until the van came to a full stop. Before he could grab her, she jumped out and stood in the road, her hand on the door, ready to slam it shut.

"What the fuck are you doing?"

"Goodbye. No cops for me. At least not for a while. I need some time first."

He looked in the rearview mirror, expecting headlights to be bearing down on them any second.

"You've got two goons trying to kill you."

"What are they gonna do—shoot me down in a public place? They missed me. Now they'll crawl back into whatever sewer they came from. The way I see it, I don't have to go to the cops. I'm not a witness to anything. Nobody's even got a right to ask me any questions."

"Well, I'm a witness."

"Then do what you think you've gotta do. I'll give you directions to the sheriff's office."

They both glanced back, looking for headlights coming.

"Get in here," he said. "You go wandering around out there by yourself, those guys'll make mink food out of you in about five minutes. Get in here before I drag you in here."

"And you're not just a witness," she said pointedly. "You're a burglar too, and maybe a kidnapper."

"You sweet thing," he said.

"I just want a little bit of space. A little space and a little time. Give me that. My father would want you to give me that. You're working for him, aren't you?"

She looked back down the road. Still no headlights.

O'Keefe thought about her father asking him to take care of her and Harrigan telling him not to take his eyes off her. Not that he wanted to do that.

"There's a nightclub at the resort up at Silver Lake. It will be crammed with people. Even if they're still around, there's no way they would do anything there."

"Get in here."

But she felt him relenting and stood there holding the door.

"Please, get in."

"You can't make me. Not without committing another crime. Promise me."

"Promise?"

"Promise me. No police. Not for a couple of hours anyway."

She knew her man. A promise meant something to him.

"I promise," he said.

He would keep the promise. She had asked for only a couple of hours. Jane and Roy were beyond succor. Tag was here beside him. Pray for the dead, but comfort the living.

CHAPTER 12

BACK AT THE car, they changed hurriedly out of their suits and into the country-and-western duds they had brought with them. By the time they finished changing, the guy in the van was long gone. If he wasn't a cop himself, he was probably heading for the sheriff's office lickety-God-damn-split. Time to vamoose. The Boss would be very unhappy because Parker's wife still breathed. Tough tit. The lady might know something, she might know nothing, another wild card waiting to be played, but it had to be smarter to let her go for now than hang around the house where the cops might show up any second. They needed to haul ass into the next county to the rented farmhouse, stash the car in the barn for someone to pick up next week when things had cooled down, and drive the pickup truck back to the city.

"So long, Minksville," said Fatso as they reached the outskirts of town.

The wild card came to him a few miles down the road as he slowed down to obey the 20-mile-per-hour speed limit sign in front of the *Silver Lake Resort*. There it was all of a sudden. The van. *The guy climbs out of the driver's side. And what's this? A broad gets out of the passenger side. Lenny Parker's wife. Carrying a backpack.*

Fatso, dumbfounded, said, "It's the lady. What's the deal?"

He clubbed Fatso in the side of the head with his fist. "You dumb fuckin' sweathog. She must've been in the house all the time."

HE STOPPED FOR gas though the gauge showed three-quarters full. His head ached from having to think so much. Job stress. Decisions, decisions. What the guy and the gal were up to he didn't know, but, obviously, they had not gone to the cops. The bodies probably hadn't even been discovered yet. Another chance to get the girl and maybe the soldier in the van too, at least if they could catch him without his rifle. This isn't the movies, so you can't just go sauntering into the resort and blow them away in front of God and everybody. *How long will they be in there, and where will they go next? Wait and see.*

Parker's wife must have been hiding in the house the whole time. Had she seen them? If she did, would she recognize them in the shitkicker clothes? Well, if she recognized somebody, let it be the sweathog sulking next to him.

He would have to smooth things over.

"Hey, Otto," he said, "I'm sorry."

"God damn it, she wasn't in the God-damned house. I looked every fuckin' place."

Except the hot tub, Otto thought. *Better not say anything about that. Couldn't be. Even if the bitch wrestled that lid around somehow, she'd have drowned inside that thing.*

"She must've been in the van."

Bullshit, Karl thought, but he kept his counsel. The situation called for some diplomacy.

"No harm, no foul," he said. "If she was in the van, that means she didn't see us. So you go in and look for her."

"What about you?"

"See that little shit-food joint there across the road? I can see the van from there. They come out, you get your ass right out behind them."

"You ever been in there?" Fatso asked, pointing at the Silver Lake Resort with his dwarfish paw.

"Yeah. They got a nightclub in there. Food and booze and a band. And they've got this pan-fried lobster they're famous for."

"Fried lobster?"

"Yep, fried."

"Dumb fuckin' hicks down here don't even know how to cook a God-damned lobster, huh?"

"You'd be surprised. It's pretty damn good." *Fatso's chomping at the bit to get in there now.* "Sit at the bar. But don't drink anything. I need you to be sober."

He chuckled as he watched Fatso cross the highway and wobble across the gravel parking lot in his new cowboy boots.

Fuckin' boots, Otto was thinking. *And fuckin' sweat, too. I sweat like a pig even in the dead of winter. Sweathog! That's what the sonuvabitch called me.* Otto had resented the insult more than the blow. His ankle turned on a rock and he almost fell down. *Cowboy boots! Brilliant! The big guy was fucking brilliant!*

Well, at least Karl seemed to believe him now about the fox not being in the house. *If she was in the house, maybe she saw me,* he thought. *Nah. Not possible. The only place she could've been was in the hot tub, and she sure as hell didn't have a periscope with her if she was.* Just the same, Otto stopped at the gift shop in the resort and bought a pair of shades.

Sunday night or not, the nightclub was jam packed and swinging with people eating and drinking and dancing to the music. Guitars, drums, saxophones, a trumpet, even a frigging trombone. The singer was a pasty-faced little white twerp who wailed and jumped around like he had mistaken himself for James Brown.

"Ya know you're all right!" the singer rasped. "Ya know you're outta sight!"

Food smells. He could use a good meal. Lobster sounded good, but none of that fried-up shit. He wanted it boiled with lots of melted butter like city people ate it. Karl had told him not to drink, but what would that look like, sitting at the bar not drinking anything? He would go a little easy though.

"Gimme a beer," he said. "A draw."

The little snatch was right there across the room, sitting in a booth in the corner with the guy from the van. A tall guy, even taller than Karl. He hated tall guys. The tall guy swallowed his drink in a couple of gulps. The girl had ordered a bottle of white wine. It looked like she intended to drink it all.

SHE HAD BROUGHT the backpack inside with her and put it on the floor underneath the booth.

"Why did you bring that inside?" O'Keefe asked.

"Because it might be the last thing I have in the world, and I'd like to hold onto it. What money and clothes I've got left are in it. I'll give you the money if you want, but do you think your investors will want to grab my clothes too?"

"Come on," he said, feeling unfairly accused.

"I don't feel sorry for any of them," she said. "They wanted to get rich quick, make a bundle the easy way. They deserve a guy like Lenny."

"Even your father?"

"Especially my father. My adoptive father, by the way."

That explains a lot, O'Keefe thought, and silently applauded this particular triumph of heredity over environment.

"Why all the hostility to him?"

Her eyes narrowed into hard and vicious little slits. "You really want to know, or are you just flapping your gums?"

Taken aback by her vehemence, he wished he hadn't asked.

"I want to know," he said.

"Because he's been trying to get in my pants since I was twelve years old."

There were just some things that life did not prepare an Irish Catholic boy to hear. Such a thing was incomprehensible to him.

"I don't believe it. The little insurance man with the American flag in his lapel?"

"What's the matter, O'Keefe? Don't you believe a girl can tell when her dad has the hots for her? Well, believe me, it must have taken every bit of strength and Christian fortitude he had to restrain himself sometimes. I'd be in the kitchen, or my bedroom, or in the backyard. Dressed, half-dressed, undressed. And all of a sudden I'd turn around and he'd be watching me."

He wondered if she wasn't a little crazy.

"Did he ever try to do anything?"

Inappropriate question. He thought for a moment she might cry, but she covered it with the tough pose. Just like Harrigan so often did.

"He came into my room one night when I was in the 8th grade. I had this terrible earache, and they'd given me some kind of drug, and I didn't really know what was going on."

She inhaled deeply.

"He 'comforted' me," she said, husky-voiced now, quavering, using her voice to stifle the cry flowing into her throat and the tears welling into her eyes. "Stroking me and rubbing me in places that didn't hurt."

With great difficulty she had managed not to cry. O'Keefe was overcome with pity and desire.

"The next day I kept trying to convince myself I'd dreamed it or hallucinated it. But I didn't. It happened."

"Did you tell anyone?"

"My mother." She spat out the words.

"And?"

"She slapped my face. I never mentioned it again."

"It is hard to believe."

"It's always hard to believe. I didn't believe it myself for a long time after my mother slapped me. For a long time I thought I was crazy. For a long time I did whatever they wanted me to so I could make it up to them. But I knew deep down. I knew by the way he looked at me after that night. He wanted it. He wanted it all. I didn't let that sink in until a few years ago. It couldn't sink in until I got away from them for a while."

"Your mother did nothing?"

"No. Because there's nothing there. The bastard ground her to dust a long time ago."

"How'd you get hooked up with Lenny Parker?"

"I can thank dear old Dad for that too. He sent me to this little, church-affiliated college close to home. At that place Lenny was the cream of the crop. And what did I know? All I was ever raised with was God and country and making money and him watching me. I didn't know any better. Lenny looked like a guy who was 'going places,' as my father used to say. Lenny and my dad became like father and son. From the day I introduced him to Lenny, he had me married to him. And that was a way to get away from him looking at me all the time. So one day I looked around, and that's what I was. Married to Lenny Parker, the mink-farm tycoon."

She drained her glass. The gold bracelet on her wrist slid down onto her forearm as she drank. She quickly poured herself another.

"Like I told you, I don't think I ever made a decision of my own in my life until now. I let other people make my decisions for me."

"So it was somebody else that decided on the big palace on the hill and the Jag and the trips and all the other little things it seems to take to keep you going?"

"I'll tell you what. If you don't have anything else, you'd better have all the 'little things' you can get your hands on." She smiled. "And what are you, a socialist, or just jealous?"

He smiled back. "Probably some of both."

Now he drained his glass.

"Jane said Lenny changed this last year."

"Like Jekyll and Hyde."

"That's what she said. Her very words."

"One day he'd be strutting around like he was king of the world; the next day he thinks he's the scum of the earth. He'd disappear for two or three days, then he'd come home and wouldn't go out of the house for a week. It got so he wouldn't even answer the telephone or go near a window."

"Jane said it didn't make any sense that he'd take off without you. She said he worshipped you too much for that."

He had hit a nerve. Was it hurt in her eyes? Sadness?

"Will you quit the interrogation bit? Give it a rest. You've nabbed me. I'm caught. Now how about giving me a little relief for just awhile, before my life becomes hell on earth."

"I'm sorry," he said, and he meant it.

She held up her glass for a mock toast.

"To what might have been," she said. "A clean escape. A girl in her Jaguar touring the country."

"Roll me away," he said.

"Yeah. Roll me away."

She took a long drink of her wine as O'Keefe remembered some more of the lyrics to the song:

"I too am lost, I feel double-crossed
I'm sick of what's wrong and what's right"

The song ended with Bob on his motorcycle speeding alone across the high country at sunset:

"Gotta keep rollin'
Gotta keep ridin'
Keep searchin' 'till I find what's right
And as the sunset faded
I spoke to the faintest first starlight
And I said,
'Next time . . . We'll get it right'"

She was calling him out of his reverie. "Hey, Pete. Where are you?"

He came out of it and gestured with an upward lift of his head that he was paying attention to her.

"I know you saved my life today. Don't think I'm not grateful for that."

CHAPTER 13

OTTO ORDERED HIS second vodka tonic. The beer just didn't hit the spot. *Party time.*

"Hey," he barked at the bartender. "Can I get some food up here?"

Some places wouldn't serve you at the bar.

"Sure."

"How 'bout some lobster?"

"Sure thing. Want a salad with it?"

"Nah. Save that shit for the rabbits, huh?"

The bartender grinned.

"Potato?"

"Yeah. Baked. Lots of butter and sour cream."

"How 'bout some broccoli?"

"You gotta be shittin'."

The bartender grinned again. He was a good guy.

"Now don't be stickin' that lobster in no fryin' pan. I want it boiled like it's supposed to be."

"You really oughtta try the pan fried. You'll never be the same."

Well, not true. He'd always be the same. *But shit, I might as well try it. I don't know nobody here. Nobody'll be the wiser. Like they say, when in Rome, do as the Italians do.*

"Tell you what," said the bartender. "If you don't like it, I'll take it back and trade it for some boiled."

Nothing wrong with that deal.

"How 'bout some wine with your dinner?"

"Sounds good. You got half bottles?"

"'Fraid not."

"Gimme a whole one then. Chablis. You got Chablis down here?"

The grin seemed to mock him this time.

"Sure do."

"Okay. And another vodka tonic while I'm waitin' for dinner, huh?"

Party time. It didn't look like the big guy and the honey pot would be going anywhere for a while. They seemed to be getting along awfully well. He wondered if Lenny Parker knew that his wife was diddling with this big guy on the side. Then Otto had a good idea. If he got the chance, he'd tell Lenny Parker all about it just before he put him out of his misery.

I'll be a sonuvabitch if this isn't the best lobster I ever tasted. The hicks really stumbled onto something here. Well, what do they say, even a pig finds a walnut once in a while.

All of a sudden the lovebirds were leaving the booth. "I'll be right back," he yelled to his friend, the bartender, but he left a fifty-dollar bill on the bar just in case. No use having the cops after him because they thought he had walked out on the check.

It turned out the lovebirds were just heading for the john. Otto weaved as he walked back to the bar to reclaim his stool and the plate of lobster. He blamed the cowboy boots, not the vodka.

THE RESORT'S OWNERS had hung a pay telephone in the men's bathroom, and O'Keefe wondered how many lies had been told in that room. And he thought about Jane and Roy. And the cops. It had been more than the couple of hours he'd promised her. There were corpses out there. But she was here. Magic. Perhaps a compromise. A telephone call.

"Sheriff's office."

The dispatcher slurred his words, and O'Keefe wondered if everyone in the county was as drunk as he was.

"There's a place out on State Road 6 called Prosperity Farms."

The dispatcher said nothing.

"You know where I'm talking about?"

"Yep."

"There's two dead people out there. They've been murdered."

"D'you do it, buddy?"

"No sir, I didn't."

"Sure. What's your name?"

He wondered if he should tell.

"Peter O'Keefe. I'm a private investigator."

"Where are you?"

No answer.

"I said, 'Where are you'?" But the guy who said his name was O'Keefe had hung up the phone.

SHE WAS STANDING outside the bathroom waiting for him as if he were in her custody and not the other way around. She smiled. She moved closer to him, a rather tall girl but small compared to him.

"You know," he said, "we ought to go to the cops right now."

She laid her hands flat against his chest. "What difference does a few more hours make? I don't know what's going to happen to me now. I'm not wanting to rush to face that."

THEY'RE GETTIN' AWFUL chummy, Otto thought. Back from the john, they sat on the same side of the booth, facing him. She was on the inside, leaning back against the wall, smiling. The guy was doing most of the talking. After a while the lovebirds got up and ducked out a side door onto a patio. "Gotta get a little fresh air," he told the bartender and, affecting casual, sauntered after them. *Whoa!* He was a little woozy. He grabbed the top of a chair to steady himself. *Fuckin' cowboy boots. All the same, better go easy the rest of the way. Try some coffee. Maybe have the bartender put some brandy in it.*

The part of the patio close to the door was crowded with people having a good time. The lovebirds sat off by themselves on a bench at the empty end of the patio next to the lawn.

"AND THAT'S HOW I ended up chasing deadbeats and con men," O'Keefe said, finishing his story. "See, I'm no different than you. Just drifting. Letting things happen to me."

She leaned back against the wall and looked up at the sky for a while. "Look out there," she said. He followed her gaze up into the sky. Stars everywhere. He couldn't tell one from another. "Out there's Andromeda," she went on, "the Chained Princess. And Perseus, the Champion. Maybe that's us? And will Pegasus, the Flying Horse, come to our rescue? If there's any hope left anyway."

He had thought she might be too tough for crying, but she was crying right now. He reached for her, but she shook her head, telling him "No." She hunched up her shoulders and bowed her head and cried on her breasts, attaining a kind of privacy despite him sitting there next to her.

The band played *Harlem Nocturne.* The wail of the saxophone, the soul's yearning lament.

"I love that song," she said.

"So do I."

She seemed to be drunk. So was he. He didn't care.

"Let's have a dance."

Her palm sweated a little. He rubbed his thumb across the top of her hand, which he held just below his chin as they danced. At least pretended to dance. Her body accommodated him when he pressed against her, molded itself to him.

She pushed back from him so she could see his face when she said, "I bet you believe in love at first sight."

"It's the only kind."

She was smiling again. "Well, maybe it was second or third sight—after that subtle come-on of yours, pinning my arms to the floor like that."

She took in his tongue. The fingers of her right hand pressed on his lower back, bringing him in to her. She rocked back and forth, moving slowly up and down, massaging them both. The hunger in her pulled at him like a whirlpool, and he gladly let it take him down because he sensed how deep her hunger was, as deep as his own, and what it was, the same as his own, a hunger beyond any momentary desperate thrusting of sex into sex, a hunger for some other kind of incarnation, some other word made flesh.

Despite her protests, he made her let him carry the backpack to the check-in desk.

"No. 424," the desk clerk said, handing him the key. "It's one of the cabins."

He pointed out the front window to his right.

"Down at the end of the drive. Down the hill. Very private. And be careful. There's fog in the valley."

Back at the van she couldn't seem to wait. She moved quickly into him, finding his mouth, pressing him back against the van, bringing his hand to her breast. A little shock wave jolted him. A revelation. "Let's go," she said, opened the van door, and jumped in.

FROM THE DARKENED interior of a black car across the road Karl saw O'Keefe and Tag emerge from the front door of the resort, followed shortly after by Fatso, wobbling on his cowboy boots. *Jesus, is he waving at me? He is, the dumb fuck. Waving eagerly, like he's attending his high school reunion or something. Ignore him.*

Karl drove out of the parking lot fast and turned onto the highway like he was heading home, leaving Fatso gaping in his wake.

The sonuvabitch is leaving me here, Otto thought. *Nah. Can't happen.* He needed somewhere to go. His worldview had narrowed considerably. It was dark out, but Otto moved through a special darkness of his own, a darkness painted over with a neon-yellow haze. He considered walking to the other side of the parking lot and sitting down under some trees just beyond the lot, but he could muster no confidence that he would make it that far. The main reality for him right now was that he had to puke. This very second he had to puke. Right inside this old white Caddy convertible here. He leaned into the driver's side and learned once again why they called it "urping."

When he finished, the inside of the Caddy looked a lot worse, but he felt a lot better. He snorted, thinking about the guy coming out of the nightclub with his date and finding his ghetto cruiser had turned into a barf-wagon. A breeze sent his own sour breath wafting back in his face. Karl would really be pissed now. No drinking, he had said. *Well, fuck him if he can't take a joke.*

He needed to move along, so he staggered toward the highway. Karl came back from wherever he had gone, pulled into the far side of the parking lot, and continued slowly on into the interior of the resort. The barf session had cleared Otto's head a little. Not knowing what else to do, he trotted after the car, hoping nobody would see him or bother with him if they did.

THE ROAD TO the cabin dipped down into a valley carved by a creek that meandered through the resort. The temperature had dropped, and the warmer air rising from the creek had mixed with the cooler air in the night wind to steam up a cauldron of fog in the valley. The headlights of the van hardly penetrated the foggy blackness. Fallen leaves swirled in slow motion in front of the van like ghosts searching for a final resting place.

"Remember," O'Keefe said, "the first time's always the worst time."

"No second chances," she teased.

But he was serious. You were always too excited, or too drunk, or didn't know each other well enough, the orifices and crevices, the wants and the needs. One-night stands did not interest him at all.

"That's it," she said, looking back out the window at a small wooden sign in the shape of an arrow that pointed to 424. O'Keefe skidded the van to a halt.

"Geez," she said, "you can't see your hand in front of your face out there."

She jumped out with her pack. O'Keefe walked around to the passenger side, opened the sliding door, and climbed into the back of the van.

"Got to get your little toothbrush?" she joked.

"Not quite."

He carefully replaced the M-16 in its holder and grabbed the shoulder holster that contained his .38 pistol.

"You really think you need that now?"

"I doubt it. But I haven't been ready for one damn thing that's happened on this trip, and I'd like to reverse the trend."

When he climbed out of the van, she pulled him to her and kissed him, opening her mouth wide, inviting him all the way in.

"It's been so long," she said.

They felt their way through the fog down a narrow, concrete path. The desk clerk had described the cabin as "very private," and in the all-enveloping darkness they wouldn't have known it if there had been another cabin sitting right next to them and they failed even to see their own cabin until O'Keefe almost tripped over the stoop at the front door.

He had trouble persuading the key to open the lock. The key fit but would not turn. He twisted it back and forth. "Careful," she said, "you'll break it off," and laughed. She put her arms around him from behind, molding herself to him again, tucked her hands underneath his sweater, pulled the tail of his shirt out from his pants and began undoing its buttons. He did not know that all the buttons of her jumpsuit were already undone.

CHAPTER 14

OTTO DID NOT stop running until he reached the top of the steep hill that dropped from the parking lot down into the little valley. Sonic booms exploded in his chest, and he thought he might puke again. He surveyed the world of fog below him. For the first time he could remember, he was scared—scared because he thought he might be suffering a heart attack. But nothing to do now but go on. Karl could not have gone anywhere else except into that world of fog down the hill.

Not far down the hill he found the black car parked in a cul de sac. Karl was nowhere in sight. Hell, there was nothing in sight. He couldn't have told a bush from a baboon in that fog. Was that the sound of someone walking on gravel, and was it in front of him or behind him? He pulled out his pistol and aimed it at the fog. This was right out of a vampire or werewolf movie from his childhood. *You need silver bullets to kill those bastards.* The crunching footsteps kept coming closer, closer, then, suddenly, someone knocked him down from behind. He waited for the werewolf to pounce.

Karl—standing over him, pointing his pistol at Otto's face. Otto started to laugh, but Karl looked more than pissed off this time, and Otto knew a killer's eyes when he saw them, even in the dark. Karl seemed to catch himself and moved the gun away from Otto's face. But Otto made a mental note. *I'm watching you from now on, Big Dick. You can't be trusted, not for a minute.*

"What now?" Otto asked.

More questions. But Karl turned the tables this time.

"You know what you're gonna do now?"

Otto shook his head; he didn't have the foggiest.

"You're gonna go find the biggest fuckin' rock you can carry, that's what you're gonna do. And you're gonna bring it right back here and show it to me when you've found it."

"In this fog?" Otto complained.

"Come on, get movin'. We don't have much time."

Luckily, this part of the world included a very large number of very big rocks, so he didn't have to go far from the car to find one. But lugging the sonuvabitching rock back to the car was another thing. If he kept this up, his swollen-up heart would surely pop like a kid's balloon. Clasping the broad flat rock to his chest, weary as Sisyphus, he struggled back toward where he hoped to find the car. When he finally reached it, after shuffling the last few steps and dragging his feet rather than stepping with them, he could not summon any more breath from his lungs. He thought about dropping the rock but was afraid it might break in two, and then he would have to go dig for another one and carry it all the way back. He set it down and wondered if he would ever be able to stand straight up again. He grabbed the front fender of the car and gulped in the foggy night air as he slowly straightened himself upright.

Karl was fiddling with something in the trunk. A hose drooped out of the gas tank, looking slightly obscene. Despite the circumstances, Otto couldn't help himself, he chuckled. *Looks like a guy's dick hanging out of his fly. A little long though.* He remembered the old joke about how a one-armed man counts his loose change and almost laughed out loud. He couldn't tell what Karl was doing, so, despite Karl's aversion to questions he had to ask.

"What's the deal?"

Karl said nothing but turned around and showed Otto something in his hand. Otto craned his neck, straining to see. A bottle of liquid with a rag stuffed in the top like a wick. *Must be gasoline in the bottle. A Molotov cocktail?* Karl was a regular inventor. Otto remembered the chemistry set they had given him on his twelfth birthday. Worthless God-damned thing. Just a bunch of funny-colored vials of liquid and some sandy-salty-looking grains of stuff in plastic bags. He had mixed all the stuff together and fed it to the dog one night with the regular dog food. The dog didn't even throw up.

"Now," Karl said, "pick up that rock of yours and follow me close. They're in a cabin down at the end of the road. There's a front window in the cabin. There's a back door too. When we get there, you're gonna throw that rock through the window and I'm gonna start firin' in. Then you're gonna hustle your ass to the back door. When they come out, blow them away."

O'KEEFE COULD NOT make the key work. "I wonder if the guy gave us the wrong damn key," he muttered. They would have to trudge back to the van and drive back to the check-in desk. He could always break in, as he had into the house earlier in the day. He wondered what the world would be like now if he had refrained from committing that felony.

"Let's just stay in the van tonight," he said.

"Let me try it."

He made way for her. She did not imitate his frantic and furious jiggling. She worked the key very slowly, listening carefully, like a safecracker, for one metal groove to slide into another. In a few seconds he heard the lock click.

"Got it," she said, and pushed the door open. "You need to learn something about putting your key in a lock, my friend" flashing a tease of a smile.

There was a moral there somewhere, and he thought it might be wise to remember it.

She started to go in first, but he held her back, grabbed her pack, and forged on ahead of her like a grunt walking point in 'Nam. The light switch on the wall behind the door turned on a small lamp next to the bed. The "cabin" was really just an oversized motel room suite, unusual only in that it was free-standing and had a back door.

He crossed the front room, flipped her pack onto the bed, and proceeded across the room to a glass sliding door, which he unlocked, slid open, and went outside. Fog. He bumped into something. Feeling along the wall outside the door, he found a light switch that turned on an ugly, yellow light bulb above him. Outdoor furniture, the iron kind. He was standing on a small porch. Maybe it had a pretty view of something in the daytime.

Back inside the cabin, he refastened the security chain and looked into the bathroom. It was larger than most motel bathrooms, and the full-sized window added a different touch. Otherwise, it was the same old thing. Fluorescent light over the sink. Stainless steel Kleenex dispenser in the wall, a piece of Kleenex sticking out of it like a tongue. Small bottles of cheap shampoo and body lotion. Heat lamp in the ceiling, controlled by a timer device on the wall. Noisy fan. Heavy rubber shower curtain. Strip of paper below the toilet seat stretched over the toilet bowl like a footbridge.

"Hey, O'Keefe," he heard her say behind him, "you're looking in the wrong place."

She was standing between the bed and the front door, the jumpsuit a discarded heap on the floor at her feet. The weak light from the lamp by the bed barely revealed her—half-darkness, half-light, the obscurest of revelations, like truth itself. He thought he knew what she wanted him to do, so he took off the shoulder holster first and then the rest of his clothes and walked past the foot of the bed toward her as she glided a few steps into the room to greet him. He stopped in front of her, an arm's length away, not knowing whether to reach out for her or just keep standing there a bit wonderstruck. Behold a vision. No goddess here. A coil, thoroughly mortal. Flesh, solid but yet so incredibly soft. Her long hair flowed over her shoulders and hung down the front of her, covering the tops of her bare breasts. Skin, translucent where the light touched it just right. Veins, the blood coursing through them, streams with no outlet. Her breasts relaxed there before him, waiting for his hands to touch them, excite them, tease her to tautness, the skin of her belly and thighs and arms and breasts and shoulders a slightly flawed whiteness, honey-tinged, golden-toned. Here too were colors ineffable, another process at work, another essence entirely. How could you describe with words the luxuriance of her hair, the beckoning of her bare shoulders and breasts?

Finally, he could stand it no longer. His hands reached for her. He did not hurry, recalling the moral of the key and the lock. She closed her eyes in a silent moan. You had to think of the Other, uniquely of her, of Tag, this profound humanscape that life would never again repeat. Somehow they were on the floor, and he cradled her in his arms and caressed her with his hands and tongue. She kept uttering small gasps of breath and saying "Oh, God." A prayer. He was about to lose all control of himself just from touching her with his tongue and mouth and fingers, his hand gripping the strong sinews of her shoulder.

He stopped for a moment, drew back and beheld her again. Flesh abounding, and grace too. Like a mother lays a child down softly on its back in the crib, he laid her back down on the floor and knelt between her legs. Their eyes met. He guessed they shared the same emotions now, the same ecstatic agony of indecision, whether to prolong the pleasures of the foreplay or move toward the climax, letting yourself go, surrendering, finally out of control for once, reveling in that surging, leaping delight, precious and soon gone, among the most memorable moments of your whole life. Whatever it was she wanted from him, he hoped he was able to give it, at the very least not spoil it completely for her—with clumsiness, or causing her fear or needless pain, or the bitter regret of having given without taking.

His hands kneaded her breasts, so ample and pliant, and moved down to her ribcage, holding firmly against the rib bones so small and brittle that they might break like dry twigs if not handled with the utmost care. He kissed the soft flesh of her stomach and made a trail with his tongue all the way down, and he felt her flinch in rebellion against the almost-unbearable pleasure his tongue gave her. He paused, heightening the delicious suspense for her, and for him too. On his knees, bent over in supplication, worshipping in a way. If there was a Grail to be found, he had found it right here. She brought her knees up and her feet back, giving him all the room he could ask for. Tiny explosions jolted her. She closed her thighs against the sides of his head and grabbed his hair with her hands. When he came up to look at her, she still had not opened her eyes. Tears wended their way lazily out of her closed eyelids. Then she was looking at him, the sheen of tears making the aqua eyes seem impossibly bright and clear.

"Are you ready for me now?" he said.

She moved her head up and down. Yes. And he vowed to live the rest of his days in affirmation joyful and constant, wallowing in life for all he was worth. Again she moved her feet back and sideways and flat down on the carpet, welcoming him. He put his hands flat on the floor next to her hips and pushed himself up like a gung-ho Marine and slid easily into her as she arched upward to receive him. His vision left him for a few seconds, and it was lovely to see the stars bursting before his eyes. The damp walls of muscle inside her gripped him and held him fast. He did not move any further—she did the rest, a small churning movement of her hips. His breath burst out of his lungs, and he groaned behind it. His arms quivered and then gave way, and he let himself down gently on her.

Sail on now. Right on through. Into the next phase, the next enfolding. It did not take long to again find her flash point. She wrapped her arms around him and dug her manicured nails polished smoothly in pink into his scarred back, and they moved in perfect rhythm together until she came, and, to his surprise, he too was ready again.

When he pulled away, they both shuddered and flinched from the shock of separation, as if these bodies, once joined, really were not to be put asunder. When he pulled her up to him, he saw that she was silently, softly crying still. He did not understand why and did not want to inquire, but he could not square it with the tough pose she had presented to him earlier in the day. He put his right arm around her and pulled her face to his chest, leaned back against the bed and petted her hair with his left hand and admired her naked shoulder while she wept on his breast. Gentle moment most solemn. A consecration of sorts.

In a little while she looked up at him. That smile. "Bang!" she said in a throaty rasp.

"Bang!" he echoed her.

She shyly wiped the tears from one of her cheeks. She stood up and threw back her head, hair flying back over her shoulders, breasts bouncing like unbreakable bubbles.

"I'll be back in a minute," she said, heading down a narrow hallway that led to the bathroom. "We might as well try the bed too," he heard her say as she closed the bathroom door. "Tag, you're it, O'Keefe."

Well, he wasn't ready for an encore just yet, in the bed or anywhere else. He left his underwear on the floor but grabbed his jeans, tugged them on and fished a crushed pack of cigarettes from one of the pockets. All but one of the cigarettes were broken. He lit the unbroken cigarette and sat on the edge of the bed looking at the pack. He reached to open it.

Another kind of bang. A detonation. The window exploding, glass flying. Something bouncing with a thump on the floor. A rock. Then something aflame. BOOM! Shards of glass tearing into his shoulder and the back of his head. *Dive for the floor. Crawl down the hallway.* The telltale ping of the silencer. Bullets rocketing all around him. Fire and smoke. *Where was the shoulder holster?* There—on the floor in front of him. A bullet nicked his foot, ricocheted against the wall beside him, whizzed past his face. Another bullet gouged a chunk out of the wall next to his head. Someone was pumping rounds in through the broken window. He found the pistol, sat up and swiveled his body toward the front of the cabin, grabbed his right wrist with his left hand, pointed the pistol at the smoke in the direction of the window, and fired three rounds.

O'KEEFE HAD FIRED two rounds and was squeezing off the third before Karl realized that the soldier inside the cabin had a pistol of his own—a loud sonuvabitch too—and was trying to kill him with it. Death did not cross his mind, as always it seemed an impossibility, but capture did. The soldier's pistol had no silencer attached to it. People would hear. They would be running to check out the source of the disturbance. Fatso was in the back. Should he go back and get him? No, the dumb shit might start shooting at him in the fog. And the Molotov cocktail had worked. Smoke poured from the cabin window, flames sprouted behind it. They could not stay in there. They would have to go out the back, just as he had predicted. If anybody but Fatso were waiting for them back there, they would be dead soon. But Fatso could not be trusted at all. Yet you had to work with what you had. *Que sera, sera. Go back up the concrete path to the road and wait to see what happens.*

TAG, ON HER knees, opened the bathroom door and watched O'Keefe fire the pistol into the smoke. When he turned around, his eyes were bloodshot and ragged looking, and he was gasping for good air.

"Are you all right?" she said. "Where's my pack?"

"Screw your pack."

He crawled into the bathroom with her and pointed at the window.

"Wait 'til the smoke gets so bad you can't stand it, then break the window and climb out."

"I need my pack."

"What for?"

"I have clothes in it, for one thing."

"Forget it."

"I'm gonna get it."

She was heading out the bathroom door, but he pulled her back and went himself. He fought through the billowing smoke and groped blindly on the bed for the pack, hoping the bed had not yet caught fire. It had. But just then he bumped into the pack, pulled it off the bed, stomped back down the hallway, and thrust it into her hands.

"Thanks," she said.

"Thanks?" he said in disgust. "After I go, close the door before the smoke gets in."

What he most certainly did not want was death by fire. He pulled open the bathroom door and dived back into the hallway, expecting to be shot at. Nothing. He moved quickly back down the hallway, around the foot of the bed and across the main room of the cabin, dived out the back door, and drove his head into a piece of the iron furniture, which stunned him for a few seconds. Someone was shooting at him, he could see the pistol flashes, and, jumping up, he fired a round in that direction. A groan of pain. *Lucky hit.* Heavy footsteps running hard away from him. He fired toward where he thought the sound was. *Only one more bullet.* He ran around to the front of the cabin where he thought the footsteps had gone.

KARL HAD PULLED the car around and pointed it up the hill. Leaving it running, he got out and listened. He heard footsteps scratching along the gravel road. It would be either Fatso or the soldier from the van. He pointed his pistol where he knew the runner would appear. A rounded shape that looked like a giant potato stumbled in front of him and fell on its face.

"I'm hit," Otto said. "Help me up, for Christ's sake."

"Well, Otto," said Karl, "what the fuck do you suppose we do now?"

Karl picked Otto up, dragged him to the passenger side of the car, and dumped him into the backseat.

O'KEEFE STOOD BAREFOOT and bare chested on the gravel road. He thought he heard a car up ahead spinning its wheels on the gravel; the wheels caught, and the car screeched off fast. Gone. At least he hoped so. But then he heard running footsteps in front of him somewhere in the fog. He fired his last bullet in the direction he guessed the footsteps were running, but he had already been vouchsafed his lucky hit for the night, and the footsteps carried on and away. He looked back at the cabin. The flames were eating their way out the front door now.

Tag!

"Tag!" he kept calling but got no answer as he ran around the side of the cabin. The bathroom window wasn't broken. She had not come out that way. *Is she still inside? For Christ's sake!* He circled around toward the back door. The back door stood open, smoke gushing out of the aperture. He held his breath and hurled himself into the cabin. She was not in the bathroom. The smoke knifed into his eyes. The front of the cabin was a carnival of flame. He stumbled back out the door to the porch, choking and gagging back the smoke.

"Tag!" he bellowed into the empty night, just then understanding that it had been her footsteps he had shot at in front of the cabin. She had run away from him.

He suddenly realized that he had no shirt or shoes on and that he was very cold. In the distance he heard sirens, and they seemed to be playing his song.

CHAPTER 15

THE SHERIFF WAS not taking the situation kindly.

"What kind of a puke are you anyway, O'Keefe? You find two people brutally murdered. Whoever did it is after the lady too. And what do you do? Do you report the crimes right away so maybe we can catch the killers before they crawl back under whatever rock they came out from? Do you bring the lady to the police so maybe we can protect her? No! Not you! You shack up with the God-damned gal! Let's stop the world while Mr. O'Keefe boffs himself a piece of ass! What were you thinkin' with? Your dick? You're sick, you know that? You're sick!"

Harrigan had been leaning against the interrogation-room wall affecting boredom, a studied indifference to the sputtering rage of the demented yokel across the room. *City mouse and country mouse,* O'Keefe thought. Harrigan pushed himself off the wall and stubbed out his cigarette in the ashtray on the table.

"If all that made you feel better, Sheriff, fine. But now let's cut the shit. Either charge him and let him make bail, or let him go."

"Maybe I think this puke killed them himself."

"Then charge him, Sheriff. Right now. But if you don't either charge him or let him go, right now, then I'm goin' across the street for a writ of habeas corpus. And I'll tell you what else I'm gonna do, Sheriff. I'm gonna sue you for violating Mr. O'Keefe's civil rights."

The Sheriff's neck and head lunged forward, and he seemed to be having a hard time keeping his body from following. For a second O'Keefe thought the lawman would leap over the table and grab Harrigan by the scruff of the neck with his teeth and shake him quickly to death like a dog kills a rat. But the Sheriff may have suddenly thought of his pension, of ending his life as a security guard trudging around dark office buildings all night for five dollars an hour.

"You scumbag lawyers just fuck up the world, you know that?"

He turned to his deputy. "Book this puke on two counts of failing to report a crime. That's a felony, ain't it?"

"Yes, sir."

"Just a minute, Sheriff," said Harrigan. "Maybe you ought to talk to the county attorney first, since I guarantee you I'm gonna sue you for malicious prosecution if you don't make those charges stick. Have you looked at your liability insurance lately? How much does it cover you for if you ruin Mr. O'Keefe's reputation and therefore his business? And it *will* ruin him, Sheriff. And it's a thriving business, I assure you. Or maybe this county doesn't even have any liability insurance on you, Sheriff. Is that possible?"

The Sheriff looked as if this was not only possible but quite probable. "Come here," he said to his deputy who followed him out of the room.

"He's not stupid," Harrigan said. "If he goes off half-cocked and charges you himself, he's got exposure. If he gives it to the county attorney, the county attorney goes to the grand jury and gets an indictment. Everybody's immune from my lawsuit then. I may not be able to stop the indictment, but I've got a lot better chance of talking sense to the county attorney than to this guy."

O'Keefe wasn't sure that he cared. Let them throw him in a cell if they wanted as long as there was a bed in there. He just wanted to crawl off to a dark place somewhere and die like a dog. They had kept him awake, not even letting him doze in his chair. He remembered his first night in the Marine Corps, when the drill instructors had marched him and the other new recruits around all night on the parade ground as the Southern California monsoon dumped rain on them incessantly, and he had been disappointed at how easily his spirit could be broken.

Harrigan observed O'Keefe closely. "Well, you're about the sorriest looking thing I've seen in a while," said Harrigan, "except maybe in my shaving mirror in the morning."

O'Keefe forced a smile, but he would rather have cried. He thought about what the Sheriff had said. The Sheriff was right. He made a mental note to read something about the process of intoxication turning into hangover. He had always been asleep before. Now he was, so to speak, an eyewitness. He had watched it all night, a transformation something like Lon Chaney turning into the Wolf Man. His heart worked furiously, pumping his polluted blood into his throat and face and temples. He had a hard time breathing, and when he did breathe, it just made him want to throw up. His hands shook as he lit what seemed like his millionth cigarette. He bent over and gagged. There had been a time when he could just throw up and feel immediately better but not anymore. Was that a signpost on the low road of creeping alcoholism? He stubbed out the cigarette in the dingy metal ashtray already chock full of other partly-smoked butts. He didn't need another cigarette. What he needed was another drink.

When the country mouse returned, he smiled at the city mouse and said, "Mr. Harrigan, I've taken your suggestion to heart. Mr. O'Keefe, someone'll be knockin' at your door real soon with a piece of paper from the grand jury, so you'd better get your bail money ready."

Not asking for permission, Harrigan said, "Let's go, Pete," and walked out of the room. But O'Keefe hesitated, waiting for the Sheriff to give his frowning blessing to their departure, which the Sheriff did with a rude jerk of his head. O'Keefe stood up and almost fell back down again. The Sheriff expelled a snort of a laugh from his nose.

"Hey, O'Keefe," he said. "I don't know if we'll make that indictment stick or not, but I've got friends up at the state capital, and no matter what, I'm gonna have your license revoked. So, how do you like that shit, Mr. Private Eye Puke?"

Harrigan's style was to cover his fear with anger. O'Keefe knew an instant before Harrigan did it that Harrigan would now move his head backward and tuck his chin into his throat like a turtle ducking into his shell, but this was a snapping turtle with the fiercest of eyes and the sharpest of tongues. "Deputy," he said, "I want you to remember what your boss said just now, because real soon I'm gonna be asking you to repeat it under oath in a courtroom. You just fucked up, Sheriff. You just fucked up real bad."

Harrigan whirled on his heel and headed for the door. The cross-examination was closed. "You always need to end the cross-examination on a high point," Harrigan had once told him. "Take whatever victory you can hold onto and get the fuck out of there."

"Pukes!" yelled the Sheriff at their departing backs.

As they walked across the parking lot to the van, O'Keefe said, "I haven't been called a 'puke' since I was in the Marines." Harrigan laughed and patted him on the shoulder, an attempt at reassurance and solidarity.

In the van O'Keefe asked, "You want me to drop you off at the airport?"

"Not so easy, my man. I'm riding back with you. Maybe we'll have time enough that way for me to figure out why you turned into such a fuckup all of a sudden."

On the way out of town they stopped at a motel and rented a room. Harrigan changed into the same kind of clothes that O'Keefe wore—Levis and sweater and topsiders, the uniform of the aging preppie. O'Keefe took a long shower that did not make him feel clean. Bending over the toilet, he crammed his fingers down his throat, but he could force nothing up except a long, quivering rope of yellow bile.

O'Keefe admitted he was in no shape to drive. When they stopped for gas, they bought a case of beer and iced it down in the big built-in cooler that also served as a console between the two front seats. O'Keefe popped a top and chugged half of his first beer even before the gas tank had filled up. Inside him the beer lapped gently at his despair, nudging his dried-out, throbbing cells, smoothing them out a little, perking them up a little. He remembered the advertisement for the hangover medicine, the song of triumph: "Oh, what a relief it is!"

"Hair of the dog, huh?" said Harrigan, and he said nothing else for many miles, and his silence constituted an accusation.

Finally, O'Keefe could not stand the silence any longer. "I gotta stop drinking, Mike. I lose my head." As if to emphasize this statement, O'Keefe took a long drink of his beer. "I feel like the world's a mortal sin and that I'm the one who committed it."

Harrigan laughed. A forgiveness. "Pete, you might be the only guy in the world that a guy paid to take his daughter to bed." He paused for a few seconds, waiting for this barb to sink in all the way. He was pure-blooded Irish, which had bestowed upon him a three-fold birthright—a poet's tongue, a drunkard's heart, and an unerring ability to shrivel his victim with shame. "Was she that good? That she could make you turn into such a dumb shit all of a sudden?"

"Look who's talking. "

"Not on duty. Never on duty. First things first."

"What 'first things' are those? Chasing deadbeats and scumbags? Injunctions and bankruptcies? Playing the badass with whoever your opponent happens to be at the time? 'Every man for himself and God against everybody'? Is that what's important to you now? Is that what's first in your life? What happened to you? What happened to us?"

It was Harrigan's turn to be ashamed now, for O'Keefe was Irish too.

"I don't know," he said. "I wish I knew."

"It's real simple. You can't swim in garbage every day without having some of it stick on you."

O'Keefe took another long drink.

"I think I fell in love with that girl back there."

"Come on. The Sheriff was right. You're thinking with your *shvantz*."

"No. She was the one. The long-haired girl."

"You mean the one we were always looking for? The answer to our question? The one who never showed up? The one who was always at the next party or the next bar?"

"You got it. Her. I had her, the very one, for just a minute, and then she was gone."

"Well, you can bet those Keystone Cops back there aren't going to find her. They couldn't find their ass with both hands."

"Can you believe they didn't even search the van?"

"You got that M-16 in here?"

"Sure do. And some other little things that are even worse."

"What?"

"Grenades."

"You're kidding."

O'Keefe shook his head.

"Get rid of those things. You can't afford more charges if they catch you with those. Those illegal weapons are gonna cook you someday. Get rid of them. You think you're Rambo or what?"

O'Keefe did not answer. He did not know what he thought he was.

"Are those grenades stable?" Harrigan asked, looking around nervously, as if he expected the van to explode any second.

"So what's your prediction? Am I gonna be serving time on that indictment soon? Can he get my license?"

Harrigan looked at him, and O'Keefe knew the look. Harrigan was trying to decide whether to be entirely honest with him. As always, at least always with his old friend O'Keefe, Harrigan opted for honesty.

"At best it's a tossup. You did call them. You took a long time, but you did call them. And you did give them your name when you called. The problem is that the criminal laws of this country are so damned broad that the prosecutors can get damn near anything to a jury. If it gets to the jury, who knows? You never know with a jury. But the bottom line, my friend, is that this is the deepest shit you've ever been in."

The van climbed the low mountains and glided down through the valleys, but the marvels of nature that had so moved O'Keefe only a day before, at the beginning of this fiasco, failed to move him now. This splendor had been created for someone else, Harrigan perhaps, but not for him. Yet the more beer he drank, the better he felt. They were both half-drunk before they were halfway home. And it was in their nature to linger. Back in the city there was only frenzy and duty. The city was a machine made to make money change hands, and they both well knew they were just slogging grunts in the machine's army of tenders, easily expendable, easily replaced. But here was a river, not far off the road, a pleasant walk back through the woods, where they sat on a cliff, legs dangling over the side, and watched the stream course below them, the only thing in the world that seemed to be going anywhere worth getting to. O'Keefe resisted the urge to hurl his empty beer can out over the cliff and watch it sail down into the river below.

"Mike, I don't think those killers were just a couple of angry investors. They were pros. But I can't figure out what the underworld would be doing in a pissant deal like this mink farm. I mean, here we've got this Mickey Mouse hustler Lenny Parker. I just can't see him moving in those circles. But then there's this 'Mr. Canada.' Whoever killed those people was after the books and records and eliminating anyone who knew anything about the money going through there. You think the underworld could have been using that mink farm to launder money somehow?"

"That's not so farfetched. I could see them trapping Lenny boy that way. At first they're just another investor. Then, all of a sudden, they've got their claws wrapped around his neck."

Harrigan paused to carefully insert the remainder of his cigarette into the top of his empty beer can. *Harrigan the environmentalist*, O'Keefe thought. That's what Harrigan should do with the rest of his life. Find a foundation somewhere dedicated to saving the environment and start suing the world, do what he could to stop the world from devouring itself.

"But I'll tell you what," Harrigan continued. "I'll never know the answer to your question, because this is where I stop. The retainer's all used up. There's no money to feed the minks. The bank's got a lock on everything. It's time for the cops now, not me. And not you either."

"What about my long-haired girl?"

"If she was ever there at all, she's long gone now. Forget her if you can."

A cold wind blew through the trees, announcing the coming of winter, and O'Keefe remembered that he had not done his exercises today.

WHILE THE TWO men talked in the woods, in the city two other men were talking.

"You want a pizza?" Mr. Canada asked Karl who was just sitting down across the table from him. Karl looked tired and worried and shook his head.

"So you didn't find my good friend Lenny Parker?"

Karl shook his head again.

"And the wife neither?"

"Lost her too."

"Nothin' to show for one dead soldier and two dead civilians. Nothin' to show for all that risk and all that blood."

"I got the books and records."

"It's Lenny we need. And the wife in case she knows anything. And what about the guy in the van? He owes us a life."

"A private detective named Peter O'Keefe. Local guy. I can deal with him tonight if you want."

"Not yet. If he and Parker's wife got the hots for each other, maybe she'll come to him. Or maybe he'll lead us to her. And Lenny too. You can bet they're together. The shit's too deep for either of them to go it alone now. So then we'll have all three of 'em in a bag together, and then we'll drop a big fuckin' rock right on their fuckin' heads."

Mr. Canada stuffed half a piece of pizza into his mouth. His mother had taught him no manners. He talked with his mouth full.

"So watch him. Follow him. After a while, if it looks like he ain't gonna help us find the Parkers, Si-yo-na-ra."

Mr. Canada's jowls wriggled as he chewed the pizza, reminding Karl of Otto, who had so lately departed from this world of tears. Then he was confronted again with a mouthful of half-chewed pizza. "You fuck up again," the mouthful of pizza told him, "there just might be consequences."

ALL THAT NIGHT and the next day he thought about just killing the Boss. *Who did that bloated-up old windbag think he was? We'll see who suffers consequences from whom. We'll see who's really the muscle in this operation.* It would be the simplest thing in the world to do away with the fool, and everybody in town, including the Boss's wife, would only thank him for it. Yet he was neither a hasty nor an ambitious man. Killing the old souse might provoke a nasty little war of succession. The cops could put you in jail, but those other guys wanted to hack you into pieces while you were still conscious and then stuff you into the trunk of a car. Let the Boss talk tough and make all the foolish, idle threats he wanted. *No muscle there anymore, just fat, a fat mouth stuffed with gummed-up gunk from fast-food pizza joints.*

The old man was slipping. Bringing Otto in on the job was more than sufficient evidence of that. He had lied to the old pizza face about Otto, telling him that O'Keefe's bullet had punctured Otto's lung and that Otto had died in the back seat of the car before they had reached the farmhouse. But the truth was a little different.

Otto was hurt all right, but not fatally. All the way back to the farmhouse Karl had to listen to the little sweathog moan in the back seat and wondered what he was going to do with him. You couldn't exactly take him to the emergency room of the local hospital. So Otto had become a question mark, and it did not take Karl long to think of the answer, especially after he recalled finding Otto earlier in the day standing with his pants down over that woman. Anybody as miserable as that didn't really want to live anyway.

"I need a doctor," Otto grunted as the car eased to a stop inside the barn next to the pickup truck. There were no neighbors within a quarter of a mile. *Still, use the flashlight, don't turn on the overhead bulb, you never can be too cautious.*

"Where you goin'?" Otto gasped when Karl left him in the back seat and headed for the house.

When Karl returned to the barn with a blanket, Otto had struggled up onto one elbow. His eyes looked like a cow's eyes must look just before they conk it in the head with the sledgehammer.

"What you doin'?" Otto asked.

Questions. Always questions. He wrapped the blanket carefully around Otto so no blood would drip on the floor when he carried him out of the barn. The little man's fear turned into gratitude then, but Otto was always missing the point. Otto started getting the point again when Karl hoisted him over his shoulder and headed not for the house but for the field behind the barn. Otto tried to struggle, but he had lost too much blood to do much more than whimper and kick a little bit. In the middle of the field Karl laid down his burden, back first, on the ground.

He shined the flashlight on Otto's face. They weren't cow's eyes at all. They were toad's eyes.

"Any questions, Otto?"

Otto had no more questions, and life had no purpose when you stopped asking questions. "Don't," Otto whispered to the pistol in front of his nose. The pistol jumped in Karl's hand, and he saw the toad's eyes no more. He returned to the barn for a shovel. It took him a long time to dig a deep-enough hole, and it was almost dawn by the time he finished. He rolled Otto in and heard him thud on the bottom.

And that was how he had disposed of Otto, the Boss's most recent mistake. Most recent. The whole thing with Lenny Parker and the mink farm had been a mistake from beginning to end. Creativity got you nowhere. Stick to the old ways, the tried and the true. If you could. You did have to change with the times sometimes. The Boss did have some gray matter left. The idea of O'Keefe leading them to the Parkers seemed smart enough. They had no real way to find the Parkers otherwise. It wasn't like they were the cops or the FBI, with every conceivable resource at their disposal.

Watching O'Keefe might not be easy. The man was a snooper by profession, which might make him more sensitive than most people to the possibility of being snooped on himself. But it was not the target itself that usually noticed you. It was usually somebody else, some other snooper, the amateur kind, who would watch you watching and somehow blow the whistle on you.

But O'Keefe turned out to be surprisingly easy to keep track of. After a day or two, he hardly ever even traveled to his office, hardly ever even left his apartment. When he did go out, it was almost always to a bar. The guy was some kind of a flake or a drunk or both. After more than a week of that, he could only pray that the Boss would lose patience and let him kill this goofy bastard, who wasn't going to lead them anywhere except maybe eventually to that street down in the bottoms where all the winos hung out.

CHAPTER 16

WINTER SEEMED TO have come already, far too early, even before Halloween. Cold winter nights without snow made her feel lonely and sometimes scared. She stood in the darkness in the living room and stared out the big bay window, clutching her overnight bag to her chest, waiting, waiting like her mom had waited through so many nights in the old days. Late, almost an hour late. Maybe he wouldn't come tonight at all. She had tried to make time move along faster by counting the cars driving by, but there had been no cars for quite a while. The whole world seemed to have been abandoned, left alone with nothing to do.

A man in a dark ski jacket came walking down the street. When he reached the front of her house, he looked up, right at her. She wondered if he could see her standing there in the window in the darkness. The man hesitated, looked as if he might come up to the house but then strolled on down the street out of sight. She had not been able to make out his face to know whether he was neighbor or stranger. She wondered if he had really been thinking of walking up to the house. "That's just your imagination," her mother always told her when she voiced her fears.

Something moved in the bushes outside. "Mom!" she yelled and darted away from the window. She heard the ceiling creak above her, her mother's footsteps responding to her call. The footsteps stopped at the top of the stairway. She could see the bottom of her mother's white terrycloth bathrobe and the tennis socks covering her feet.

"What is it?"

"I saw something moving in the bushes outside."

"Turn a light on down there. And turn the front porch light on. Stare out into the dark long enough and anybody would start seeing things."

The tennis socks walked away from the top of the stairs. Kelly peeked out the window at the bushes and had to admit that there was probably nobody there. She switched on a lamp in the living room and walked to the front entry hall to turn on the front porch light. She avoided looking at the small, diamond-shaped pane of glass built into the front door for fear of seeing there, in her imagination or otherwise, some horrible face. Which made her think of the door that led from the basement to the kitchen. She ran back to the kitchen to make sure that door was locked. It wasn't. Her mother was so careless. And Kelly was certain she heard something behind the door. She stood there listening, frozen in place a few feet from the unlocked door, trying to screw up the courage to make one quick movement to the door to lock it. But what if someone opened the door just as she reached for it? She could turn and run as fast as she could to the stairway and up the stairs to her mother, who would only tell her again to stop imagining things.

She only needed to take a couple of steps, reach out and turn the lock, and she would have been able to, had she not heard again, she would swear, that shuffling sound behind the door . . .

Another sound made her jump. The blare of a horn. Out front. Her dad. At last. She quickly ran to the door, turned the lock, yelled goodbye to her mom, and was soon tearing across the front lawn toward the headlights of the van waiting for her in the driveway.

"Dad, where have you been?" she reproached him as she struggled up into the front seat of the van.

"Sorry. My meeting lasted longer than I thought it would."

"You could have called."

He knew where she had heard that line before. A hundred times before probably.

"I said I was sorry."

That tone of voice, that guilty defensiveness, a slight slurring in his words, the drink he held in the plastic cup in his hand, all told her that he was lying. There had been no meeting, or if there had been a meeting, it had been more about drinking than business. And she sensed that he did not even really mean her to believe the lie, that the lie and the threatening voice he told it in were just his way of escaping, of moving the conversation on to something else, that he did not really expect her to believe but to accept it anyway, to act as if he had done nothing to hurt her until he could make it up to her somehow.

They rode on in silence for many seconds, the lie choking off the possibility of communication. She knew he hoped she would speak first, but she did not intend to give him that satisfaction.

"Well" he said, finally, "what would you like to do tonight?"

"I don't care. Whatever you want."

"Well, what I'd like to do is rent a movie and buy a pizza to eat while we watch the movie."

She knew he did not care that much for pizza, or movies either. He was trying to make it up to her. She decided she would let him.

"How about two movies?" she said. "And popcorn during the second one?"

He laughed. A deal.

YES, HE HAD lied to her. But it could have been so much worse. He could still be sitting there in the bar alone, so close to severing the line, cutting the cord, even the cord that linked him to Kelly. The other day, on waking with an excruciating hangover, he had considered finding some cocaine to cure it.

The night they arrived back in town, Harrigan had wanted to keep on going, run the bars for old time's sake, but O'Keefe had declined. It wasn't that he was tired or sick anymore—in fact, he was drunk all over again. But the idea had kept building in him all the way home that, when he walked around the side of the house toward the front door of his apartment, she would be sitting on the stairs waiting for him. When he turned the corner and beheld the stairs—empty stairs—he instantly convinced himself that she had gotten inside his apartment somehow, that she would be sleeping, exhausted, on the couch, or curled up in his bed, hair wet and body fresh from the shower. That didn't happen either. Surely then she would call him from wherever she was hiding. He even bought a telephone-answering machine in case she called when he wasn't home, but her voice had not graced his telephone line.

She must have been terrified when she had run away that night in the fire and smoke and the fog-painted darkness, having abandoned any hope that he, her supposed protector, would be strong enough or cunning enough to save her from Mr. Canada's men, the fiercest of warriors, like the little men in the black pajamas on the other side of the globe. He had lost that war too. He tried to accept the fact that she might be dead by now. If not, then death must be stalking her always. He waited for some notice from someone, an obituary perhaps, that would end the waiting and push him into another phase of his grief.

He had considered another possibility—that she had ensnared and deceived him, used him to keep the cops at bay for a while until she could make good her escape.

Harrigan had called him on Thursday about the indictment.

"They handed it down this morning. I have to surrender you on Monday morning. The bail hearing is set for early Monday afternoon. I've chartered a small plane. We'll fly down Monday morning and be back Monday evening. You'll only be locked up for a couple of hours, until the bail hearing."

"Sounds too easy. You find a soft spot in the old Sheriff's heart or what?"

"Not a chance of that. I hired local counsel down there. A guy named Hugh Carruthers. He's one of the most respected guys in the area. He worked it out with the county attorney. The Sheriff didn't like it one bit. He wanted to come up here and grab you himself."

"So what's the prognosis?"

"Hard to say. The Sheriff's pretty powerful down there, more powerful than the county attorney, so the county attorney can't afford to tell the Sheriff to go to hell. So we probably won't be able to talk him into a dismissal. But he'll cut us some slack along the way. Like maybe give us a little time, and time usually favors the defendant. I'm preparing half a dozen motions to try to get the judge to dismiss the case, but why should he go out of his way to do anything for us? If it goes to the jury, I've got a story to tell them, but the other side's got a story too."

"Great system, huh?"

"Don't tell me that comes as news to you. You've worked in it long enough to know."

"Yeah, but it seems different when it's my nuts in the vise."

Harrigan laughed. "I know it's not funny, but if I didn't laugh, I'd cry, and I wouldn't be much good to you then, would I?

Maybe we are swimming in a shithole like you say, but then we'd better be the best God-damned swimmers around."

"What about the murder case?"

"Nobody seems to be getting anywhere. The county attorney issued warrants for Lenny and Tag as possible material witnesses, but that doesn't mean shit, especially if they've left the state."

"How about the FBI?"

"They won't come in unless the Sheriff calls them in, and he doesn't seem to be willing to do that, at least not yet."

"The Sheriff seems to be more interested in putting me away than in catching those killers."

"Catching those killers would be too much like work. You're in his net already. He doesn't even have to bend down to pick you up."

"How about Anderson and Lufkin?"

"Case closed. The old misers didn't like spending the money in the first place, and now they're scared shitless to boot. They told me to turn the thing over to the state and federal securities people. Which I did. Which means they'll just put it on the bottom of the pile underneath all the other con schemes and rip-offs that hit their desk before this one did."

"I wonder if I ought to call Anderson. Maybe he'd want me to find his daughter. Maybe I'd do it for nothing."

Harrigan hesitated, then sighed and said, "My gut tells me this is a snakebit deal for you all the way. Let it go. Let the whole damn thing go. Go back to work and let me do the rest."

"It's not so simple."

"I know that, but, for once, let's try and make something simple."

"I haven't done a decent hour's work since I got back in town. I don't think I give a crap about it anymore. I'm not sure I ever did."

"Well, all you've got to do is stay thinking that way for a few weeks, and there won't be any business there to give a crap about anyway. Unfortunately, we're both in the service business, and we don't have much capital to keep us going while we indulge our manic-depressive tendencies."

"I've turned a lot of things over to Jarvis this week."

"Did you tell him this indictment was coming down?"

"Yep."

"Better watch out. He'll be looking for another nest to roost in."

"Maybe not. I hinted I might sell him the agency on pretty good terms."

"And what then? Retire? I don't think that business of yours is worth all that much."

"I'd be happy just to get out from under the debt. You know how much cash I have to collect every month just to keep these doors open? And for what? I don't even like what I'm doing."

"I don't remember you ever liking anything you did."

O'Keefe's jaw clenched in anger. Harrigan, the archer, barbs of truth in his quiver.

"Maybe that's it. Or maybe it's wanting to live for something besides cash flow. Maybe I haven't forgotten what we wanted to be when we were in high school, Mike."

"What was that? Seekers of the true way? Knights of the Grail?"

"Something like that. To be real. To do something worth doing, to be something worth being."

"'Real.' What the fuck is that? It's time to grow up, Pete."

"Yeah, that's what I've been telling myself for years, but it isn't working for me anymore. I feel like I've amortized my life. I've pledged it to pay for something I didn't even really want in the first place."

"You know what I think, Pete? I think you're slipping back into the asshole of the world again. 'Turn on, tune in, drop out,' and all that shit." Harrigan's voice had caught, had nearly broken. O'Keefe wondered if there were tears building behind his friend's eyes and who it was that he wanted to weep for. "All I can tell you is to keep going. Keep going, and maybe something will happen to make you want to keep going."

"And what if we're going in the wrong direction? What about that?"

"I'll see you at the airport Monday morning," Harrigan said and hung up the phone.

KELLY LOADED THE first movie into the VCR, then skipped to the kitchen to help him cut the pizza and pour the drinks, Coke for her and beer for him. She frowned when she saw that he had already drunk two beers at the apartment. His face was flushed, and whenever he moved, he lurched a little bit as if he had to concentrate very hard to make his body do what his brain intended.

"I thought you were gonna buy me a bicycle this week."

"I forgot. I'm so sorry. Maybe tomorrow."

But she knew it would not be tomorrow. He would sleep late tomorrow and probably be lazy and crabby the rest of the day. She wished she could make him happy. He was unhappy so much of the time. She wondered why she couldn't be enough for him. He was enough for her, he and the movies and the pizza and the evening. She thought of what her mom always said about him. "He'll never be happy. Nothing's ever good enough for him. There's always gonna be something better over the next hill."

"Dad?"

He must have sensed what she was thinking from her tone of voice. He looked at her furtively, as if he were an animal and she were hunting him down.

"What's wrong, Dad?"

He shook his head as if trying to shake off her question. "Nothing," he said. "At least nothing I know how to explain."

"Couldn't you try?"

He looked down, like a schoolboy who had been caught doing something wrong. No, he could not, not in a way so that she would understand. Even trying to form an answer for her made him feel ashamed of himself.

Kelly fell asleep during the second movie, and he decided to go to bed himself before he ended up too drunk to rise up from the couch at all. It seemed too much trouble to make her take her clothes off, so he just put a pillow under her head and laid a blanket over her. For a long time he sat on the edge of his bed, drinking beer, smoking cigarettes, and looking out into the night. The door to his exercise room had stayed closed all week and would stay closed again tomorrow. The last few days had been one long, bleak hangover, and he seemed to be drinking now for no other reason than to keep the hangover going. He had still trudged dutifully to the office each day, but he just sat there, letting the phone messages pile up on his desk, postponing or canceling appointments, delegating everything, whether the person he delegated it to could handle it properly or not, avoiding Sara's gaze so he would not have to answer the fierce question mark flashing in those dark eyes. Days of torture, of minutes seeming like hours as he resolved each minute to plunge himself into the work but being held back by an invisible yet mighty opposing force, a mental force but too powerful for him all the same.

Meanwhile, the walls kept closing in. The licensing people notified him that they had initiated an investigation of the mink-farm incident, which they told him in the official notice they mailed to him, could lead to the suspension or revocation of his license or other "appropriate action." Harrigan promptly threatened the licensing board with a lawsuit, warning them that they had better have the most solid of grounds before they undertook any adverse action against his client.

O'Keefe discovered that he could still laugh when the constable served Preston's suit papers on him. Preston's lawsuit advanced the theory that O'Keefe and his employee Sara had invaded Preston's privacy in the hotel room that day. The suit named Sara as a codefendant, which added more guilt to all the other guilt.

"Preston's really grasping at straws now," Harrigan said. "Take those papers home and use them for toilet paper." Still, his liability insurance company presented a problem. Another claim would surely cause the company to cancel his policy. So he considered not making the claim. He would pay for the defense himself. But even if he did not make the claim, the policy required him to report the claim. When the claim was reported, the company might cancel the policy anyway.

The crisis in his life that he had long been expecting, perhaps even perversely hoping for, had crashed down upon him. He had gone along for years playing the business game, negotiating his dreams away in driblets, always hoping for some kind of rescue, some kind of escape, some marvelous epiphany that would infuse him with the knowledge and the courage to do such things as he needed to do to be his truer self instead of stumbling about on the stage of his life playing some poorly conceived role in a script he had neither written nor even deliberately chosen.

He thought of Kelly. What did he owe that little girl sleeping in there on the couch? Did he owe her the standard of affluence to which she'd become accustomed, to which he had accustomed her? But it was another man's daughter—the girl who had wanted to climb into that Jag and roll herself away—that he thought most about, and he cursed himself for that too, but he could not seem to avoid it. Still, every circumstance of his present situation told him it was folly to pursue her. He had no idea where even to begin the search for her. And even if he found her, what would he find—was she Rapunzel, as he had imagined that day as he stood outside her house, gazing up at the forbidding slabs of dark-tinted glass, or was she really Rapunzel's witch mother deceitfully cloaked in Rapunzel's exquisite form? And there was an indictment to be defended against, a licensing investigation to be faced, a business to run, employees to care for, amends to make, Jane's and Roy's murders to be avenged, a daughter to father.

There were those things, but then there was another. A vision. A vision of achieving a treasure hard to attain. The words of the Yeats poem came to him:

I went out to the hazel wood
Because a fire was in my head . . .

It had been one of his and Harrigan's favorite poems:

Though I am old with wandering
Through hollow lands and hilly lands,
I will find out where she has gone,
And kiss her lips and take her hands;
And walk among long dappled grass,
And pluck till time and times are done
The silver apples of the moon,
The golden apples of the sun.

KELLY WOKE IN the middle of the night. She still had her clothes on, and she could not remember where she was or how she had come to be there. Maybe she had died and this was her grave. They had all left her alone and forgotten. Then she remembered she was at her dad's apartment, on his couch, with her clothes still on, without a fresh, clean sheet beneath her. He had just stuck a pillow under her head and laid a blanket over her. She heard a drunken snoring from his bedroom. And she thought she heard the sound of someone walking softly across the front porch. Just her imagination again? Or the man in the ski jacket, the man without a face? And if it wasn't her imagination, if it was the man in the ski jacket or some other monster coming to get her, would her dad be able to wake up from that snoring sleep to protect her? She pulled the cover over her head and pressed her hands against her ears. *Go away,* she prayed. *Go away, imagination. Go away. Go away, whatever you are.*

CHAPTER 17

MONDAY MORNING CAME far too quickly. They hardly spoke on the flight. Harrigan seemed to be deliberately avoiding conversation, as if he felt his words could only do his friend harm, that a tight-lipped silence punctuated by sputters of awkward small talk was the only true gesture of friendship he could offer at this difficult time. He marked furiously with his gold-plated mechanical pencil on the documents he kept pulling out of his briefcase while O'Keefe stared out the tiny window on his side of the airplane and wondered why perfectly rational people like Harrigan and himself so blithely entrusted their lives to a puny, little, whining machine and a pilot they had never even laid eyes on prior to the flight.

"I've got the usual dilemma on an out-of-town deal," Harrigan said, as the pilot traced his pre-landing pattern over the tiny rural airport. "Do I let my hometown boy Carruthers do the job and wish I'd done it myself because nobody can do as well as this particular prima donna, or do I do it myself and hope the judge hasn't just been waiting for the chance to nail some smart-ass, big-city lawyer to the cross? And the only thing that's riding on my decision is your ass. So this bail hearing might be a bit of a rehearsal today, so I can see whether it's me or Carruthers who should handle the trial."

"That's fine, but I wouldn't want you to forget the job at hand. This bail hearing's definitely one of the high points of my life.

I'd like not to spend a night or two in that calaboose down there while somebody's trying to raise the bail money for me. This cow ain't stump-broke yet and doesn't want to be."

Harrigan tried to keep from smiling. "Not a chance," he said. "Carruthers has a bail bondsman standing by in case we need him. I'm betting we don't need him. If we do, that's gonna be a real bad sign."

"What's the problem?"

"The county attorney wants a hundred thousand dollars bail."

"Jesus!"

"I'm sure the Sheriff insisted on that. What we want the judge to do is let you go on your personal recognizance, no bail money at all."

"Just show me where to sign."

The Sheriff greeted O'Keefe with handcuffs.

"Come off it, Sheriff," Harrigan said, his head tucked back into his neck in that involuntary, snapping turtle motion of his.

"Standard procedure," the Sheriff said, grinning maliciously, displaying a snaggled, tobacco-stained front tooth as if it were a medal he'd won somewhere. "I can't treat your friend here no better nor no worse than any other criminal we got down here."

The Sheriff exercised his prerogative to exclude Harrigan from the arrest, booking, fingerprinting, and mug-shooting process. The process reminded O'Keefe of the Marine Corps, as did the Sheriff, who never took off his Smokey the Bear hat and looked like a boot-camp DI gone to seed. Some of the DIs used to make offending privates kneel in front of them with their hands to their sides while the DIs aimed side-thrust kicks at their bellies, going for a square hit in the solar plexus. O'Keefe thought the Sheriff would be very good at that.

"Were you by any chance a Marine, Sheriff?"

"Sure was."

"So was I."

"I hear the Corps's gone soft. I hear all kinds of trash and shitbirds make it through nowadays."

"Any leads on those murderers, Sheriff?"

The Sheriff showed off his tooth again and advised O'Keefe that he had the right to remain silent and perhaps the obligation to do so.

"You know those were professional hits, don't you, Sheriff?"

"Didn't look too professional to me. The way the woman was left, it looked to me like a sex murder. Like something one of those serial killers might do. That's probably what it was. One of those serial killers roamin' the country. Just got hungry when he was passin' through."

"Come off it, Sheriff. You think it was a serial killer that threw that Molotov cocktail into that cabin?"

"Who knows what kind of enemies you've made, Mr. Private Eye?"

"You know that's bullshit too, Sheriff. They were after the lady, not me. Maybe you should remember that they were looking for her at her house earlier in the day."

"All I got is your say-so about that, and I'm not sure your say-so is worth spit. I'm not so sure you didn't do both of them yourself."

"You planning to call in the FBI, Sheriff?"

"Hell, the FBI wouldn't piddle with this little ol' deal in this dinky ol' town even if I did call them in."

"Sounds to me like there isn't a chance in hell of catching those killers."

"I wouldn't know about that. All I know, Mr. Private Eye, is that whatever chance I had to catch 'em, you fucked it up."

"One more question, Sheriff."

"Boy, I thought I told you that you had the right to remain silent."

"I just wanted to know if you were born an asshole or just studied real hard to get that way."

O'Keefe had never seen a portly man move so quickly. A leaden fist in his solar plexus collapsed the air from his lungs, and a boot nearly crushed his testicles. He staggered around in a drunken dance before he fell to the floor, curling up in a ball, trying to summon enough breath to be able to vomit.

"Now, why don't you see if you can prove I did that?" the Sheriff said and walked away.

Harrigan decided that Carruthers should handle the bail hearing. The judge set bail at twenty-five thousand dollars and let O'Keefe sign for it himself.

"So when might you fellas be wantin' to try this case?" the judge asked the lawyers at the end of the hearing.

"First date open on the criminal docket in January," said the county attorney. "Isn't that our agreement, Hugh?"

Carruthers stood up and mumbled his agreement. Harrigan, who during the hearing had not said a word, not even whispered in Carruther's ear, who had only watched and listened to everything with his fanatic's gaze and the concentration of a mongoose sizing up a cobra, suddenly stood up and addressed the judge.

"Your Honor, I'll be filing some motions this week. We think this case ought to be dismissed. I'll admit every item of evidence they have, without objection, without even cross-examination, and they still can't make a submissible case with it."

"Well, Mr. Harrigan, we've got a good deal of respect down here for the good sense of a jury. They usually do the right thing. Don't you think so, Mr. Harrigan? Don't you think juries usually do the right thing?"

"They probably do, Your Honor, but I know I've won cases I should have lost and lost cases I should have won. And I think Mr. O'Keefe here has the right to rely on you to keep him from having to endure a trial if a trial is not justified in this case. And Mr. O'Keefe and I fully intend to rely on you to do your duty in that regard, Judge."

O'Keefe winced at Harrigan's last remark and hoped Harrigan knew what he was doing.

"Well, Mr. Harrigan, you file your motions, and I'll see what kind of duty I think I have. And, by the way, Hugh, have you told Mr. Harrigan I don't read anything that's more than two pages long?"

Carruthers and the county attorney chuckled with the judge like courtiers fawning upon their king.

Good old boys, O'Keefe thought. God save me from the good old boys.

"I try to be to the point, Judge," Harrigan said, "but I don't think two pages will do justice to my cause." Harrigan had paused a beat after the word "justice."

"Well, Mr. Harrigan," the judge chuckled, "I guess you've been fairly warned. I can't remember the last time I read a motion more than two pages long."

"Well, Your Honor," Harrigan said, smiling himself for the first time, "I guess I'll just have to take my chances on that. And I'm sure it won't go completely to waste. Because I know there's an appellate court that will read it."

Later, as they walked out of the courthouse, Harrigan said, "I hope I didn't fuck up with that judge today, but I've never gotten anywhere by kissing a judge's ass. If you do, all he does is make you kiss it some more."

"I guess I'd rather have you than those good old boys," O'Keefe said. "Those good old boys have to live with that guy every day of the week, so they're not gonna push anything too hard, including my cause."

"Just know, Pete, that I'm going to pull out all the stops for you on this including bringing to bear all the political clout I might have developed up to now. If you go down, it won't be because I didn't give it all I've got."

"I don't deserve you, Mike. Never did."

"What the fuck am I living for if not to rescue fuck-ups like you?"

They laughed.

"Just try to help me out a little bit, please. Try not to dig this hole any deeper than you already have."

They were careening down an otherwise empty highway toward the airport in a black Lincoln Town Car that seemed considerably larger than the airplane they had flown down in and that waited now on the little strip of runway to take them back to the city.

"I'm gonna stay down here for a while," O'Keefe said as they pulled up to a wire-mesh fence that separated the parking lot from the airport runway.

Harrigan started to protest vigorously but then seemed to think better of it, shrugged, and said as mildly as O'Keefe had ever seen him muster, "Do I have to tell you I think that's a dumbass idea?"

"Save your breath. I'm not letting it go. And 'reason' is just one of the multitude of important things I won't listen to."

"Is it the lady?"

"Maybe her testimony will help my case."

"Bullshit. They see her in front of them, they'll know damn good and well why it took you so long to report those crimes."

They laughed. Just like good old boys.

Harrigan climbed out of the car and looked back in the window with a melancholy smile.

"If you do find her, I hope she's worth the trouble."

O'Keefe watched Harrigan struggle into the cockpit of the tiny plane. The plane wobbled and bumped down the runway and lurched off, miraculously he thought, into the darkling, late-afternoon sky.

An enclosed metal hangar beside the runway contained one person, a straw-blond tomboy sort of girl who performed all airport functions, from air traffic control, such as it was, to auto rental, such as it was. She wore greasy overalls, a red-and-black flannel shirt, and a pair of mud-caked, waffle-stomper hiking boots that looked elephant size. She regarded O'Keefe with suspicion, and he wondered if she had been appointed Mistress of the local Xenophobia Brigade.

"Not goin' back with your friend, huh?" she said, eyeing him as if she would as soon knock his block off as give him a dollar's worth of change.

"Guess not. Do you have a pay phone?"

"You know that car's s'posed to be back here by five o'clock today."

"Does somebody have it reserved?"

"Nope. Just s'posed to be back, that's all."

"And what happens if I keep it past five?"

"Nothin'. If it ain't in by ten in the mornin' though, it'll cost you an extra day."

"I plan to have it back by then."

"How you expectin' to get outta here now?"

"I don't know."

"Ain't no commercial airplanes come in here. Closest place for that is Elrod. One plane a day. Eleven-thirty every morning to St. Louis. That's it."

"What if I want to leave the car in Elrod?"

"Drop charge. Big one."

"But I can do it? Leave it up in Elrod?"

"Long as you let me know that's what you're gonna do."

"Good. Well, I guess I'll do that."

"You leavin' tamorra?"

"Not sure yet."

"I guess you'll have to let me know then."

"Guess I will. See you later."

"Hey!" she yelled as he walked out the door, "I thought you wanted to use the phone."

She watched the black Lincoln drive away, then reached for the phone to use it herself.

He stopped at a service station and used the pay phone. He remembered the banker's name, Jerald Ullman, but he had forgotten the name of the bank. Bank names all sounded the same. Luckily, the town contained only two banks, and Ullman worked at the first one he called.

Ullman answered on the first ring, like he had been sitting there waiting anxiously for a call.

"Mr. Ullman, my name is Peter O'Keefe. I'm a private investigator hired by the directors of Prosperity Farms, Inc. to check on some things down here."

Ullman snorted a laugh. "I know who you are."

"I understand you were the company's banker here locally."

"Who told you that?"

"Jane, Lenny Parker's secretary."

O'Keefe heard a slight hiss on the other end of the line, a sharp intake of breath, then utter quiet as if some monstrous secret had just been revealed.

"So what do you want with me?"

"I need to ask you some questions."

"Well, I don't know if I can answer them. There's privacy laws and rules about that kind of thing."

"The corporation was your customer, right?"

"I guess so."

The lie came to him easily. "I've got a signed statement from the board authorizing me to investigate and waiving the benefit of all privacy and other applicable laws."

"How do I know who the board is?"

"I guess I need to talk to your boss. What's his name? Can you transfer me to him?"

"Mr. Tolliver won't want to be bothered with this."

"Well, I've got to bother somebody. I'm just a working stiff doing my job, Mr. Ullman. A few simple questions and I'll be out of your hair."

"When did you want to talk?"

"Right now. I need to leave town tonight."

"I'll be waiting."

O'Keefe hung up and reluctantly called his office. Everyone, including him, had to check in daily. If an operative failed to call in at least once a day, the police were called immediately, and people were sent out to find him. Yet he had considered breaking the rule. He did not want to deal with Sara.

"It's me," he said when she answered. "Just checking in."

"Do you want your messages?" she asked.

"Only if they're urgent."

"Herman Sanders is upset that you haven't returned his call. He says, if you're so busy, maybe he ought to stop sending you business for a while."

Tell Herman Sanders to stuff his business, O'Keefe thought. *Let Herman Sanders threaten some other idiot with the loss of his favor.*

"Do you want to tell me where you are?"

"Down in the lake country."

An awkward pause.

"Jarvis wants to talk to you."

"Okay."

"Pete?"

"Yeah," he said impatiently, trying to intimidate her with his tone of voice, keep her from prying.

"When are you gonna get around to telling me why you're doing this?"

"What makes you think I'm doing anything?"

"Save that for somebody else. How can anybody help you if you won't let them?"

"Why are people always under the illusion that they can help? Usually they can't."

She said nothing else, just transferred him to Jarvis.

"That you, Pete?"

No, it's your fairy godmother, he thought. "That's me," he said.

"I picked up a helluva new piece of business today."

You're confusing me with someone who cares, O'Keefe thought.

"Don't you want to know what it is?"

"Sure."

"It's from Zeitzman Corporation. Their union contract is coming up for renegotiation, and there's been some threats of sabotage. They want us to put one of our men in the plant and see what kind of scuttlebutt we can pick up."

"Scuttlebutt? You mean 'spying.' Are they trying to bust the union?"

"They say not. They say they just want to protect themselves from violence."

Several seconds passed; the men said nothing, as if a barrier had come between them.

"This is a major breakthrough, Pete. It'll be our single largest fee this year, and there's a ton more business where this came from."

"I was just thinking, when I was a kid, all my people were union people. Everybody."

"So were mine, but it's a different world out there now."

"I suppose it is."

When he arrived at the bank, Jerald Ullman's secretary told him that Mr. Ullman had been called out of the bank on an emergency matter, and that just before leaving, Mr. Ullman had told her to tell Mr. O'Keefe that he apologized that he had to break their appointment and could Mr. O'Keefe call tomorrow to schedule their appointment for another time.

"I need to talk to Mr. Tolliver then," said O'Keefe.

"I'm afraid he's gone for the day, too."

"Did he leave before Mr. Ullman did?"

She hesitated, he could tell the impertinence of the question shocked her, but she seemed to see no alternative other than to answer it.

"Well, yes he did. Just a little while ago, in fact."

So, O'Keefe thought, *Ullman had seen Tolliver leave, knew that Tolliver would not be around to answer my questions, and then ducked out himself. A mistake to tell Ullman that I was leaving town tonight. Or maybe it wasn't. It led Ullman to reveal himself.* O'Keefe had not expected the interview with the banker to yield much of anything, but the banker kept acting like a man with something to hide, and that was itself a revelation of sorts.

He found Ullman's phone number and address in the telephone directory. He let Ullman's phone ring ten times, but Ullman was either not home or not answering the phone. A family that delivered newspapers out of a rust-red minitruck topped with a camper shell gave him precise directions to Ullman's house.

CHAPTER ▶ **18**

THE HOUSE WAS a tiny box of peeling, dirty-white paint at the dead end of a dead-end street. A detached garage, stripped of its doors, seemed almost as large as the house itself. The house looked abandoned, but there was a five-year-old Chevrolet in the garage. O'Keefe knocked intermittently for several minutes. He intended to keep knocking for a very long time, until Ullman's nerves were on the verge of screaming out loud, until he would do anything, even confront O'Keefe, to stop that knocking.

"Who is it?" a voice said from the other side of the door.

"Peter O'Keefe. Sorry to disturb you, but I couldn't wait 'til tomorrow."

Several seconds passed in silence as the man on the other side of the door tried to decide what to do. O'Keefe hoped Ullman would realize that this was best—an interview at his home, away from the prying, busybody eyes of his coworkers at the bank.

"I promise I won't take long," O'Keefe said.

"Just a minute," he heard Ullman say through the closed door. "I was sleeping."

A few moments later Ullman let him in. Ullman wore a washed-out and wrinkled white shirt, unbuttoned down the front and exposing a gray-white T-shirt, a dark pair of suit pants, no shoes, and a droopy pair of dark socks that looked like they had been worn for several days. The man tried to smile, but he could not quite pull it off, as if he no longer could summon the will to play the various parts the world expected of him. The failed smile only made him look more hungover and bedraggled.

"Sorry I stood you up," he said. "I was sick. I've been sick a lot lately." And Ullman looked sick too. O'Keefe wondered if he had been wrong about Ullman having something to hide other than a drinking problem and a numbing despair.

"Hey, no sweat. And I'm sorry to bother you at home. But I gotta leave town, and I just have to talk to you for a few minutes."

Ullman only shrugged, turned away, and walked into the house, leaving O'Keefe to close the door and follow. One glance and you had seen half of the little house, which consisted only of a kitchen, a bedroom, a bathroom, a dining nook, and a living room, with a small back porch appended to it like an afterthought. On a small table in the dining nook there was a quarter-full bottle of *Jim Beam*, a glass that had been drunk empty, and an ashtray containing a half-smoked cigarette broken in two because it had been stubbed out so hard. Ullman had not been sleeping. He had been sitting there drinking whiskey and smoking, and when O'Keefe had knocked on the door, Ullman had jammed the cigarette down into the ashtray in anger.

"You want somethin'? Coffee? A drink?" When Ullman said the word "drink," his voice lifted, a lilt of hope. He was not talking about *Coca-Cola.*

"What do you have?" asked O'Keefe, pretending he had not seen the bottle of Jim Beam.

"Bourbon."

"Bourbon's fine."

"Anything in it?"

"A little water."

"Have a seat," Ullman said and shambled off into the kitchen.

The furniture looked like it had been picked up at garage sales from people down on their luck. There was a tan, vinyl easy chair, mottled with old stains of grime and maybe sweat, next to it a tiny end table and on it a shadeless lamp with a pull chain of tarnished metal beads dangling from the naked bulb, underneath the lamp an old brass ashtray, scarred and scratched, half full of ashes and cigarette butts smoked down to the filters. There was a dull-brown couch littered with newspapers, in front of it a glass-topped coffee table whorled with fingerprint stains and on it another ashtray stuffed tight with cigarette butts, a wooden pencil sitting on top of a half-finished crossword puzzle, a beer can that looked empty, a plastic plate containing a dried-out crust of white bread, a smear of mustard, a half-eaten pickle. No windows. No pictures on the wall, just water stains.

He heard Ullman struggling with an ice-cube tray out in the kitchen. A color photograph on a dusty, chipped, and battered credenza attracted the eye because it provided the only real colors in the room. Ullman, looking very different than he looked now, posed with a woman and two children—a teenaged boy and a little girl. *What had happened between them? What will happen to me and Kelly?*

"Fucker!" he heard Ullman mutter, then a banging, probably the ice tray against the kitchen sink. O'Keefe decided to sit at the little table in the dining nook, where Ullman would have to sit directly and intimately across from him. The table wobbled when he rested his elbows on it. The Formica tabletop, though covered with some kind of fake walnut treatment, was metal-hard with sharp edges, not made for skin to touch it.

Ullman came from the kitchen carrying a glass half full of ice and a pitcher of water. He sat down across from O'Keefe and pushed the bottle of Jim Beam across the table.

"Help yourself," he said. "That way you'll get it right, the way you like it."

"Sorry about the cheap shit," Ullman said as O'Keefe mixed the bourbon and water. "The good stuff is a little beyond my budget these days."

When O'Keefe finished, Ullman took the bottle and poured himself a straight shot. His hands shook as he brought the glass to his mouth. You could tell he was embarrassed about that but not enough to keep him from taking the drink. O'Keefe thought Ullman must be in his late forties, but there lingered a boyish look to him, as if he had not really grown to manhood but had leaped in one jump from a dewy, lithe boy, pretty like Lenny Parker, to a bloated and blowsy middle age. The confident, elegant, and supple youth still lived on in that partly inflated balloon of flushed and sagging skin. The prince was turning into a frog. No country boy here, O'Keefe thought, this boy grew up in the grassy suburbs, at country clubs, on golf courses and tennis courts, and in frat houses. Wisps of the blond hair of his youth still clung precariously to his scalp. He also had blue eyes and soft, white skin, but the eyes were streaked and the complexion spotted with red from too much whiskey. O'Keefe noticed a tiny patch of blond stubble under the banker's chin that he had missed when shaving that morning, the sign of a drunk or a man in too much of a hurry or both. His teeth were stained, like his easy chair and his coffee table and the walls of the rooms in his house.

"They repo'd it," Ullman said, and O'Keefe's face signaled confusion. "The house," Ullman clarified. "The bank repo'd it, and nobody would buy the dump and so they let me live here for just the price of the taxes and the insurance and the upkeep." He laughed a little death of a laugh. "Not much upkeep though, as you can see."

"Sounds like a good deal."

"Yeah," Ullman said bitterly. He took another drink. "So what can I do for you?"

"All I'm trying to do is figure out what happened."

"Join the club."

"You loaned Lenny some money, right?"

"No."

O'Keefe's look showed Ullman that he did not understand. Ullman smiled triumphantly, as if he had made an important point, then said, "I loaned the money to the corporation. The corporation's assets were the collateral. I looked at the file after you called. Got a corporate resolution and everything. The money was supposed to be used for corporate business. If Lenny did something else with it, I can't help that."

"Mr. Ullman, I want you to understand I'm not here to go after the bank or you or try to get out of the loan or anything else. I'm just trying to figure out what happened down here."

"Well, like I said, join the club. My God-damned job's on the line over this deal. The collateral won't even come close to paying off the loan."

"How well did you know him?"

"Too damn well."

"Did you know him socially?"

Ullman nodded his head.

"How about the business, the mink farm? What did you think of that?"

"I thought it was a dumbass business, but he had all that equity, all those investors. And he lived like a king."

"Is that why you made him the loans?"

"Maybe that was it. And maybe it was because I was tired of the same old dull shit down here. Trucks and tractors and farms and cows and women that look like cows."

O'Keefe thought of Tag, what her presence would have meant in a town like the one Ullman lived in, and Ullman seemed to divine O'Keefe's exact thought.

"Hell," Ullman said, "I probably had it in the back of my mind that if I loaned him some money, I could get myself into his wife's pants."

Ullman laughed, and O'Keefe tried to laugh with him so Ullman wouldn't see any outward expression of the wound he had just inflicted.

"Well, I'll tell you this, Mr. Ullman," O'Keefe said, desperately trying to play along with the joke, "you may have just proved yourself to be the most honest banker I ever met."

"Well, it's not hard to have honesty when you don't have anything else."

O'Keefe looked puzzled again.

"You see, they're gonna fire me over this loan, I know they are. I've been in this position before. Scapegoat. That's me. The scapegoat. They just use you, then spit you out. Well, fuck 'em."

"Ought to be plenty of other jobs in banking, huh?"

Ullman swallowed the last of the bourbon and set his glass down too hard on the table. "Not for me. Like I said, I've been in this position before. Wrong place, wrong time." O'Keefe quickly drained his drink to catch up with Ullman, and they poured themselves another round.

"Where were you before this?"

Ullman smiled, fox-like, as if he suspected O'Keefe of laying a trap for him.

"St. Louis. Other places."

"Never worked up in my city?"

"Nope," he said casually, but O'Keefe could sense though he could not see, a movement somewhere underneath the skin of Ullman's passive face.

"No family here?"

"Nope. Families are like bank presidents. They don't like to have failures hanging around."

"I don't mean to pry."

"Then don't."

O'Keefe took a long swallow of the bourbon and water. He needed it to steel himself for the next question.

"Did you?"

"Did I what?"

"Get in her pants?"

Ullman changed into the other half of himself then, the teenage boy boasting of his female conquests, real or not, to his leering companions.

"I'll take the Fifth on that," Ullman said, his smile tainted with cruelty. "What's the deal? You jealous or what?"

"What's that mean?"

"Well, in your case I understand there's no doubt about who got into whose pants."

"So the Sheriff's been talking around, huh?"

"It's a small town. What do you expect?"

"I'm trying to find them. Lenny and Tag. Either of them or both of them. Any ideas?"

"None."

"I thought you were a friend of theirs."

"Not really. Just some weekends at their pool and cruising around the lake in their boat sometimes. No big deal."

"No trips out of town?"

"No trips out of town," Ullman answered by carefully repeating O'Keefe's question, and his face changed, as if an invisible hood had been drawn over it, and O'Keefe suspected Ullman was lying.

"I hear they traveled to Florida a lot. And Arizona."

"I hear that too, but I never went with 'em."

"No guess where they might be?"

"Well, from what happened out at that mink farm, I'd guess if they're not dead, they'll be dead soon."

Ullman seemed to enjoy that idea, and O'Keefe wanted to reach over and grab him by the throat and squeeze hard. Not kill him, just terrify him so he would think he was dying when he passed out for lack of oxygen.

"Why do you say that?"

"Obviously they got involved with the wrong people."

"How would the 'wrong people' ever have found this little town?"

"Lenny raised money in the cities, not here. That's where he found them. Or they found him. Same difference. Trapped either way. Once they've got you, they won't let you go."

"You talk like one who knows."

"I know business. There isn't much difference. They're just businessmen with guns and garrottes."

"You ever heard of someone called 'Mr. Canada'?" O'Keefe asked and watched the invisible hood drop once again over Ullman's face.

Ullman just shook his head, his face impassive, but O'Keefe thought he detected a muscle twitching somewhere in some deep part of Ullman's face, and the fact that Ullman said nothing more, asked no questions, showed not the slightest curiosity about the man with the odd name—that absence of reaction, like the dog that failed to bark in the night- told O'Keefe a very important story.

"I understand that most of the money you loaned Lenny was borrowed in just the last few months."

"That's right. He worked it perfectly. Just like a bust-out."

"Bust-out?" O'Keefe said, as if he didn't understand.

"You know, just like the criminals do when they take over a business. Buy all they can on credit, pocket the money, then fold up the business. I've seen bust-outs before, but I never thought I'd see one in this burg."

"People tell me Lenny changed a lot in the last year. Did you notice that?"

"I noticed he wasn't around as much as he used to be."

"Nothing else? No personality change?"

"What personality? The pious little fucker didn't have a personality. He was a robot who wasn't programmed for anything but separating fools from their money."

"I don't see you as a fool, Mr. Ullman."

"I was talking about the investors, not me. And if this," he said, gesturing around the room, "doesn't look like a fool's paradise, I don't know what would."

"Maybe you've had some rough times like you say, Mr. Ullman, but a fool you're not."

"That's your opinion," Ullman said, as if O'Keefe had insulted him.

"What about her?"

"Tag?"

"Yeah."

"What do you mean, 'what about her'?"

"You think she was in on it with him?"

"Who knows? I'd say no, but she was a mystery. I mean, what the hell was a piece of ass like that doing with a twerp like Lenny in the first place?"

O'Keefe was afraid he really would reach over the table and grab Ullman by the throat if he stayed any longer, so he too abruptly stood up to leave. Ullman stayed in his chair and poured himself another drink.

"Thanks," O'Keefe said.

"Thanks for what? I'd say I didn't tell you anything you didn't already know."

"Thanks anyway."

Ullman shrugged, drained his whiskey glass and, his fingers twitching toward uncontrollability, took a long drag off his cigarette.

"How about telling me where to get some good food around here? I hear there's a place called *Angie's* that's supposed to be good."

Ullman had not expected the question. He forgot to drop the invisible hood this time. He looked nonplussed.

"No. Not here . . ." He caught himself then and looked like he wished he hadn't said that.

"Where is it then? Is it close?"

"No. Who told you about a place called '*Angie's*'?"

"I don't remember. Maybe it was Jane or Tag."

"Well, there's no *Angie's* around here."

"Where is it then?"

Ullman hesitated and then said, "I think there's a place in St. Louis called that. I really don't know.

"The place to go around here," he said, trying to recover himself, "is the Silver Lake Resort. Try the fried lobster. You won't believe how good it is. Or maybe you tried that the other night?"

"Why are you trying to get yourself beaten up, Mr. Ullman?"

But there was no use in that. He was in enough trouble already; he couldn't risk another charge, especially assault.

STANDING AT HIS front window Ullman watched O'Keefe turn the Lincoln around in front of the house and drive off down the street out of sight. He guessed he would not see the private detective again. The guy didn't seem all that smart, despite that cute little trick about Angie's. He looked at the telephone hanging on the wall in the kitchen as if he were considering calling someone. Then he thought he heard a noise, a thumping sound from the direction of the back porch. He considered going out there to check things out but instead returned to the table and his bottle of Jim Beam. His ears had taken to hearing things lately.

CHAPTER 19

WHEN O'KEEFE ARRIVED back in town the next day, he knew he should go to the office, but he went home instead. The message light blinked hopefully on his new telephone-answering machine. He pushed the button beneath the blinking light to rewind the tape. A small, nervous cough. Then a hesitation, so much a part of the man that it amounted to a character trait, revealed his identity even before he spoke. "Pete," the voice said, "this is Ernest Anderson. I want you to call me. I want you to find my daughter. I think I know where she is."

Ernest Anderson's house was as far out in the suburbs as it possibly could be, in the middle of a street without trees—standard cookie-cutter Colonial, white Doric columns, reddish white brick, white trim—here in late autumn the lawn still green as if it had been painted onto the front yard. *Zoysia grass, the grass with no soul.* No flowers, just evergreen shrubs planted in little, white pebbles looking like they had been carefully scrubbed clean one by one.

The sky had darkened on the drive to Anderson's house, and thunder exploded above him as he reached for Anderson's doorbell. Fat little pancakes of rain began to fall. Anderson opened the door with an insurance man's smile on his face. He wore white shoes, light-blue pants, a white belt, and a white knit shirt. He looked like a retiree heading for Florida.

"Good to see you, Pete. Come on back to the great room."

O'Keefe followed Anderson through a house full of Early American reproductions standing against the most ornate wallpaper he had ever seen. Light green carpet. Fake rubber plants spotted around. He could not believe she had grown up in this house, that anything could grow in this house.

When they entered the great room, O'Keefe thought for a moment that Tag herself was there. In a way she was. The room itself, uglier even than the other rooms he had come through—knotty pine on the walls, hooked rugs on the linoleum floor. But she was in there too. Everywhere in there. The walls of the room were covered with photographs, some of them blown up to poster size. Like a gallery. Like a temple. Tag on horseback, Tag the school spelling champion, Tag holding a string of fish she had caught, Tag accepting a prize at a horse show, Tag in a boat, Tag in her convertible sports car, Tag as a little girl opening presents, Tag and Lenny at college, Tag in her wedding gown, Tag stuffing white cake into her new husband's mouth, Tag in her cut-off jeans shorts and T-shirt, Tag in her low-cut prom dress, Tag in her tank top, Tag in her white bikini sunning by the pool.

Dark testimony. Testimony to a bewitchment, an indecent obsession. She had been telling the truth about one thing at least. He accompanied Anderson to the far end of the room where a round, wooden table sat in front of a fireplace. Above the fireplace hung a huge portrait of Tag. She must have been eighteen or so then. She had not changed much since. Every time he saw her it seemed like some small sinew snapped in his heart. From the portrait she looked down on the two men, both obsessed with her in ways they should not have been.

"Would you like something to drink?"

"Coffee?"

"How do you take it?"

"Black."

Anderson lifted the receiver from a fancy telephone console on the table and punched a button on the console.

"Mr. O'Keefe would like some coffee. Black. And I'll have some too."

O'Keefe wondered if Anderson had servants.

The rain had become a deluge, pounding on the roof of the house and the ground outside. O'Keefe plucked his pen from his pocket and laid it on the table, then zipped open his brown leather portfolio and removed a simple spiral notebook, the pages empty and waiting—a clean slate. Anderson sat there for a few moments staring at him, and O'Keefe remembered the awkward pauses in the conversation that day in Harrigan's conference room and the hesitations in the voice on the telephone. As if explaining himself, Anderson said, "Let's wait for the coffee."

As long minutes dragged on while they waited for the coffee, they made the smallest of talk, endured long, uncomfortable pauses, and listened to the rain pounding on the roof.

The woman stepped uncertainly into the room, looking down at the tray in her hands. *What had Tag said in the nightclub?* "The pious old bastard ground her to dust a long time ago." The woman dressed exactly like Donna Reed used to dress in her television show. One of his favorites from childhood. O'Keefe had always wished his mother could be more like the lovely, bright, fresh Donna instead of the foul-mouthed harridan she actually was, but then whatever beauty may have once shined in Tag's mother existed no more, all allure in it long gone, being unanimated by any discernible spirit whatsoever.

She set the tray down on the table.

"Pete, this is Tag's mother," Anderson said, as if he were announcing a rather boring home slide show.

"Nice to meet you, ma'am," O'Keefe said earnestly, standing up and extending his hand. She seemed confused, looked at his hand as if it meant her some harm, and quickly withdrew her own hands behind her back.

"The pleasure is mine," she said and averted her eyes before his could meet them, busying herself pouring cups of coffee from the pot on the tray. When she finished, she looked around as if searching for a chair to pull up to the table. Apparently she intended to stay. O'Keefe moved to offer her his chair, but Anderson waved him back down into his seat.

"Thank you, dear. That will be all." He had dismissed her, banished her from his presence as he would a servant. She hesitated for a moment, and O'Keefe thought he detected the tiniest quiver of rebellion far back in her eyes, but she wilted quickly under Anderson's glare and left without saying another word.

"This has been a terrible thing for her to endure," Anderson whispered as they watched her leave. "She's dying right before my eyes."

O'Keefe wanted to tell him she was already dead.

The thunder sounded as if it intended to rip open the sky. The lights dimmed and then came up strong again. Something, probably a tree branch, thudded against the house.

"Terrible storm we're having," said Anderson. Then he sat in silence for several long seconds. The man seemed to thrive on awkward pauses.

"Nice house," lied O'Keefe.

"Thank you."

Another awkward pause.

"The nicest thing about it is that it's paid for. No mortgage. In fact, I have no debt whatsoever."

"That's very impressive, sir," O'Keefe lied again. "Especially in this day and age."

"Our world is only what we make it."

You can say that again, you rotten old bastard, O'Keefe thought.

"When I was a young man, and we lived on the farm, in terrible poverty and want, even then, through the grace of Jesus Christ, I was able to see that America was still, and would continue to be, a land of plenty, and that the things of this world would come to those who worked hard and lived right and kept an eye out for the main chance. And since then, my life has been blessed in every way. At least until now."

You're never safe until it's all over, old man.

A pause. Anderson coughed his little cough.

"Have you found Jesus Christ as your personal savior, Pete?"

"No, sir," he said, embarrassed, trying to play the man straight. "No, I haven't. Not yet," he said, trying to leave the impression that this great transformation might, indeed, someday happen even to him.

"I hope you find Him, Pete, and soon. It seems to me that your life has been blessed too."

"How is that, sir?"

"Well, the war for one thing. How many miracles happened every day to save you from death in that war?"

"I guess I never thought of it that way. I think more about the others, the ones who died. Where were their miracles? It seemed like dumb luck—who lived, who died."

"And that, Pete, is the most terrible and foolish of all the terrible and foolish delusions of this modern world. That everything is left to luck, to chance. God has a Plan, Pete, a Plan for each human life. All we have to do is help Him by living in such a way that His Plan may unfold for us."

Anderson summoned up another awkward pause and presided over it like a god.

"Do you have life insurance, Pete?"

O'Keefe wanted to laugh, but Anderson was too eerie to laugh at. "Some," he responded. "thirty thousand dollars of term, I think."

"Do you have a family?"

"A little girl. I'm divorced."

"I'm sorry to hear that. Not sorry that you have a daughter, of course, but that you're divorced, and that you have such a small dab of insurance. Think of your daughter's future, Pete. If God claimed you early, and look what almost happened to you down there, thirty thousand dollars wouldn't even be enough to pay for her education."

O'Keefe squirmed. *Just pull out the paper. I'll sign up for any amount.*

"How old is your daughter?"

"Ten."

"And I'm sure you love her very much."

"I do."

"Then maybe you can understand what I'm going through now. Imagine how you would feel if, despite everything you could do, your daughter somehow fell into an evil web."

Anderson paused again and pawed with his hand at the photo album on the table in front of him.

"I was just sitting here looking at this album, her life spread out before me here. I said to you that my life has been blessed. And she was the greatest blessing of all. A gift from God, a perfect child in every way. And I prepared her in every way I could for an abundant and prosperous life. Yet she has fallen into an evil web."

"You mean Lenny?"

"I mean those men who were trying to kill her down there. And I guess Lenny too though it's hard to believe. It seems that Lenny has given his soul to the Devil. When he was a young man in college, there was no finer young man in this world. When I first shook his hand, I knew he and my daughter were destined to spend their lives together."

"Did Tag think that way too?"

The question had a bitter edge, and it took Anderson back a little. O'Keefe could tell that whatever she'd wanted had meant nothing to her father until she'd escaped him and rejected him, which must have been the greatest shock of his life.

"It was always hard for me to know what she was really thinking. She's quite a mystery. But you've met her. You know that."

I do know that.

"Mr. Anderson, I think Lenny started out believing his own story, but then he figured out that the mink-farm deal just wasn't going to work. But he, and Tag too, had grown too attached to the lifestyle to give it up. And then the evil, as you say, came along. I'm sure Lenny didn't seek them out. But they found him, and he was weak. The same old story."

"But why? What would they want with Lenny?"

"I think they were using Lenny's operation to launder their dirty money."

"And Tag?"

"Like you say, sir, she's a mystery."

"You have to find her. You have to protect her. My wife couldn't go on living if something terrible happened to Tag."

"It's a big country, and I don't even know where to start."

"I think I know where she was two days ago."

Anderson presided over another pause, heightening the suspense.

"For many years we've vacationed in southern Arizona. Tucson and that area. That's where Tag learned to ride horses. She's quite a horsewoman. She won many prizes when she was younger . . ."

Anderson must have sensed O'Keefe's impatience and dispensed with the rest of the biographical detail. "Anyway, we have many friends out there. One of them called me two days ago and said he thought he had seen Tag in a grocery store there. And there's no mistaking her, as you know. If he thought he saw her, I'm sure he did."

"Did he talk to her?"

"No. He said he made eye contact with her once, that it seemed like she recognized him but didn't want to acknowledge it. She was halfway across the store from him. She went down an aisle. When he went to find her, all he found was her basket, abandoned half full of groceries."

"Does anyone else know this?"

"No one."

"I guess I should tell you that you should tell this to the police."

"Would that help Tag?"

O'Keefe considered this for a few moments. Anderson was really asking him another question—if the police caught his daughter, would they end up protecting her or arresting her?

"No," O'Keefe said, "it probably wouldn't."

"It seems to me it ought to be handled more discreetly than that," Anderson said. "Privately."

"Privately," O'Keefe said, echoing Anderson, nodding in agreement.

O'Keefe remembered Jane had said that Tag and Lenny visited Arizona often and now Anderson had told him the family had frequently vacationed there. He quizzed Anderson about all the places they had stayed the places she had especially liked. What were her favorite landmarks and sight-seeing places? Could she speak Spanish? Did Anderson know where Tag and Lenny stayed when they visited there? O'Keefe scribbled Anderson's memories in his notebook. Something Anderson said would end up being important. Or the separate pieces would come together for O'Keefe in a kind of gestalt. Your history made you. You might vary it some, but you would likely repeat most of its essentials. Something in those notes could lead him to her if only he had brains enough and time to figure it out. When he could not think of any more questions, he closed the notebook and said, "If you think of anything else, no matter how trivial or stupid it may seem, get hold of me, and let me know what it is."

"I'll get you your retainer check," Anderson said.

He didn't tell Anderson that he would have done it for free. That would have seemed like a confession of some kind, what the lawyers called "an admission against interest." Anderson left the room to go to wherever he kept his bag of gold. O'Keefe scanned the picture album on the table and the photographs on the walls. She gazed down on him from all over the room, especially from the portrait on the wall above him. Those eyes. The expression in those eyes stirred a memory he couldn't quite catch. Where had he seen that look before?

O'Keefe was still staring at her portrait when Anderson returned. "Pete," he called, standing in the doorway, waving the check. *A temptation,* O'Keefe thought. *Not gold. Thirty pieces of silver.*

O'Keefe took several photographs from the album, grabbed his portfolio, and left the room without looking back though the pictures on the wall beckoning him to stay. He wondered how much time Anderson spent in that room. At the front door Anderson handed him the check. And hesitated. After the customary pause, he said, "And Pete, I don't believe in keeping secrets. I think I know what happened between you and Tag down there."

O'Keefe closed his eyes. Guilty as charged.

"And I just want you to know that I forgive it. Because I understand. She is such a wonderful girl, and in a moment of weakness, just a moment, anything can happen. Let it be a lesson. We have to maintain control at all times. At all times."

Since Anderson did not believe in keeping secrets, O'Keefe considered telling the old man the secret he knew about him. But he kept it to himself. The keepers of secrets possess great power but also great guilt. Later, brooding over that meeting in Anderson's house, O'Keefe could not keep from thinking that his own guilty knowledge had somehow made him an accomplice to Anderson's crime, and that he and Anderson had made some unholy covenant, the subject of the contract being Anderson's daughter, and it seemed like an obscure and unspoken arrangement to share the booty and divide the spoils.

"I'll report to you whenever there's anything to report," O'Keefe said, sealing the covenant.

He started to go but remembered something he had forgotten to ask. "One more question. What made you name her 'Tag'?"

Anderson hesitated, put his hands in his pockets, examining his shoes and the light-green carpet on the floor.

"That's not her real name. Her real name is Constance. Tag is just a nickname. When she was a tiny little girl, she loved to play tag. Everywhere. With everyone. All the time. It almost drove us crazy. 'Tag, you're it!' she'd say. So we started calling her 'Tag,' and the neighborhood kids did too. She liked it and started calling herself that, and it just stayed with her."

O'Keefe walked away from the tears streaming down Anderson's face.

CHAPTER 20

NIGHT HAD FALLEN by the time he left Anderson's house and the rain had subsided to a thick and misty drizzle. Back at his apartment, he did not go in but donned a windbreaker and a pair of Sportos he kept in the van and walked through the haunting, rain-ravaged streets. The storm had blown down huge tree branches and even whole trees, and had littered the streets with sticks and branches and leaves that had been crimson or golden just a few hours before in the glory of their dying but now lay in dark and forlorn clumps, sodden and forever expired. The streets were empty of people and even cars, as if all creatures but him were cowering in their burrows. There was no dark as dark as this, no loneliness as lonely as this, and it seemed this night had been created for him to wander in.

He walked through the little park near his apartment. A tree had toppled over onto the swing that he and Sara had swung gently back and forth in not very long ago. He remembered how he had wanted her that night, but it did not occur to him to want her now. An even greater wanting drove him now, an even deeper wound he sought to salve, but for a few moments he managed to forget even about the wanting and the wound as he lingered there in the shrouded womb of that ruined night that doom itself had seemed to come to, leaving behind it a devastated but satiating peace, as if truth could be found only in defeat. Finally, reluctantly, he walked back to his apartment, for there were things it seemed he had to do.

He called Harrigan at home. Mary answered.

"Hello, Mary."

"You remembered. Good for you. Hello, Pete."

"Is Mike in?"

"You're joking, aren't you? Is it two o'clock in the morning yet? Have the bars closed already?"

She stopped. He guessed she was crying. He did not know what to say. After a few seconds, she hung up the phone.

He tried Harrigan at the office, and he answered on the first ring.

"What's goin' on with you?"

"Just sitting here wondering what the fuck I'm doing here."

"Hey, you oughta call Mary. She thinks you're out boozing."

Harrigan said nothing. O'Keefe could tell he would not call her. Their marriage had settled into a bitter stalemate, a small, sad, cold war of the nuclear age.

"I need a favor."

"What favor?" asked Harrigan, sounding more wary than willing.

"You've got connections in St. Louis, don't you?"

"Sure. Some."

"How about bankers?"

"Some."

"I want you to check on a guy who used to be a banker there. It was a few years back. His name is Jerald Ullman. My guess is he was fired or resigned suddenly from his last job."

"Okay. I'll check on it. It might take a few days. I'm busier than a one-legged man at an ass-kicking contest."

"It can't take a few days, Mike. I need to know tomorrow."

"Shit. What's so damned important about this guy?"

"He was Lenny Parker's banker down in the lake country."

"Shit, Pete . . ."

"Spare me the lecture. Just try to find out about him, okay?"

"Why should I help feed this obsession of yours? Maybe I should tell you to go fuck yourself."

"I'll just find out some other way. But it'll take a lot longer. And meanwhile there's a life at stake."

"Whose? Yours or hers?"

Before O'Keefe could answer, Harrigan an expert at getting in the last word, had hung up the phone. The answer to his question was "both."

He had not eaten anything since breakfast, but it didn't seem to matter to his stomach. He poured himself a Wild Turkey on the rocks, sat down at the kitchen table with an ashtray, a pack of cigarettes, a lighter, and his notebook. It occurred to him that Ullman might be sitting at his own table now down in the lake country, not that much difference between the two of them, except that Ullman could only afford Jim Beam and had come a little closer than O'Keefe to the end of his rope.

He read the notebook over and over. She loved Chinese food, ice cream, and barbecued ribs. In her childhood she had possessed no household pets and few friends. In college she had majored in foreign languages, and she was fluent in Spanish. Her only hobby was stargazing, her favorite color, purple. At age eight she had been hit by a car while playing in the street and spent a week in the hospital. She had never wanted to be a movie star. Until junior high she had been taller than all of the girls and most of the boys.

She had been a champion diver in high school—her specialty was the high dive, the big board. He imagined her in a royal blue tank suit, water droplets beading her skin, strong bare feet gripping the board, three or four confident, graceful strides to the edge, right leg up and poised for the spring, her calves suddenly, surprisingly bulging with muscle as she springs, up, so high, the audience gasping as she folds backward toward the board into a gainer, two-and-one-half somersaults in the pike position—marvelous, impossible, the water not protesting her entry at all. Champion.

Facts. Facts but no meanings. The maze of biographical detail thwarted his quest. The only intelligible messages the notebook imparted were "southern Arizona" and "horses." The lady was crazy for horses. Her parents had given her a fine palomino.

"I'm sure she still has it," Anderson had said, "pays someone to keep it for her out in Arizona. And she has another one too, I think, one she bought for Lenny to ride. The palomino's name is Pegasus. She calls him 'Peg.' I don't know what the other one's name is."

"Do you know where she keeps it?"

"I'm afraid not."

"Well then, all I have to do is contact all the places out there that board horses. I find Pegasus, I find her."

"It's not that easy. Maybe she'd leave it at one of those commercial places, but I doubt it. I rather think she would have found a rancher or someone like that, someone she could trust to care for the horse like it was his own. That horse could be anywhere in southern Arizona."

"How about veterinarians? There shouldn't be all that many veterinarians out there."

"Horses aren't taken to vets very often."

"And," said O'Keefe, thinking out loud, "even if we find a vet who's treated the horse at some time or other, that won't necessarily tell us where it is now."

"That's right."

Still, you had to work with whatever little you had to go on. Unless he could come up with a better idea, he would have to go talk to the horse doctors. But where should he start? Southern Arizona. Anderson's friend had seen her, or thought he had seen her, in a place called Green Valley, a town full of retired people located a few miles down the interstate highway from Tucson. That might be the logical place to start. Yet Green Valley might be just a red herring. She was certainly plenty smart enough to shop or make any other essential public appearance a very long way from the place where she was hiding.

The family had vacationed in many places, from Tucson south to Tubac, east clear to Douglas. There had been dude ranches and resorts. There had been camping trips and wilderness treks. After her marriage, she had continued going there, three or four extended trips a year, sometimes with Lenny, sometimes without him. As an adult, she repeated the experience of her childhood, going to many different places, often separated by a hundred miles or more, peripatetic wandering, in no particular direction, forming no pattern. The only thing very meaningful he could lock onto—Tag seemed to like things remote, the remoter the better. She seemed to want to be near wilderness. And that would be a necessity in her current situation. But then there was wilderness all over southern Arizona, or at least what passed for wilderness in the late twentieth century. The government seemed to own half the state.

He had never been to Arizona so he pulled out his road atlas. *South, a long way south, to Tucson. South from there on Interstate Highway 19 to Green Valley. A few miles farther south to Amado and Tubac. Then Nogales on the Mexican border. Border. She speaks fluent Spanish. Horses. On the run. She likes things remote. At home in the wilderness. What would you do if you were a woman on the run? No, what would you do if you were this woman, Tag, with her particular wants and hopes and talents and fears?* The gestalt was forming unconsciously in his head.

Back up to Green Valley. Due west the Papago Indian Reservation. He had never heard of the Papagos, they had never made it into the movies. *Nothing due east except the Coronado National Forest. Forest? Pine trees in the sand? South and east, Sonoita, and Patagonia. Ranch country, according to Anderson. Did the cows munch on sand? Farther east, Sierra Vista, Tombstone, Bisbee, Douglas. There's neither time nor money enough to cover all that ground.* Frustrated, he cast the map and the notebook aside. He had drunk too much whiskey too fast and felt like throwing up. He would need help in the search, and the help he wanted was George. George had skill, but better than that, seemed to have been vouchsafed a supernaturally large allocation of dumb luck. O'Keefe could use some of that. It seemed like he himself had used up his lifetime quota.

He had picked up the phone to call George when the doorbell rang. *Too late for someone to be dropping by.* His hackles lifted in sudden fear. He paused at the door, curiously uncertain, debating whether to look out the peephole. *Booze is supposed to make you brave, but it's making me afraid.* Then the doorbell rang again, seemingly insistent and angry. Finally, he looked through the peephole. Sara. He hesitated even more now, wanting to see almost anyone but her, hoping she would go away. But she wouldn't. Maybe she had noticed the peephole darken when he put his eye up to it. She glared at the door as if she could see through it. *Shrink. Shrink away. Lovely lady, but no eros there, only disapproval and scolding.*

"I'm not going away. You're gonna have to talk to me, so open the door."

When he opened the door, she did not try to conceal her anger and disgust. He stepped back, and she walked past him into the living room, the smell of her perfume dazzling him a little as she passed. She sat down on the couch without taking off her raincoat.

"We need to talk."

He sat down on the Queen Anne chair across from her. She was as angry as he had ever seen her, but she was too gentle for real anger. Her eyes, deep brown wells of sadness, betrayed her. *Be careful, Sara, or I'll fall into your eyes.*

"George quit today," she said.

He tried to conceal his shock, tough this out like the tough guy he was supposed to be.

"Jarvis tried to make him do that union spying job, and George told him to stick it. He said for me to tell you that you could stick it too."

"So Jarvis is a dumb shit. I'll talk to George."

"It wouldn't have happened if you'd've been there, if you hadn't stopped giving a shit about everything."

He shrugged. She was right. He didn't care about it anymore. Even the news that George had quit had failed to move him much.

"You haven't been in the office for days, and even when you're there, you might as well not be. You're losing your clients. Even Harrigan's ready to write you off."

"Good. I'm sick of it anyway. Let Harrigan find himself another money grubber."

"So is that what you're doing? Making some kind of protest against the system or something? If you don't like the system, why don't you just close those doors and go off to the mountains or an island somewhere? This way doesn't show any brains at all, or any guts either."

Truth. But he was beyond truth.

She stuck her hand in her coat pocket, pulled out a piece of paper and thrust it at him.

"Here. It's my resignation. I'll stay for another month. You know, for old time's sake, like you and Harrigan, but then I'm gone."

There did not seem to be anything to do except to take it. She had emptied the shallow pool of her anger. One soft, slow tear meandered down her cheek. Then she seemed to be leaving. *It would be polite to open the door for her.* At the door she suddenly turned to him, grabbed his hand, and squeezed it. Tears shined in her eyes.

"I read the book."

"What book?" said the look on his face.

"Malory's book," she said. "*Morte D'Arthur.*"

He smiled suddenly, oddly, a little embarrassment of a smile.

"Do you remember it?" she asked.

"Not very well."

"Then maybe you ought to read it again. Those knights did what they called 'marvelous deeds.' Maybe you do 'marvelous deeds' yourself, but something broken in you won't let you see it. It was only the worthiest knights that received the gift. Only the worthiest ever got to see the Grail. It's inside you, not out."

She opened the door and let herself out as he tried to concentrate on what she had said, leaving him nothing except the fading scent of her perfume. Had he remembered it? Yes, that's what she had asked him. No, he had not remembered it. He had forgotten all about it.

GEORGE OBJECTED TO O'Keefe calling him so early in the morning, and he had plenty to be surly about already. "If you're gonna try and talk me into coming back, forget it. This rat ain't staying around for the ship to sink."

"I've got a job that only you can do. Besides, you'll like it."

"Is it sabotaging some union?"

"Come off it, George."

"I'm not believing you, Pete. You forget where you came from or what?"

"I wasn't thinking straight."

"It seems to me you ain't been thinking much at all lately."

"Will you take the job or not?"

"I told you I'm not coming back."

"You don't have to come back. Just do this one job and do what you want after that."

"I'll tell you what. Maybe I'll let you hire me as a consultant."

"Consultant?"

"Independent contractor all the way. You don't take out no taxes or nothin'."

"Yeah. And then you won't pay them and the IRS'll make me pay twice."

"That's how it's gotta be. You're hiring a consultant."

"Well, aren't you hot shit? All right. How about coming over here and 'consulting' right away?"

IT CAME TO him as he waited for George. He wondered how long it had been right in front of him. The gestalt. That's the way the gestalt worked. Now you don't see it, now you do.

"Tomorrow you're getting on a plane to Tucson," he told George. "And when you get there, you're going to the public library."

"If it's all the same to you, Boss, they've got more books than I can read right here in town."

"You're going to be reading local newspapers, George—the classified sections."

"How exciting."

"If you were a lady trying to hide, what would you do? You wouldn't go to a dude ranch or a resort. If you were smart, you wouldn't go anywhere you'd ever been before. You'd try to find some inconspicuous place, some remote place, to hole up in. If you're that lady, maybe you already know of such a place. Maybe you even have an old friend who owns such a place or knows of such a place. But the last person you want to contact is that old friend. They might be able to trace you easy that way. No, you need to avoid the old contacts and find some place new."

He sipped his coffee and took a drag off his cigarette. George was sniffing at the bait.

"If you were that lady," he continued, "what you might do is read the classified ads, the section that says "Farms and Ranches for Rent." You're looking for someplace way out in the boondocks. You leave a trail that way too, because you have to rent it from someone, the owner or a real estate agent, probably an agent. You can't help but leave some kind of trail, but this one's at least harder to follow. And meanwhile, you'll try to figure out how to get really lost, no trail behind you at all. You don't exactly know how to get out of the country, but you speak fluent Spanish, and the border's right there next to you, and you've got lots of time to figure it out, at least you hope you do, and there are smugglers all over southern Arizona, people smugglers, except they're usually bringing the illegals in from the Mexican side, not from the American one. And if you can get into Mexico, all Spanish-speaking America opens up to you then. So if those classified ads give you any kind of choice at all, you choose a place as close to that border as you can."

"So, George, you start reading those newspapers. We're interested in everything from Tucson on east and south. But we focus first on the remotest possible places and the places closest to the border. You copy down the ads and the phone numbers of the people who've placed the ads. You go see them and take these pictures of Tag and Lenny. If we're lucky, we find them pretty easily. If we're not lucky, we start talking to the horse doctors."

"Horse doctors?"

"It's a long story that I hope I never have to tell you."

"What about you? You coming out there?"

"Soon. But I have to do some trick-or-treating first."

"What?"

"See you later. Leave as soon as you can. I figure you can get done with the newspapers tomorrow and be talking to the real estate people first thing Monday morning. I'll be driving out. I should get there sometime on Monday or Tuesday."

"Why drive?"

O'Keefe looked evasive. "Thought I'd see the country," he said.

George knew O'Keefe was lying, but he left it alone, quickly downed his drink, and left. One little spark and he knew they might come to blows.

HARRIGAN DID NOT call for two days.

"It's about time," said O'Keefe.

"Actually, it's pretty good service when you give me bum information and send me on a wild goose chase."

"What's that mean?"

"That guy Ullman isn't from St. Louis. He's from right here in town. He left about five years ago."

"He sat there and lied to me. He must have hoped I wouldn't check."

"And the guy's apparently a snake. He was a real wonder boy for a while. For a while he was Carter Kendall's fair-haired boy over at First City Bank. Big corporate accounts, the best country club, wonderful family, all that shit. But Ullman had a taste for booze and broads and BMWs, and everybody was wondering how he could do all that on a banker's salary, especially when his wife finally got fed up and divorced him and he's got no assets left and has to pay all that alimony and child support. Then, all of a sudden, a couple of his accounts turn bad. Real bad. A couple of equipment-leasing scams. Lots of paperwork, lots of money going out, some coming in too for a while, then nothing; and then, when they go to find the equipment, it isn't there; it never was there. He says he trusted the borrower, didn't bother to check on the equipment after a while, just took the borrower's word. The borrower whose word he thought was so good turns out to be a small-time mobster who goes to jail for the scam, but everybody knows there's somebody bigger involved."

"So Carter Kendall quietly unloads his former wonder boy Ullman on another unsuspecting bank. A tiny bank, and Ullman's no less than the president of that tiny bank. And, after a year or so, all of a sudden Ullman's in the middle of a couple of bust-outs again. So Ullman resigns and moves out of town. All very quiet. Nothing left of him but ugly rumors. Because the little bank has done the same thing that Carter Kendall did to the little bank, unloaded Ullman on another unsuspecting bank, an even smaller bank down in the lake country. Where he is now. And there you have it. The Pilgrim's Progress, late twentieth-century style."

Later O'Keefe called Ullman's bank down in the lake country, but they said he had left, didn't even give any notice, just up and left—didn't just leave the bank, left town too, no forwarding address. When O'Keefe hung up the telephone, he reached for the local phone book, looking for a restaurant or a bar whose name began with the letter A.

HE WONDERED HOW the place had escaped his notice all these years. Not that it was the kind of place that would attract any attention—a decrepit little building at the bottom of a bluff in the bottoms area of town between the railroad tracks and the river. It looked like someone had rolled it down the hill and left it where it happened to land. Yet two black Cadillacs were parked in the back of the place and a Lincoln Town Car and a couple of sports cars out front.

The food was awful, bad American-Italian mainly. O'Keefe tried to eat a few bites of spaghetti and meatballs topped with a gloopy sauce that must have come out of a can. Another customer examined with suspicion a greasy-looking plate of sausage and peppers; another surprisingly seemed to be relishing a microwaved pizza. There was a bar, a few tables and booths, and a pool table in the center where slick, young men drank Seven & Seven and gambled at eight-ball in tight-fitting pants and shirts open to show the gold chains on their tanned and hairy chests. When O'Keefe came in, they stopped talking and talked no more until he left. At one point a little man, nearly as broad as he was tall, appeared from somewhere in the rear of the place and gestured to one of the pool players, who followed the man back to wherever he had come from.

O'Keefe pushed back his chair and casually asked the bartender the location of the john, which, as he had hoped, turned out to be in the general direction from which the fat man had emerged. On his way he passed through a large room with an old bowling machine and an old shuffleboard. He guessed the machines were only for show as the room looked unused.

At the far end of the room, barely visible in the darkness, was a door, from under which a gleam of murky, yellow light oozed into the room. Standing there in the big dark room, looking at the door and the sinister shaft of yellow light, O'Keefe fought the impulse to flee from that place and not look back until he had covered a great deal of intervening ground. He looked back over his shoulder and saw that one of the pool players was watching him like a housecat studying a mouse.

He returned to his table, tossed down the remains of his drink, left too much money on the table to pay for his dinner and drinks, and left. He walked quickly to his van, looking back over his shoulder in the darkness a couple of times. When he got into the van, he locked the doors, something he could not remember ever having done before, and he kept the doors locked until he reached his apartment, for his city seemed changed, full of menace, a menace that emanated, it seemed to him, from a crack beneath a shabby door at the far end of a dark back room at a nondescript place in the bottoms called *Angie's*.

HARRIGAN TOLD JULIA to hold his calls, took a drink of his coffee, lit a cigarette, looked across the table at O'Keefe, and said, "Okay, what's the deal?"

"You ever heard of a place called '*Angie's*'?"

Harrigan shook his head.

"There was a note scribbled on one of the deposit slips down at the mink farm. It just said '*Angie's*.' Nothing else. Well, Angie's turns out to be a dump of a bar and restaurant down in the bottoms, but where you'd expect winos to be lying around, there's black Cadillacs parked instead."

"You went there?"

"Sure did. Even ate dinner there. The food was conclusive evidence of the banality of evil."

Harrigan laughed.

"Then I go check on the ownership of the liquor license, and guess who owns it?"

Harrigan shook his head, refusing to guess, and waited for the answer.

"Donald Praeger."

"The lawyer?"

"None other."

"Oh, shit."

"And Donald Praeger means . . .

"Carmine Jagoda," said Harrigan, very softly.

"None other. I think that's who 'Mr. Canada' is."

Harrigan stood up and walked around the desk to the window and looked down at the city. The smoke from his cigarette curled back over his shoulder.

"It didn't seem so scary until now," said O'Keefe. "Until it ended up right in my own backyard."

"How about now, Pete?" Harrigan said.

"Meaning?"

Harrigan whirled around, and the ash from his cigarette dropped and splattered on the carpet at his feet. This time he was unable to disguise his fear with his anger. "Meaning how about now you stop this shit? There isn't a more vicious sonuvabitch in this country than Jagoda. He likes to have people carved up into chunks and stuffed in the trunks of their cars."

Harrigan turned and looked out the window again. For several seconds they remained silent.

"How the hell does Jagoda get hooked up with a weenie like Lenny Parker?" Harrigan said to the window.

"I think Ullman was the link," said O'Keefe. "Ullman was 'The Man Who Corrupted Hadleyburg.' And guess what? Ullman's disappeared. Off the face of the earth, it seems."

"Disappeared into the earth probably. Have you told this to the Sheriff down there?"

"Yes, I have. I called him today. And he's still not interested. He seems to think I'm making all this stuff up so I can get myself off the hook."

"You've got to go to the cops here then."

"Okay, I'll go to the cops. Call 'em up right now, Mike. But what are they gonna do? Not a damn thing, that's what. They've never been able to touch Jagoda. And what do I have to give them? A name on a slip of paper, and the slip of paper doesn't even exist anymore."

"We'll go to the strike force then."

"And about a year from now they might indict him for tax evasion or something."

"What're you gonna do then? Play vigilante? Track him down yourself?"

O'Keefe shook his head. "The truth is I have no idea what I'm gonna do."

CHAPTER 21

ALL SOUL'S DAY. The festival of the dead.

"Let me do it, Mom," Kelly said.

They stood on the front porch in the gathering dark. Her mom struck the blue-tipped, wooden match against the side of the box and quickly handed it to Kelly. Kelly stuck the burning match into the skull of the jack o' lantern that she and her mom had carved out a few hours earlier. The match almost burned her hand before the wick of the candle caught fire, and she had to drop the match inside the pumpkin. She pulled up the long skirt of the white dress her mom had given her for her costume and maneuvered awkwardly down the front porch stairs to gain a head-on look at the jack o' lantern.

"Be careful, you'll trip," her mom said.

The flame danced behind the jagged eyes and the yawning mouth.

"Geez, it's really spooky!"

"Okay, come on in, and get the rest of your costume on," her mom said as she put the top of the jack o' lantern's head back on. "Your dad'll be here any minute. That is, if he's on time for once."

"I wonder if it's going to rain again," said Kelly, looking up at the sky. It had rained most of the afternoon and had cleared up only an hour ago.

Her mom had a date that night, so her dad would take her out trick-or-treating and she would stay all night at his place. She put on the halo that she had fashioned out of white coat hangers, and her mom pinned on the wings they had created from metal rods, rubber foam, and white cloth. Her treats bag was a white pillow case, shining bright from the washer, dryer, and hot iron. Her mom's old white dress and a pair of white ballerina shoes completed her outfit. She marveled at how inventive her mom could be. Her dad could not have accomplished anything like her mom had so effortlessly managed. He had no skill with his hands. He would have just gone out and rented her a costume.

"What did they think of your costume at school today?"

Kelly shook her head as if to shake off the memory, and her mom thought for a moment that her daughter was going to cry.

"They didn't like it. They thought it was dumb to dress up like an angel for Halloween."

"Well, what do they know anyway?"

"Nothin'. That's what they know. Nothin'."

The doorbell rang.

"Okay," said her mom. "Here's your goodies bag. See you tomorrow."

The doorbell rang again as she stepped carefully down the stairway. Her mom had forgotten to turn on any lights downstairs. She had to hold on to her halo to keep it from falling off. Her mom hadn't turned on the porch light either. She reached for the light switch as she opened the door. Something was wrong. A hulking, rounded shape lurked there in the darkness, and when she reached to turn the light on, the thing lunged to grab her. She screamed as loud as she could. Then all kinds of things seemed to happen at once. A light turned on overhead, her mom came running down the stairs, the thing grabbed her arm and kept saying "Kelly, it's me. It's me! Kelly!"—and although she realized after a few seconds that it was her dad's voice coming out of the thing, she still couldn't stop wailing.

"Hey, I'm sorry. I didn't mean to scare you."

Her mom grabbed her and hugged her tight.

"The hell you didn't," her mom said to him over Kelly's shoulder. "You always thought that scaring people was so cute."

"I really didn't!"

But he had meant to surprise her, and maybe even scare her too, just a little bit, not the way it happened. Another bad idea.

"God, Dad! You scared me to death!" Kelly said, turning around. She knew she had to get out of there with him fast or there would be an even uglier scene. "Bye, Mom. See you tomorrow."

She took his hand and pulled him after her out the door.

"Jerk!" she heard her mom hiss as the door closed between them.

Once she got over the scare, Kelly was delighted with her dad's costume.

"That's neat, Dad. Where'd you get it?"

"I rented it. I always wanted to be a gorilla."

She laughed and put her angel's hand in his gorilla's paw, and they walked off down the sidewalk, she pulling him along eagerly toward the next-door neighbor's house where three little devils were knocking at the door.

Kelly's mom watched them through the front window as they moved off down the sidewalk, shaking her head angrily at the way Kelly had forgiven him so quickly and easily, as quickly and easily as she herself had forgiven him so many times over the years.

"Don't stay too close, Dad," Kelly said. "I don't want them to think I'm a little girl."

When she walked up to the front doors of the houses, he stood off in the darkness, as she had sternly instructed him to do, so the people could not see that she was chaperoned.

A fog had descended on the misty night. They could not see more than half a block.

"Geez!" she said. "It's really spooky now."

It was like a ballet in a dream, half full of foreboding, half full of wonder. The yellow street lamps emitted only a wan and distant light, vague and blurred and ebbing. All about them, up and down the sidewalks and crossing the streets and standing on porches with their treat bags, the little graveyard people moved through the night amid the mist and the fog. A witch, a vampire, and a bloody corpse walked up to them.

"Hey, Kelly," said the witch.

"Who's that?"

The witch cackled. "Guess who? Trick or treat."

Kelly watched them walk past and off down the street, trying to figure out who it was.

"I don't know who that was. Next year I wanna go out trick-or-treating with my friends. Can I do that? Will I be old enough then?"

"We'll see next year. That's a long way off."

He supposed this would be the last time he would trick-or-treat with her. Another letting go. Letting go, and letting go, and letting go again. That seemed to be what being a parent was mainly about sometimes. He remembered that he had begun to go trick or treating without his parents by age eight or nine. But everything was so different now. Brownies laced with strychnine. Razor blades in caramel apples. Real goblins and demons stalked the night these days, and the wolves had emerged from the forest and were hunting in the streets.

They had entered a cul de sac of only a few houses. She had forged ahead of him about ten yards. "Look, Dad," she said, pointing across the street. An executioner, much taller than the other trick-or-treaters, in black hood and cape and brandishing a bloody ax, marched slowly, portentously across the street toward her. O'Keefe started to laugh, but the laugh caught in his throat when he saw the executioner bearing down on her with what seemed like harmful intent. The blade of the ax looked so real. Something in his body told him to move very fast.

He had covered half the distance between him and Kelly when the executioner saw the gorilla running toward him, stopped, abruptly dropped his ax, and yelled. "Hey, Kelly, it's me. It's just me, Kelly," as if she were the only court of appeal from the galloping gorilla. Then he turned and ran away.

Kelly was laughing. "I know who you are!" she yelled at the running figure. "That was Stevie. Caroline's brother. I guess we showed him."

"Hey, Stevie," she yelled at him again. "You better watch out, or I'll sic my gorilla on ya."

"What an idiot," O'Keefe muttered, his heart still racing. *I'm getting scared of my own shadow.*

As they walked farther on, she said, "I don't think they ought to allow big kids to trick or treat."

Her sack was soon almost full.

"What kind of stuff do you have in there?"

"Mostly just those little miniature candy bars. It seems like everybody gives you the same thing."

"You had enough yet?"

"Just about. Can we just finish this block?"

The elderly Ryans' house, the spookiest house in the neighborhood sat far back off the street, surrounded by hedgerows. The

Ryans couldn't afford to keep the place up anymore, so the paint on the wood trim was nearly peeled off and the yard was more weeds than grass and always needed mowing. The only yard work old Mr. Ryan ever managed to accomplish was to hack futilely at his hedgerows with an ancient pair of shears. One of the shutters hung crazily down from one of the upstairs windows, half on and half off. It had been hanging that way for years, and the kids always wondered what kept it from falling all the way off. An old wooden swing on the front porch often moved slowly back and forth by itself even on hot and windless summer nights.

The kids in the neighborhood had made a mutual dare at school that each one of them would walk alone up to the Ryan house and ring the doorbell and wait in the darkness for old Mrs. Ryan to shuffle slowly to the door, creak the door open, and reach out her gnarled, claw-like, liver-spotted hand so she could drop two measly, little candy kisses into your bag. Anyone who didn't have the courage to do it had to pay each of the other kids a dollar, and Chris Larkin claimed he had a way to know if anyone cheated.

"I'd skip that place if I were you," said O'Keefe.

But she apparently meant to go up there.

"You want me to go up with you?" he asked.

"No," she said sternly. "You have to stay right here." She disappeared between the hedgerows.

Walking along the narrow path with the bushes scraping at her on either side, she imagined a hand reaching out from the thicket of branches. She kept looking straight ahead, never to the side, for fear of seeing a pair of red eyes peering at her. One of her wings caught on a branch and wouldn't let go. She pulled away hard and heard the wing tear.

"You'd better not be there, Stevie," she muttered. "You'd better not try to scare me."

It seemed to take forever to get to the porch. She rang the doorbell and tried not to look toward the shape in the darkness to the left of her, the old wooden swing, the scariest thing about that scariest of places. Mrs. Ryan was not answering the door. Maybe the doorbell didn't work anymore. Maybe the Ryans couldn't hear it ring. Maybe they had died in there and wouldn't be coming to the door at all. She reached out to knock when the door opened and she almost fell forward into the house.

"Trick or treat," she whispered, hardly able to get the words out. "Well, aren't you the sweetest thing!" said Mrs. Ryan. "Herbert!" she screeched. "Come here and see what the Good Lord's put on our doorstep tonight. You don't mind if Herbert comes to see you, do you?"

Kelly shook her head. No, she didn't mind. Yet she couldn't help but think of Hansel and Gretel and the old witch who lived in the forest and fattened up little children so she could roast them in her oven and eat them up. But she could also tell that these were kindly old eyes she was looking into. A fierce-looking old man came shuffling up behind the old woman, but he brightened as soon as he saw the angel on his doorstep.

"Well, well, Katherine," he said to the old woman. "Ain't she the very picture of heaven?"

He stuck out his old hawk's face and said, "What's your name, little angel?"

"Kelly O'Keefe," she said, stepping back on the porch, preparing to turn around and run if she had to.

"And an Irish angel at that," the old Irishman said, affecting a brogue.

"And look, Herbert," the old woman said, "she's an angel with a broken wing."

"Why don't you come on in here and have some hot apple cider," the old man asked, "keep us old folks some company for a few minutes?"

"My dad," she mumbled. "He's waiting for me out at the curb."

"Well," the old lady said, "let's have him in too."

She started to say "No." If her dad came up to the house, she might lose the bet with the other kids. *Would that nasty Chris Larkin call that cheating? Where will I get the money to pay all those dollars?* But the old couple stood there beaming, and she did not see how she could tell them "No."

"Dad," she yelled. "Dad, come up here a minute."

She heard him rustling along the hedgerow. "Don't be afraid," she told the old couple. "He's a gorilla."

"THEY WERE NICE," she said as she and her dad came out from the Ryans' yard onto the sidewalk. There were no trick-or-treaters left on the streets, and most of the porch lights had been turned off.

"Will you carry my bag for me, Dad? I'm tired."

"Heavy," he said. "I think they gave you all the candy kisses they had left."

"That's what I'll show the kids tomorrow. All those candy kisses! I'll bet nobody else went inside," she said proudly. But she thought she would leave out the part about her dad coming in with her.

"Look, big kids," she said, and shrank toward him. Down the block two skeletons, both of them taller and broader than children, taller and broader even than teenagers, walked toward them. They did not seem to have much in their bags. They were almost walking in step, not like teenagers out on a lark, more like soldiers out on a march. They said something to each other, then, at the very same time, each of the skeletons reached into his bag.

Kelly lost her grip on her own bag of treats when her dad suddenly snatched her up, hoisted her over his shoulder, and started running back toward the Ryans' place. Her candies scattered all over the sidewalk. From over her dad's shoulder she could see that one of the skeletons had dropped to one knee and was pointing something at them. Soundless flashes of fire jumped out from the skeleton's hands, and she guessed it was bullets that were whizzing all around them and crashing into the bushes. Then her dad fell down, and she spilled hard onto the sidewalk. The fall knocked the breath out of her, and when she looked up, he was on his knees and crawling toward her, struggling to his feet. He swept her up again and they plunged through the Ryans' front hedgerow. She cried out when the spike-like branches jabbed and scratched her face and arms and legs. Now he had dropped her and was pulling her along the ground, and she thought he might pull her arm clear out of its socket. The pain kept her from seeing the pistol muzzles flash on the other side of the hedgerow, kept her from hearing the skeletons crashing after them and cursing because they had a hard time struggling through the thicket.

Now her dad was dragging her into some kind of hole that she later realized was the big window well of one of the Ryans' basement windows. He covered her up, crushing her with his big hairy gorilla's body, and whispered for her not to make a sound, but he was breathing so heavily and choking and gagging that she just knew the skeletons would hear him. She waited for them to come and fire the soundless bullets into their huddled bodies, and it was only then that she started to cry.

They told her later that she had gone into what they called "shock." She did not really remember very well the footsteps of the skeletons running past the window well or the long minutes after her dad passed out on top of her and she thought his bulk might smother her. She only vaguely remembered the flashlight shining down on them and old Mr. Ryan standing above them and saying, "Oh, my God, oh, my dear God," or the policeman carrying her to the ambulance. But she remembered too vividly seeing them pull the gorilla's head off her dad and the blood that covered his head and face and how she screamed and how they had to hold her down for a while after that until they gave her a shot of something that made her fall asleep.

O'KEEFE SAT ON an examining table in the emergency room with the bottom part of his gorilla suit still on and twelve new stitches in the back of his head.

"You daughter's fine," the intern said. "She's sleeping. She'll be ready to go home tomorrow. You're lucky you had that gorilla's head on. I think it deflected the bullet so it only grazed you. Lots of blood, but not very deep. Without that ape head, I'll bet it would've taken the whole back of your head off."

"Can I go now?"

"Yeah. The cops are waiting outside to talk to you. And one very angry lady."

He saw her through the window of the emergency waiting room, pacing and sobbing. She was dark-haired and dark-eyed, and her eyes grew even darker when she was angry. She had fought hard in aerobics and exercise classes to keep the thickness of approaching middle age off her and had succeeded admirably. She wore a sleeveless red dress that looked so good on her that he forgot for a moment why their marriage had broken up.

She came charging in as soon as the intern left. "You bastard," she said. "That little girl was almost killed tonight because of you. You should have seen her, you bastard. She was scared almost to death. Trembling and shaking and sobbing and screaming until I thought she was going to go crazy."

It surprised him when she reached out and slugged him and tried to slug him again. He caught her arm and held her away from him. She sobbed and shook her arm from his grip.

"Well, if I have my way, you're never going to see her again without a police escort. I've already called my lawyer, and he'll be filing something tomorrow. No court in the world is going to make me give my daughter up to a man who endangers her life!"

He started to say she didn't have to file something, he would do whatever she wanted, but she turned and stomped off before he could say it. He didn't want to yell after her, it seemed hopeless.

"Geez," said one of the cops, watching the woman in the red dress stalk out of the emergency room door. "I think if I was you, I'd rather get shot at."

THINGS WERE BAD, real bad, but Karl couldn't help being amused though he took care not to show it. The Boss had sent boys to do a man's job. They sat there now, looking sheepish and resentful, pouting like the spoiled children they were. The Boss had been amazingly patient while he listened to the story, but Karl could tell that the Boss would soon blow like Old Faithful.

"It was the perfect plan," Jimmy Raymond was saying, "Legitimate disguises on Halloween, nobody can recognize you, hide the guns in the treat bags, nobody even challenges you, you're just another monster in the street . . ."

"So you thought it was just a great idea to start blasting away right in the neighborhood there when you could have killed the little girl and who knows how many other kids. No way I could have survived that. No way."

"We know how to aim, God damn it. No chance we were going to hurt the kid . . ."

"Get the fuck outta here," the Boss told them. "Get the fuck outta here before I tear both of ya apart with my bare hands."

They obeyed, a little insolently, Karl thought, affecting a casual air, slouched shoulders and rolling hips, as they walked out.

"Anymore you got nothin' but shit to work with," the Boss said.

"You shoulda had me do it."

The Boss shrugged his shoulders. "You gotta let the young ones learn sometime."

"You want me to do it?"

The Boss shook his head. "Too much heat too close to home. We need to bring somebody else in. I'm thinkin' about Joe Sola. Call him. Tell him he needs to get up here right now. Meanwhile, you keep an eye on that detective every fuckin' minute of the day and night. That little visit he made down here. What a cocky bastard. What a stupid bastard. Well, that was his death sentence. He sentenced himself to death. We're gonna chop him up. Alive."

LATER IN THE evening, when her mom had gone home to pick up some things at the house, the duty nurse let him sit in a chair by Kelly's bedside. Kelly lay on her stomach in her usual way. She slept soundly and peacefully, apparently no skeletons haunting her dream, a couple of deep scratches on her face the only marks the evening had left on her body. Yet there would be scars for sure, inside at least. It had been a close-run thing. He imagined her dead. Become nothing. Gone forever. The one thing in his life he knew he had done right, however accidentally, was helping to bring into the world this precious creature sleeping there beside him. And it was he who had put her at risk, brought terror and nearly death itself to her on that fog-shrouded street. He put his elbows on the side of her bed and buried his face in his hands. He was exactly what her mother said—a danger. He had forfeited whatever rights a father was supposed to possess. And it seemed fitting to him that he would now be cut off even from Kelly, the only thing that had been holding him to the world all these years. He fetched a piece of paper and a pencil from the nurse, scratched a note, and, left it on the table by Kelly's bed.

"Love you" is all it said.

Then he was gone. Time to tie up all the loose ends.

CHAPTER 22

O'KEEFE SPENT MOST of the next morning with the police. They seemed to care, seemed to want to do something, but like everybody else, they had a hard time believing that Carmine Jagoda was mixed up in some piddling mink-farm scam down in the boondocks. The Lieutenant called the Sheriff's office. The Deputy told him the Sheriff had gone off on vacation and that only the Sheriff knew anything about the status of any investigation that might be underway. The Deputy did not expect the Sheriff back for a couple of weeks.

"They don't know their ass from a hamburger bun down there," the Lieutenant said. "O'Keefe, I'd love to do something, but there's this little problem called evidence. There isn't any— no eyewitness identifications, nothing. If you look at this deal from the standpoint of the evidence, all it looks like is that you're some kind of human magnet that exerts a strong attraction for speeding bullets."

"What about Ullman?"

"That's the only direction we've got to go in. We'll find him. A guy can't just vanish these days."

"Tell that to Jimmy Hoffa."

O'Keefe had left a few things out of the story. He did not tell them that Tag had been seen in Arizona or that George was out there searching for her right now. At best the police might put her in jail as some kind of accessory to something; at worst they might get her killed. Mr. Canada seemed to be more powerful than the cops. Same old story. Mr. Canada could trump them at every turn because they had to adhere to law and procedure, and Mr. Canada did not. And that was fine, he knew, because that was the only thing that kept them from becoming Mr. Canadas themselves.

"And you'll have a car driving by my daughter's house for a while? No way they would be stupid enough to go after her, but still . . ."

"Count on it. For the indefinite future. We won't pull it off until you tell us it's okay. But I don't think your little girl is anywhere close to danger. At least as long as you're not with her. It's you they'll be after."

But the cops did not offer him any protection, and he asked for none. A police escort would only get in the way of what he intended to do now.

YEARS OF STALKING people had taught Karl patience, but he was getting more and more disgusted with this stake-out on the private detective. Sitting in a car in the darkness so close to the guy's apartment just couldn't be smart. It would be much easier and less dangerous if the Boss would just let him quietly ease himself on inside and put the idiot out of his misery. One way or the other, the guy was going to end up an ugly way of dead, so why not make it simple? But the Boss had not wanted the people close to him to be involved in this killing so close to home, and, as always, he followed the Boss's orders, stupid or not. They had journeyed all this long way together, he and the Boss.

The guy's lights had turned off just after ten, now Karl's clock said ten minutes to midnight. His police-band radio told him a patrol car had moved closer to the neighborhood. It might be a little tough to explain how one of Carmine Jagoda's men had come to be sitting in a parked car so close to the private detective's apartment. He knew of an all-night place on the other side of the little pocket park next to the apartment. The guy had parked his van on the street; it would be visible from the window of the all-night place, and he might as well walk over there and keep his parking space.

He had started down the stone steps that led into the park, his hands trapped in his trench coat pockets, when someone tackled him and knocked him over the railing. He thought at first it must be a cop, or a mugger. Then the cord tightened around his neck. Clutching frantically at the cord, he tried to flail out of his attacker's grasp, but his assailant was too strong. Then he realized he might be about to die. He thought he had forgotten how to be afraid, but just before he lost consciousness, he tried to scream through his closed throat, and when he couldn't scream, he shit his pants instead.

He could not believe it when he woke up. He wasn't dead, yet anyway, but he was tied up like a calf at a rodeo. The driver drove fast and wild, and he was bouncing around in the back of a van. After a while the van stopped, the driver jumped out, and the side door of the van slid open. *The fucking private detective.* It would have been so much better to have killed him right off the bat.

The detective dragged him out and threw him on the asphalt parking lot next to *Angie's*. He lay there for a long time, trying to groan and scream the pain away, wishing the crap in his pants would dry out. It surprised him that he seemed to be falling asleep despite the pain. When he woke up, the Boss and Joe Sola were standing over him.

"Anymore you got nothin' but shit to work with," the Boss said.

"Look, Boss," said Joe, "there's a note pinned on him."

"Maybe it's from his Mama," said the Boss.

Joe ripped the note off him and opened it up.

"What's it say?"

"It says, 'FUCK YOU.' That's all it says—'FUCK YOU.'"

O'KEEFE ALSO LEFT a note for Sara. When she arrived at work the next morning, she cursed herself for leaving her computer on the night before until she saw that someone had typed a message on the screen:

I'm gone out of town, and nobody but you needs to know it. I'll call in. Pete

P.S. You're a wonderful person. I didn't deserve to know you.

After she read the note, she stood there glaring at the computer screen for a moment, then reached out and pushed it off her desk, sending it crashing to the floor.

THEY WOULDN'T LET you tote an M-16 automatic, a .45 caliber pistol, and several hand grenades onto an airplane, so O'Keefe had to drive. He took the northern route, across Kansas, through Colorado Springs, down into New Mexico. The vast, empty plateaus, the far-distant ridgelines, and the endless sameness of the ghostly landscape seemed to contain a secret and to promise him a vision, but he had no time to stop.

West of Albuquerque he entered Indian country. Far off the road he could see tiny shacks, modern-day hogans, broken-down cars littered around them, a culture that had paid a high price for trying to live easy on the land, a culture that did not know how to dig in and root and burrow and cling, a culture unable to excrete itself in edifices, in suburbs and strip centers and fast-food franchise stores.

Arizona was a revelation too. He plunged down from the alpine heights of Flagstaff, the San Francisco Peaks looming above the town like white-capped breasts of rock and trees thrusting from the earth to nourish the sky. Down from Flagstaff to the desert floor. Amazingly green. Giant saguaro cactus lined the foothills like sentinels. Broad valleys full of mesquite trees and dust, mountain ridges rising from the desert floor in the distance, bordering your vision, otherwise you might be able to see forever. To his right as he rolled into Tucson hovered Baboquivari Peak where the Papagos believe the world began. He pulled off the road and called Sara.

"Pete, you're scaring the shit out of me. That note you left me sounded like a suicide note."

"It wasn't. Have you heard from George?"

"George is at a motel in some place called Sierra Vista," she said. "He says he thinks he has good news, but he has to confirm it first. He'll meet you at the motel."

George. George and his over-quotient of luck. Rather be lucky than good. Yet even luck gave you no answers if you failed to ask the right questions. O'Keefe had asked the right questions. Again. That's what had made him a success. He had learned from Harrigan the art of asking the right questions, and he wondered if there would ever be anything he would be able to teach Harrigan in return.

"Pete, you're uncanny sometimes," George said as they cruised down an isolated state road not many miles from the

Mexican border. The government owned most of the land on either side of the road, part of the national forest system.

"The real estate lady recognized your lady right away. 'All business, cold as a fish' is how the real estate woman described her. There wasn't the slightest doubt in her mind when she saw the picture. Even though the lady doesn't have that long hair anymore."

"Really? She cut her hair?"

"Yeah, I guess so." George wondered why O'Keefe sounded so sad.

O'Keefe tried to imagine her without the long hair and failed. He could not even bring her image clearly into his mind.

"It's right up here," George said.

O'Keefe drove slowly by a mailbox and a dirt road that wound through the desert and disappeared over a rise in the land.

"It's a long way back off the road," said George. "I drove up there this morning. Acted like a tourist who'd gotten himself lost. I stopped fifty yards from the house and looked around like a bumpkin. Then I stomped my foot and banged on the fender of the car with my hand like I was mad as hell and drove off."

"Did you see anyone?"

"Not a creature was stirring, not even a mouse."

"What's back there?"

"A tiny little house and a barn backed up against the foothills. There was an old pickup truck parked in the front."

O'Keefe saw a cloud of dust billowing along the dirt road toward them. There would be a vehicle in front of the dust cloud, most likely the pickup truck George had just told him about. He jammed the accelerator to the floor. It might be her in the vehicle, and she might recognize him and spoil his plan.

"Take those binoculars back there," he told George, "and see what you can see out the back window."

George climbed in the back, and O'Keefe slowed down. "It's the pickup truck, all right," George said, "but it went the other way. You want to go after it?"

"No."

"Well, what do we do now?" George asked as he climbed back into the front seat.

"Well, what you're gonna do is go make a reservation on the next plane out of Tucson and leave the rest to me."

"Why?"

O'Keefe had not prepared an appropriate lie. He would have to tell George the truth, to the extent that he possessed any notion of the truth anymore.

"This is my deal, George. I just want to play it the rest of the way alone."

"Yeah. Real smart. You did a real good job playing it alone down at that mink farm."

"Hey, George. Fuck you."

George had to restrain himself. He was tempted to whip O'Keefe's ass right there in the car. He had achieved it twice in grade school and once in high school and was pretty sure he could do it again. Silly, self-centered asshole. O'Keefe and Harrigan were just alike. They thought they were some kind of special. Grail knights and all that baloney. They thought they had some kind of direct line of communication to the Upper Sphere or something. They tried to keep everything important to themselves and not share it with anyone. Terminal uniqueness.

"Well, fuck you too," George said. "I wash my hands of your dumb ass right here and now."

They rode the rest of the way in silence. At the motel George jumped out of the van even before O'Keefe had come to a full stop.

"I'll leave my room key at the desk if you want to use it," George said. "But maybe you want your own special room."

"Come on, George."

George slammed the van door and walked off. Maybe he should have tried to explain it better to George, but he didn't really know how. Surely George would get over it. All he needed now was some food to stow in his backpack and a good map. The food was easy enough to obtain, but he had to drive to Bisbee to secure a small-scale contour map of the area, which turned out to be so minutely detailed that it even showed the ranch house and barn. Only the one dirt road led to the house, and he did not want to approach that way. Even if she was alone, he did not want her to see him before he saw her.

National forest land bordered the ranch on both the west and south and it allowed public access for hiking, camping, and backpacking. He planned to drive as deep into the forest as he could and then strike out on foot to the east. The route would require him to climb over several steep ridges, then he would hike north a mile or more, and if he had remembered and correctly applied what they had taught him in the Marine Corps about reading a map with a compass, he would arrive directly behind the ranch house, which could be seen with binoculars from any number of hills that rose steeply behind it.

He woke up the next morning before dawn and loaded his backpack. Minimal food, the .45 caliber pistol, the M-16 disassembled into its pieces, several bandoliers of ammunition, two hand grenades. He wasn't about to let anyone catch him unprepared this time. He had heard the desert got very cold at night and wished he had room to carry a small tent in addition to his sleeping bag, but he was traveling too heavy already. Besides the backpack bulging with the heavy metal of the guns, he would have the big water bag to lug around in those mountains. It had been a long time since he had humped like a grunt, and he had never done it in a desert, which made him a little afraid, but he remembered another thing the Marine Corps had taught him besides how to read a map with a compass, which was that no matter how hard it got, you could always take worse.

CHAPTER 23

AFTER ASCENDING THE first ridgeline, O'Keefe stopped for a rest. He was breathing too hard, and his calf muscles quivered and shuddered, suffering from something like shock. If he was reading the map right, he had veered only slightly off course in the first two hours, a deviation he could correct on the next leg of the journey, which would take him down the ridge he now stood on and across the wide flat plain below.

The plain was probably a half mile across, a sea of light greens—mesquite, palo verde, prickly pear cactus, cholla, ocotillo, agave, saguaro. On the far side of the plain a series of ridges, one behind the other, each progressively steeper, thrust abruptly up from the desert floor. It looked like a staircase for titans. The map told him the land would plunge down on the other side of the staircase into another long, flat plain, the bottom of a bowl, rimmed by mountains to the south and foothills to the east, west, and north. When he reached the bottom of the bowl, he would turn left, to the north, traverse the bottom of the bowl, and then climb up some foothills from which he should be able to observe the ranch house with his binoculars.

He guessed there might not be another human being within miles. Except for her in that ranch house—or perhaps her and someone else, a painful thought, but more than possible, in fact probable. Moving through the landscape, he began to understand why Tag loved this place, Arizona, so much. This was his first encounter with the high desert, but it felt to him that he had finally come home. The blue diamond sky sat on his shoulder. The sun, a different sun than had ever shined on him, imparted to this sorcerer's kingdom a brightness and clarity so exquisite it was almost physically painful to behold. Nothing could be simpler, or more complex, than this world of sun and dust, rocks and dirt and sky, where wind and slow time had, like Bach in his fugues, worked innumerable variations on a single theme. As he stood on the ridge, seeing for miles, no human busyness to distract him, a new intuition began to stir within him, an acceptance of something he had all his life been vainly resisting, and he thought that, maybe for the very first time in his sojourn on earth, he was standing on firm ground.

Crossing the plain, meandering around the spikes of the cacti, he tried to prepare himself mentally for the long climb up the staircase of ridges, which would be an agony of plodding, lungs straining to provide air to the leg muscles screaming for oxygen. Just put one foot in front of the other. Don't look up unless you must in order to see where you are and get your bearings. Don't stop for a rest because you won't ever want to get up again. Watch where you're stepping, in this desert a sprained ankle means death. Above all remember there is nothing you cannot endure in search of a treasure hard to attain.

A few yards before he reached the top of the staircase he collapsed, too exhausted even to take off his backpack or unsling the water bag and take the drink he wanted so badly. He lay face to the sun like a turtle turned upside down with no foreseeable prospect of ever righting itself again. His stomach muscles convulsed, heaving a gag into his throat, and he turned his face sideways and retched, emptying the contents of his stomach onto the ground next to him, his quivering body achieving a kind of peace in this renunciation.

He drifted off into sleep and dreamt of Tag crying out for him, her voice constantly receding though he strove madly to reach her through fire and smoke. When he finally found her, it was not Tag at all, it was Kelly's face on the body of Tag, and she asked him if he had bought the bicycle yet.

The view from the top of the staircase bestowed worth on the pain of the climb. He thought he could probably see all the way to Mexico. The mountains in the distance shimmered in the heat and slowly swirling dust. Through his binoculars he could see the state highway and also the dirt road that meandered from the highway to the ranch house. The ranch house remained hidden, shielded from view by the foothills behind it.

He did not reach the ridgeline above the ranch house until late in the afternoon, and it took him another hour to find the best place on the ridge from which to observe the house without being seen himself—three or four square yards of flat, bare ground behind two immense boulders. He found a crevice between the boulders where he could stand, prop his elbows against the rock, and train his binoculars on the house. But he could see only the house, not the barn behind it that George had told him about. He crawled on his belly around the boulders and down the ridge until he could see the area behind the house. He sat behind an ocotillo, legs folded as if he were meditating, and studied the scene. The house was small and rudimentary, probably no more than a back porch, a bedroom, a bathroom, a kitchen, and one other room that served as both living and dining room. The barn, though he would have called it something much less than a barn, sat to his left, twenty yards or so behind the house. Back from the barn, to his right, a small corral penned in two horses. Directly across from the barn, separated by a few yards of flat ground trodden bare by boots and hooves, hunched a row of huge boulders that looked like someone had deliberately placed them there to provide symmetry to the scene.

The barn, the corral, and the boulders formed a U shape behind the house. One of the horses in the corral was brown, the other a palomino. *Pegasus.* The horses looked toward the house as if waiting for someone, and it was not long before the someone they waited for came out of the house, walking toward the corral. At first he thought it was a young boy, lean in his jeans and cowboy shirt, long hair for a boy, at least the way most boys wore it these days, hair that covered his ears and his shirt collar at the back of his neck. But it turned out not to be a boy at all. He could tell it was her by her walk—even in her cowboy boots, the walk of that girl he had first seen on the television screen, the girl wearing the mink, the girl with the beauty that stabbed you in the heart.

She fed the horses and returned to the house. Pegasus whinnied in protest, wanting her back, and O'Keefe himself had a hard time keeping from scrambling down the hill after her, but he remembered that she had once before run away from him. She was a mystery he had not yet solved, and it took a little time and a little patience to solve a mystery. From behind the two boulders he watched the setting sun color the mountains sandy-red and ate his dinner out of a can. He recalled with disgust the C-rations he had eaten in the Marine Corps. Ham and lima beans, lukewarm lumps of congealed slime. He almost chuckled, remembering they had called them "ham and motherfuckers." Before nightfall he assembled the M-16 and laid out his other equipment so he could put it on at a moment's notice—cartridge belt beaded with rounds for the M-16, a grenade on each side of the belt and a canteen hooked to its rear, first-aid kit and Swiss army knife in a pouch that snapped around the cartridge belt, the .45 caliber pistol in its shoulder holster, binoculars on a lanyard so he could hang them around his neck. He almost laughed at himself for toting all this destruction around in search of that wisp of a girl, but he kept thinking about that night in the cabin, the fire and smoke and whizzing steel, when it seemed like Vietnam had come to him instead of he to it.

Nightfall brought cold and a sky full of stars. The night sky must be another reason she loved Arizona so much. He heard coyotes howling somewhere.

He woke up before dawn and crawled reluctantly out of the sleeping bag, his cotton turtleneck and heavy wool sweater no match for the cold. He ignited fuel tablets beneath his small camp stove and heated a cup of water for coffee, which failed to warm him in the slightest. Nothing could get colder than a soldier on maneuvers. By dawn he had resumed his place behind the ocotillo. Soon after first light she came out of the house to the corral and took Pegasus into the barn. When she came out again, the horse was fully saddled. She swung up into the saddle and gently coaxed the horse into a quick trot onto a path that started behind the big boulders across from the barn and led down the far side of the corral into a small canyon.

O'Keefe crawled back to his place behind the two boulders and trained his binoculars eastward. He ducked down as she emerged from the canyon onto a ridge not more than two hundred yards away from him and skillfully guided the horse down the ridge. When she reached the bottom of the bowl, she pointed the horse in a southeasterly direction and let him walk at his pleasure. O'Keefe decided to follow her, wondering if it would be the right time to make his presence known to her. She seemed to be alone in the house.

Keeping out of her line of sight, he followed her across the bowl. He alternately lost her and found her. As he walked, he flushed lizards, jackrabbits, and cottontails, bustling families of quail, and various other birds whose names he did not know, and it amazed him how this desert seemed to burst with life. Once he thought he had lost her completely, until he stopped on top of a rise in the ground and scanned the landscape with the binoculars. Below him, about halfway across the bowl, she rode toward a stand of tall cottonwoods, which seemed out of place amid the other desert vegetation. He jogged in a beeline toward the west of the stand of cottonwoods where he might be able to see what was on the other side of the trees. When he arrived there and caught his breath from the jogging, he focused his binoculars on the cottonwoods.

It was an oasis of sorts, a pool of water no larger than a small pond, probably fed, he speculated, by an underground spring. The trees grew up to the edge of the pool and blocked his view so he could not see her, but he did glimpse the horse standing riderless on the tiny shoreline and munching on the grass that grew there. The pool was surrounded by rock except for the side where the horse was standing.

She stayed in the cottonwoods for more than an hour. When she came out, she came out at a gallop, heading back across the bowl in the direction of the house.

When he returned to his watching place behind the ocotillo, Pegasus was drinking from a trough in the corral, and he guessed that Tag must be back in the house. The old truck had not been moved since the day before. He used the long minutes and hours to try to memorize the scene below so he could traverse the area between the ridge and the ranch house blindfolded if he must.

After dark, he crept down to the house. When he passed the corral, the horses whinnied loudly in fear, and he dashed around to the back of the barn. The screen door on the back porch creaked open, and boot soles crunched on dry dirt. A flashlight beam hit the horses, then arced around the corral, over toward the boulders, back to the corral, and toward the barn. Then the light switched off, the boots crunched on the dry dirt again, and the screen door creaked open and then closed. He crawled slowly underneath the windows at the side of the house toward a window at the front that appeared to be open. Through the open window he could hear nothing except what sounded like someone washing dishes. He raised himself to the window, looking inside and back toward the rear of the house.

The house was so small you could see the back door from the front door. A waist-high breakfast bar separated the dining and living area from the kitchen. He could see her waist and chest and hands washing dishes in the kitchen. A cabinet above the sink concealed her face. He had to expose himself more to see into the living-room area, and when he did, Lenny Parker seemed to be looking right at him.

But Lenny did not seem to see him. Lenny was staring instead just above the window, an absent-minded stare, the stare of a man in the grip of depression. In his arms he cradled a double-barreled shotgun. O'Keefe froze, afraid that even the slightest movement would jar Lenny out of his reverie and catch his attention. When Lenny stopped staring at the wall and started staring at his lap instead, O'Keefe ducked back down below the window.

He had convinced himself that she was alone. He would be able to hear them talking through the window, but he did not really want to hear whatever they might say.

"You've got to eat something tonight," she said. "You can't keep going on without eating."

"I'm not hungry. What I am is going crazy. This place is driving me crazy. This waiting is driving me crazy." It was a whine, the semi-hysterical wheedle, not the gentle, schoolmarm voice he had used with the investors.

"Only two more days and we're across," Tag said.

"We're not gonna make it. I know we're not gonna make it."

"We'll make it as long as you don't turn into a basket case on me."

"This was crazy. This whole thing was crazy."

"You should've thought about that before you started it."

"I keep asking myself 'Why?' Why, Tag?"

"It's too late for that now."

"It's too late for everything now," he said, and for the first time in the conversation, he did not whine. He spoke as if he had seen the end of something and had resolved to accept it.

O'Keefe slithered up the side of the window so he could just barely peek inside. Lenny looked as if he had not shaved or even washed for several days. His hair spiked up in clumps here and there where he had been sleeping on it. He was pale and gaunt, as if he were wasting away. A bare pillow and a rough, green, army blanket were knotted in a wad at one end of the couch. Tag sat there staring at the wall. Lenny sat there staring at her. Lenny clicked the safety catch of the shotgun on and off, on and off.

"Where'd you put the stuff?" he said.

"No more, Lenny. Please, no more."

"It's all I've got."

She hung her head, despairing, in agreement with him.

"You're gonna leave me after we get across, aren't you?"

"Stop it."

"You're gonna leave me, I know it." He spoke without inflection, in a monotone, as if the human being in him had been replaced by a computer-generated telephone message.

"Maybe I should just end it now. It's not worth living this way."

When Lenny moved the shotgun from his lap, O'Keefe thought he intended to turn it on Tag, but it was himself that Lenny intended to harm. His thumb groped for the trigger. She screamed and leaped at him. The shotgun exploded. It happened so fast that O'Keefe could only stand frozen in stupefied witness. She had managed to grab the gun and turn it away from Lenny just as it fired. There was now a large hole in the wall next to Lenny's head. Lenny sat there gasping for breath, his face glistening with sweat. On her knees in front of him, sobbing hysterically, shoulders heaving with terror and grief, her right hand tightly gripping the gun barrel, her left arm locked around his leg as if she were trying to hold him to his life.

"That was it," Lenny said softly. "That was all the courage I had."

He pushed her gently aside and rose uncertainly to his feet, staggering a little.

"What did you do with the stuff? No use trying to hide it anymore. I'll ransack the place if I have to."

"In my backpack," she said. "I put it all in there." Lenny walked over to a small table near the breakfast bar to her pack and opened it. When O'Keefe saw what was in the pack, an image, a sound, and a concept flashed across his mind: angels' wings, a dying fall, paradise lost. The pack was stuffed full with bags of white powder and green cash He slumped down the side of the house. He had solved her mystery. He so wished that he hadn't.

"You want some?" Lenny asked.

"Just a little," she said in the smallest of voices. "A couple of lines."

"You want to try the needle again?"

"No," she said, her voice lifting in stress.

"You didn't like it?"

"I liked it too much."

O'Keefe struggled back up the hill to his place behind the boulders like a wounded animal crawling back to its hole. He was cold. He dragged himself into his sleeping bag. If he had been a coyote, he would have howled at the moon, but instead he lay a long time on his back in the sleeping bag, smoking cigarettes and looking out at the night, wishing it would tell him something he desperately needed to know. *Star light, star bright, first star I see tonight, I wish I may, I wish I might . . .* But he was beyond even wishing now. Out there somewhere was Andromeda, the Chained Princess, and Perseus, the Champion, but Andromeda had only herself to thank for her chains, and Perseus could not break them, try as he might. He had hoped against hope that she hadn't just used him that night in the nightclub and cabin, buying time so she could make good her escape. *Delusional, wishful thinking.* At dawn he should just walk out of this desert forever and leave Tag Parker to the tawdry destiny she had brought on herself. The object of his quest had proved unworthy. He felt like a fool and knew now that he had been a fool all his life.

He tried every trick he knew, but he could not force himself to fall asleep, and, before that long painful night ended, he had somehow come to see things in a different way. She was a damsel corrupted but in distress all the same. Anderson had not hired him to find and protect her only on the condition that she remain true to O'Keefe's illusions about her. He had always done his duty. Dreams may die, but duty lives on.

CHAPTER 24

SHE DID NOT see him sitting on top of the boulder until she had come through the line of trees into the oasis, riding toward the spring-fed pool. Frightened, she started to turn Pegasus around and gallop off. Fine with him, her decision to make. Halfway into the turn, she must have realized who she had seen, and she whirled the horse back around to face him.

"Hello, Tag."

"Pete," he heard her say faintly. She rode up to him.

"I never thought I'd see you again," she said dreamily. "It's good to see you again."

She sounded like she meant it, but surely he was just striving to delude himself yet again. Grasping at straws seemed to have become a specialty of his lately. She swung off the palomino and let him wander off to graze on the grass beside the pool. She wore jeans, a white cowboy shirt, and a pink bandana tied around her neck. He thought he would be disappointed when he saw her close up and shorn of her beautiful hair, but she was lovely still though a little boyish and slimmer and sharper around the edges, like the vegetation in the desert she seemed so at home in. The short hair gave special prominence to her aqua eyes that seemed to beckon him.

"Well," she said, looking up at him perched on the rock, "I guess the question is 'What are you doing here?' And 'Why'?"

"Your father sent me."

"Of course," she said, with doom in her voice, the aqua pools in her eyes clouding, and she looked like a prisoner suddenly aware that she had failed to escape, probably never would escape.

"I told you to stay away."

He jumped down to face her. "You just used me to get away, didn't you?"

She seemed genuinely surprised by his tone of outrage. "Yes, I used you. I used you to save my life. And what's wrong with that? What else were you there for?"

He had no answer for that.

"And whether I used you or not, I still meant what I said, and I still meant what I did, and you didn't deserve more than that. If you want perfection, you're in the wrong world."

"I'm in the wrong world, all right. It wasn't a Ponzi scheme at all. It was a real investment with real return on the money. But the investment wasn't in minks. The suckers didn't know it, but the investment was in cocaine."

"I told you to stay away," she said, trying to turn his accusations around on himself.

"Not at first," he continued. "It took Lenny a while to figure out that the mink farm wasn't going to work. How he hit on the idea of becoming a pusher I don't know. But the returns on the cocaine investment were truly fabulous, better even than the promises he'd made to the investors.

"That cocaine turned his lies into truth. There was enough money to give the investors back big bucks and plenty left over so Lenny and Tag could live high in the treetops.

"But Lenny got himself in too deep in a couple of ways. First, the people you run with in the drug business aren't exactly Sunday-go-to-meeting types. Once he got hooked up with Mr. Canada, Mr. Canada owned him, body and soul. But even that might have worked. You might have been able to go on for a long time that way, maybe even long enough to make enough money to give the investors all their money back and still have a nice pile left over, even after Mr. Canada got what he wanted out of the deal. Then it's out of the country and live the rest of your life in leisure, Lenny-and-Tag style. But Lenny fucked that all up when he started sampling the product. More and more of the product started going up Lenny's nose and then through a needle into his arm. And Lenny started thinking and acting crazy, like all cocaine addicts do. Jekyll and Hyde. I can't believe now I didn't recognize the symptoms when I heard them from Jane. Maybe that was what you were there for—to make me not see what was sticking out right in front of my face. And Lenny got crazy enough to get the fool idea that he could even rip off Mr. Canada himself. I mean, after all, hadn't Lenny's life been blessed by God? Didn't God have a Special Plan for Lenny? And then there's Tag. How does she fit into the Plan?"

He glared at her, trying to shame her, but she did not seem ashamed, only sad.

"I didn't know what he was doing until he was already in deep trouble. And then, when I found out, what was I gonna do about it then?"

"And you were afraid to lose your toys and your trips, the big-time lifestyle."

"Maybe. For just a minute or two."

She turned away from him and lifted her head toward the mountains as if asking them for forgiveness. "I held onto it for just a minute or two. And then it was too late."

"And now Mr. Canada wants your head. And you've got a paranoid cocaine addict on your hands down there, and you're starting to like the stuff a little too much yourself."

She looked toward him but not at him, still talking beyond him to the mountains, entreating them but without any real hope of reprieve. "I should have gone to the police when I first found out," she said. "Now I've got blood on my hands. Jane's. Roy's. There are some sins that there's no forgiveness for. Once you go a certain way, even just a little way, you can't go back."

He knew the line for that. Sara's. No cage you couldn't walk right out of if you have the courage to face what's outside. But he did not really believe it. That was for other people, people like Sara, not people like Tag, or him.

"You can walk away right now," he said half-heartedly.

"Mr. Canada won't let that happen."

"Then go to the cops."

"And then to prison."

"Maybe you'll have to pay some dues. But I have a lawyer friend who can probably trade your testimony for a suspended sentence. That's not a bad deal."

"You're dreaming. Mr. Canada lives forever."

He had nothing to say to this. She was right. Mr. Canada would live forever, or, if not forever, then long enough.

"Day after tomorrow we're crossing the border," she said.

"How?"

"We're meeting them out there," she said, pointing to the mountains to the south. "Our buyer arranged it. A package deal. Money and passage out of the country in exchange for the drugs. We'll have a car, and we'll cross Mexico and end up on a little island in the Caribbean where there's no extradition and we can stay lost for a long time."

"Who's dreaming now? Why don't you think you're being set up? That buyer's gonna feed you and Lenny to the vultures out there."

"Well, it's either that or Mr. Canada. At least we've got a chance with the buyer."

"Yeah. Slim to none."

"Sometimes you make a choice that eliminates all the other choices whether you like it or not."

"Then I'll go with you. At least through Mexico. Your father is paying me to protect you. I'm sure he didn't have this in mind, but then I guess if he doesn't like it, he doesn't have to pay the bill."

"Don't get in this any deeper. This is our problem, not yours. You'd be committing a crime. You might go to jail. I've got enough blood on my hands."

"I'm a survivor," he said.

"What have I done?" she said softly, desperately, more to herself than to him. "What have I done?"

He recognized suddenly where he had seen those eyes before. The wild creature imprisoned in the cage, doomed but defiant, resisting its fate and accepting it at the same time. *Tag, you have mink eyes. They wait for the knife to fall.*

She reached out to him, and he let her embrace him. They held each other.

"I'm so sorry," she said. "So wrong. So sorry."

She molded herself to him like she had that night on the dance floor. He pushed her away.

"You're married."

"Married! Somehow I don't understand your morality. That didn't seem to bother you that night in the cabin."

"You said you'd kicked him out of bed a long time ago."

"And I did. Just because I take care of him doesn't mean I love him. I'm all he's got. I can't just throw him away." Then she laughed, not a real laugh, more an exclamation of amazement, as if she had just gotten a joke. "You're unbelievable," she said. "Maybe I just don't understand you Irish-Catholic boys. Is it some kind of purity you want?"

That was probably it. That was probably it all along.

"Well, if it makes you feel any better, I've been celibate for months except for that night in the cabin. Jesus, stop this. There's no time left for this, whatever this is you're doing."

He let her come to him then, and for many seconds they just held each other, rocking slowly back and forth, and for a few moments they only kissed, not even touching tongues at first. He kissed the top of her head, her forehead, the closed lids of her eyes. He untied the pink bandana and kissed her on the neck. She gave the front of her shirt a tug, and the metal buttons snapped apart. An invitation, and a request. He cupped her breasts in his hands and watched her eyes relax and close, a gesture of release. They teased each other with their tongues and fingers and hands until she took his right arm in the crook of her left, hugged it to her side, and led him toward the grazing palomino.

She had an extra blanket tied to the back of the saddle, which she spread on the grass in front of the pool, and the horse moved away from them as if deliberately giving them room. After she took off her shirt and then her boots and jeans, he just stared at her for a few moments. She seemed to understand that, for him, just looking at her was almost enough. Then he went to his knees and fondled her inside and out with his hands and fingers and tongue until she clenched his hair in her fingers and humped and shuddered and moaned.

After a while, she made him undress too and sit down on the blanket. She knelt down in front of him and returned his favors. He placed his hands on her hair and watched her—her long, slender fingers flat against the outside of his thighs, the muscles in her back, the sides of her breasts, her rump resting like a pillow on the soles of her feet, and he could not recall ever seeing anything in the world more pleasing than that. Then he remained as he was, and she straddled him, carefully sliding down on him, gently impaling herself. She bent her head down, kissed him on the neck, and whispered "fuck me, Pete, fuck me now, fuck me forever" just before coming, and her words and her churning made him come along with her.

When they finished, she raised herself up and let him out of her, then turned around toward the mountains and sat between his legs, wrapped his arms around her, kissed his hands and let them drop to her lap. He contemplated the mountains over her shoulder.

"I want them to bury me right here," she said. "I want to spend my eternity right here."

They spent more time on the blanket and then packed up to go. She watched him strap on the cartridge belt and the shoulder holster and sling the rifle tightly across his back so it would not bump against him when they rode back to the house.

"You look like you're ready for war," she said. "And that makes me feel good. I still don't think you should come with us, but I'm glad you're coming.

"You want to do the driving?" she asked, holding out the reins.

"Yeah, I'd like to try it."

She swung into the saddle behind him and wrapped her arms around his stomach as they rode. Halfway across the bowl, she said, "I could make a cowboy out of you in no time," and they said nothing else the rest of the way.

CHAPTER 25

"HOW DO I know he won't shoot me?" O'Keefe asked, only partly in jest, as they walked toward the back door of the ranch house.

"He won't," she said. "I won't let him."

Lenny sat on the couch with the shotgun cradled in his arms, much like he had been sitting the night before. He looked even more bedraggled now than then, but he was no longer depressed; he was exalted. The source of his exaltation lay on the coffee table in front of him. He had a straw and had been snorting the cocaine directly from the bag. O'Keefe knew how Lenny felt. He felt triumphant, that he would prevail despite everything, that this shabby human form he appeared to be mantled in was only a disguise, a mere cloak that concealed a godhead.

Lenny had bestowed upon Tag a smile of triumph, but when he saw O'Keefe behind her, he looked stricken with fear, and he leapt to his feet and trained the shotgun on the intruder. Tag kept her body between Lenny and O'Keefe, advanced on Lenny and quickly, gently took the shotgun from him as if he were a small boy brandishing a toy.

"Lenny, this is Peter O'Keefe, the private detective I told you about. Dad sent him. He's here to help us."

Lenny's face changed, like a sea grown suddenly calm and ominous, a deep black pool of hatred. O'Keefe wondered if Lenny knew what had happened at the *Silver Lake Resort.*

"Help?" Lenny said. "He's here to help, all right. He's here to help himself."

"Stop it, Lenny," Tag said. "We can use all the help we can get." "You found us?" Lenny asked in amazement.

O'Keefe nodded. "It wasn't that hard either."

"That means somebody else can find us," Lenny said. He moved to the front window and stared down the dirt road. "There was that guy that drove up here the other day."

"That was my man," O'Keefe said.

"We're not gonna make it, Tag," Lenny whined. "I know we're not gonna make it."

"One more day, Lenny. We just have to make it one more day."

There's a lot more than that involved, O'Keefe thought.

Lenny looked at Tag, at O'Keefe, at the backpack, and, finally, at the bag of cocaine on the coffee table as if that was his only friend in the room. O'Keefe could tell that Lenny did not want to accept the situation but didn't know how to change it, at least for now.

"One more day," Lenny said, as if steeling himself. He slumped down on the couch and eyed the bag of cocaine. He obviously wanted in that bag very badly but was reluctant to take it in front of O'Keefe. O'Keefe considered making some kind of speech to reassure him but gave up the idea as futile. No words could halt or even really slow down the roller-coaster that Lenny now found himself hurtling along on, swooping gut-wrenchingly up and down from paranoia to grandiosity. Although he had himself many times taken that same ride, O'Keefe could muster no empathy or sympathy, only loathing for the worm-like creature on the couch, writhing in his self-pity. He turned and walked out of the house. He may have violated the man's wife, but he would not violate his privacy too. Tag followed him out as Lenny reached for the straw and the bag.

"Did you tell him about us?"

"I wouldn't do that to him."

"Well, I think he knows somehow."

"There's no way for him to know."

"If you think you can control him, you're wrong. He's out of control."

"What do you want me to do? Shoot him?"

He looked at the shotgun in her hand. It would be so simple. Lenny was more than a nuisance; he was a threat. To everything. To her, to him, to the possibility of escape, to what they might create for each other if only given a chance, if they could only overcome this last redoubt, swim this last moat, slay these last dragons. Suddenly psychic, O'Keefe saw in his mind a scene like the recollection of a nightmare, muddy and deliriously blurred, a scene in which Lenny would be the cause of some fatal undoing, some hideous demise. He recalled watching Lenny on television, bilking the suckers. Lenny had added nothing to life. He was corrupt but not even really a corrupter, only a vessel of corruption, like a prostitute who carries but herself does not suffer from a venereal disease. He remembered what Tag had said that day at her house: "I woke up one morning and realized I was living with a ferret." Tiny, bright, beady eyes. Greedy, twitching nostrils sniffing the ground. Sharp, little, needle-like teeth ripping at the throat of a baby rabbit.

O'Keefe's life had never before had in it a moment like this. There were few such moments in the world, moments that give sudden and monstrous birth, and he understood then that it was only the language of tragedy and not tragedy itself that has disappeared from our lives. Maybe if you took a man's wife, you thought you could take his life too. Maybe you thought you had to somehow.

He is at Lenny's side, the pistol leaps up in his hand, the muscles of Lenny's face distend horribly and then collapse in the ultimate stress of violent death. The bullet rips off the top of the head, and the corpse pitches sideways onto the hard-packed, unyielding ground.

O'Keefe stands there. Alone. Despite her standing there. Even she has no meaning now though he had thought he was acting for her. His life has been a search for something to fill up the emptiness in him, but now he is as empty and soulless as the creature shriveled there on the unpropitious earth. His quest is fulfilled, his life's task complete; he does not have to strain against the rein of reality anymore. To murder and create, the poet said. He has created a new self, an abstraction, utterly bereft of context, of syntax, of any language to connect him to the vibrant, suffering, striving, foolishly hopeful world.

She looked at him strangely, her brow furrowing in a dismay that would soon give birth to scorn. She had not meant to be taken seriously; she had just been making a sarcastic point. If she had fully understood what had just passed through his mind, she would have recoiled in revulsion, the same nauseated revulsion he felt now for himself. And if she kept standing there looking at him like that, she was bound to come to perceive what he had become in that moment.

"Just watch him," he said and walked away.

HE HIKED IN the foothills for hours, hoping the sweat of the climb would flush the murderer out of him. Finally, exhausted, he crawled into the shade beneath a mesquite tree, and, as if he were a boy and a believer again and kneeling in the cathedral, the light from the stained glass windows ebbing in the Saturday twilight, waiting for the priest to hear his confession, he examined his conscience. *Thought before deed*. The Church had taught him that the very thought itself was a mortal sin. And the Church had been right about that. Whatever else the Church might not be right about, it was right about that. He probed within himself for the source of his sin. His whole life had been a wanting, a search for something transcendent, as if he were entitled to a special providence, and maybe this is what came of too much wanting. Lacking a priest or even the belief in priestly powers, he would have to prescribe his own penance and seek his own absolution. He recalled how yesterday, as he watched through the window, she had lunged at Lenny to save him though he was so little worth saving, how she had locked onto his leg and held him fast to the world though he wanted only to forsake it. He had read somewhere that there were more galaxies in the universe than there were grains of sand on the earth. That made him a mere speck in the cosmos, an almost nothing of a thing that did not matter at all. Then why did he seem to matter so much? Surely it was just a trick the mind played, the ego's delusion and denial of death, but he still seemed to matter and perhaps now more than ever. He did not fully understand it until much later, but, at that moment, his view of the world shattered and then shifted, and, for the first time in his life, he and his self were not at the center of things. There were other things on the planet now to consider and care for. One of them was Tag Parker, and, O'Keefe supposed, even Lenny Parker, miserable, ragamuffin, snot-nosed child of God that he was, might deserve some caring for too.

WHEN HE RETURNED to the house, Tag was cooking dinner. Lenny had shaved and showered and changed his clothes. He looked almost like the old Lenny again, which was not an improvement. He smiled his cherubic smile, the give-me-your-money smile. O'Keefe swallowed his disgust and tried to replace it with at least a modicum of lenity, however grudging and charged through with contempt.

"Do you want to clean up before you eat?" Tag said to O'Keefe, more a command than a question. He had to go through her bedroom to the bathroom. The room was dark and cool and awash in her scent, and he felt like a hunter who had stumbled into the secret lair of the wondrous animal he had long fruitlessly pursued. The bedcovers were turned down as if in invitation. The sheets would be cool and the mattress soft enough. He imagined lying there with her in the late-afternoon shadows, watching the twilight fade into night. He had made love to her on the floor in the cabin and on the blanket in the grass by the spring-fed pool, but he wondered if he would ever be able just to lay peacefully abed with her, merely sleep with her, her back to him, her rump tucked into his groin, the flesh of her breast cupped in his hand as she slept. Her smooth nakedness next to him would be all the comfort he needed.

Dinner was waiting when he came out of the shower. She had fried cube steaks and potatoes, made salad, sliced tomatoes. A homely little meal in the country. She said nothing more than she had to, maybe embarrassed having two lovers at her table. Lenny maintained a morose silence. *As if he knew. How could he not know?* O'Keefe felt like taking his food out in the yard and eating it there.

They talked about the only thing the three of them had in common, the day after tomorrow.

"We only have two horses," O'Keefe said.

"One of you can ride with me," she said.

"What time are you supposed to meet them?" O'Keefe said.

"Ten a.m." she said. "It's three hours' ride from here."

"What's the place like where you're meeting them?"

She looked sheepish. She had no idea.

"Out in the desert somewhere," she said. "That's all I know. I have it marked on a map."

"And what happens when you get there?"

"We make the trade, the cocaine for the money, and they take us on over," Lenny said.

"And from there?"

"They'll have a car for us. It's from there to the ocean and the island."

"I hope it's that simple," O'Keefe said, trying to keep the sarcasm out of his voice. "But somehow I don't think it will be. We should get there early, as soon after dawn as we can. Lenny and I will ride in together on one of the horses. You stay behind us with the cocaine, so you can see us but we can't see you. If things seem okay, Lenny will come riding back to you for the cocaine. Give him the cocaine, and stay where you are. Don't come to us until I signal you again. We make them give us the money, but we keep the cocaine. And then I'll show them the grenade."

"The what?" Lenny said.

"The grenade. With the pin pulled."

"You have a grenade?"

"Yes, and it's going to stay in my hand with that pin pulled until you're in the car and gone. If they try something funny, everything blows. The cocaine, the money, everything. Tag, if the shit hits the fan when we first get there, before I signal you to come down, you ride hard out of there. When you get back here, get in that truck and get to where people are. And then you'd better go to the cops. You won't have any other choice then."

"And what happens to you and me?" said Lenny.

"We do whatever we have to do."

"I'm no hero."

"Neither am I. We try to get out ourselves and ride after her. But don't wait for us, Tag. You understand that? Don't wait for us. Assume we're dead."

"Jesus," Lenny said in a throaty whisper. He stood up, walked over to the television set, turned it on, and resumed his well-worn place on the couch.

O'Keefe drank coffee and smoked at the table while Tag washed the dishes. When she finished the dishes, she sat down on the couch next to Lenny. The characters on a television sit-com chattered punch lines at them, but they did not laugh. Time moved unbearably slowly, and their lack of anything to say to each other oppressed them. *This isn't escape,* O'Keefe thought, *it's exile.*

Lenny laid out four meandering lines of cocaine on the coffee table and took one in each nostril with the little straw.

"You want some?" Lenny said.

O'Keefe shook his head "No."

"Tag?" Lenny said, offering her the straw.

She looked at O'Keefe. Was she pleading to him with her eyes? He hoped not.

"No thanks," she said.

A few minutes later, she said, "I'm going to bed" and left the room without looking at either of them, and neither of them felt like saying "Good night."

Later O'Keefe stood up and said, "I'm gonna go try to sleep myself."

"Where?" Lenny said, his ferret eyes darting back toward Tag's bedroom.

"I'm taking my sleeping bag out to the barn."

Lenny looked relieved. O'Keefe felt like a villain. But when he walked out of the house into the moon-bright night, the cold, clear air seemed cleansing. His step felt firm on the hard ground. One of the horses snorted in the corral. Coyotes howled in the hills, then stopped abruptly. He could see the mountains on the moon. Everywhere a stillness. Utter quiet. The earth and its creatures, all but the human ones, seemed to be at peace. He stopped and looked back at the house, at the window of the room where she lay, and it seemed like he was telling her goodbye.

CHAPTER 26

O'KEEFE WOKE UP the next morning not long after dawn, cold and stiff and weary from another night on the ground. She had perched herself on a hay bale across from him, leaning back against the wall of the barn, sipping coffee and making fun of him with her smile.

"You were snoring," she said.

"Doesn't go very well with my hero image, does it?"

"You are, you know."

"What?"

"A hero."

He shook his head. *A clown. At best a Don Quixote. A hero, not even a little. All of the heroes had departed from the earth long ago.*

He struggled out of his sleeping bag and put on his pants and boots and a jacket. She had the horses saddled and waiting.

"Come on," she said.

"Where?"

"You sure can't be a hero if you don't know how to ride a horse. I'm gonna teach you what you'll need to know tomorrow."

LENNY STOOD ON the back porch and watched Tag and O'Keefe ride out of the barn. At first he thought they might be abandoning him there, but then he remembered that it was tomorrow morning that they were supposed to meet the buyer. Then where might they be getting to? *Probably out into the foothills to . . . Time to have another snort.* He hadn't slept all night though he had pretended to be sleeping when Tag had come into the living room that morning. He needed the cocaine every every hour or so now. *Who does she think she is, just riding off with that guy? They're probably planning something. Probably planning to dump me out in the desert. Maybe kill me first. I saw the look in that guy's eyes yesterday. The look of a killer.*

He watched them ride out of sight. He noticed that she had left the shotgun leaning up against an old wooden chair on the porch. *Good.* He would have something to protect himself with when the time came.

The mouth of the small canyon behind the corral was narrow and framed by boulders on either side. They had to ride single file to pass through it. The canyon was no more than fifty yards long. At the end of the canyon a trail switchbacked up into the foothills. The rifle bounced against his back. He had decided to bring the rifle and the pistol and the pack with the grenades in it. No use leaving anything behind to tempt Lenny. Only then did he remember the shotgun.

"Have you done much riding?" she asked.

"Quite a bit when I was a kid. Hardly any since then."

"Up the hill you lean forward. Down the hill you lean back."

"I remember that."

His horse stopped to munch on the vegetation at the side of the trail.

"Don't let him do that," she said. "Let him know who's the boss."

At the top of the canyon she showed him how to tighten the cinch of the saddle. "It loosens up after you ride for a while, and you'll need to tighten it back up."

They remounted the horses and paused to contemplate the scene—the panorama of the desert floor spread out for miles below them, the distant mountains bestowing a welcome finitude, a contented confinement, a wise limitation. They had found themselves at the center of a circle of wonder, as if the sacred-seeming vistas all around them had been created solely for them to behold. But he knew otherwise now. Their sentience so often tricked them, gave them an illusion of mastery over the vast, indifferent land. They were but specks in the cosmos. But such marvelous specks they were, charged with the magic, whirling stuff of life, comets fading toward death but shining brightly still, orbiting through the mystery.

"Ready?" she said.

He had a hard time pulling himself away from the scene. Another moment of peace, seldom come, dearly bought. Too quickly they had to ride on. He seemed comfortable on a horse and kept a good seat in his saddle, so she dispensed with the basics and taught him the few things he would need to know tomorrow. He rolled well with the horse in the gallop though once she had to stifle laughter when he pitched to the side and struggled madly to right himself, nearly falling off. Like most beginners, he experienced the most trouble in the trot. A horse could not gallop very far, but it could trot all day, and if you could not master the trot, could not keep from jerking and bouncing in the saddle, before very long your body would think it had been pureed in a blender. He could not quite get the hang of it, tried too hard, cursed himself frequently.

"It's like riding a bicycle," she said. "Once you get it, you've got it forever. But until you do, you think you're the most unco-ordinated person on Earth."

Like riding a bicycle. Kelly. Did she live in fear every night, given what had happened to her on Halloween night when the real goblins had paid them a visit?

THEY RODE TO the oasis and let the horses graze while they loitered by the pool. He tossed small rocks into the water. A hawk soared far above them. She had brought the blanket, expecting they would make love again, wore moccasins that she could quickly slip off her feet, loose fitting pants, no bra, no panties. She thought she would be eager to have him lick and fondle and fuck her again in his gentle, awed, reverent way, as if he were performing some kind of worship, but he gave no sign of wanting to, and she shared his mood. When their eyes met, he only smiled his strange, sad smile that seemed to be mocking something—him, her, the world, she didn't know what. After a while he walked to her horse and untied the blanket, placed it unrolled on the ground, and laid his head back on it, using it for a pillow. Then he pulled her down and gathered her to him, her head resting on his shoulder, moving up and down with his chest in the slow rhythm of his breathing. They lay that way for a long time.

"Last night," she said, "when you were talking about tomorrow and the car, you didn't say 'we.' You said that Lenny and I would get in the car and go on. You didn't mean that, did you?"

She thought for a few moments he was not going to answer her. Then he said, "I can't believe how I hunted you down here like you were an animal. It seems wrong."

"And I can't believe I ever ran away from you."

"I almost killed Lenny yesterday."

"What?"

"I did. I came that close," he said, holding his thumb and index finger a hair's breadth apart. "And I don't know if it's out of me even now. I don't know if I could stay around him and you and not have that feeling again."

"I don't believe it," she said, looking perplexed and a little afraid of him all of a sudden.

"I've wanted you too much."

"I don't believe it," she said again.

"I won't be getting in that car with you."

She felt like she had been kicked in the chest. He had come all this way for her, had finally conquered her and put her under his spell, only to abandon her. So much of her life had been a kind of dull hell of a life, a life of stunted emotions and a background white noise of nauseous distaste for almost everything that was not mineral or vegetable or non-human animal. Even her beauty had been small consolation, had merely made her an object of pitiless desire, coveted even by her father. She had never before suffered the excruciating, discrete hurt of a seemingly unbearable loss because her whole life seemed to have been but one long, dull hurt, one long, dull loss that had happened so long ago she could not remember what happened or how. The pain seized her in successive, silent, shuddering waves. She tried to cry out, let the pain escape out into the air of the world, but she could hardly breathe, and it took a long time for tears to come.

"I'm through drifting," he said. "And wanting."

Her eyes told him she did not understand.

"Do you remember what you said back at your house that day? That you'd been a wisp blowing in the wind. That's me, too. I've been like that all my life. Right up to now. I've been a fool all along, but I'm not drifting anymore, not even for you. I'm sorry, Tag, but I've got a daughter back there. It's time for me to make some kind of stand."

She broke off from him, not angrily, but firmly, as if she could find the strength she needed only by separating herself physically from him. She stood up, wiped her eyes, looked away from him, then back.

"I'm determined to hope," she said. "There will be a time you can come to me."

"Where?"

"That little island in the Caribbean. Where nobody will ever bother us again."

"Well, there it is. The long-haired girl and the island too."

"And that's exactly what we're going to have."

"No, it's just a dream. You're chasing a dream. It's not even a dream, it's a nightmare. Give it up."

But he could see that she was determined to chase it.

"Tag, there's nothing I wouldn't do for you here."

"I can't stay here. It's all over for me here. I have to go."

"Maybe you do," he said wearily. "Too bad for both of us."

"Yes," she said. "Too bad for both of us."

He was right about his daughter. She would never try to interfere with that. She looked away from him and toward the mountains. Just seeing them seemed to restore her strength. When she turned back to him, she seemed to have accepted the loss. She smiled at him. She had long ago given up whatever hope she had been born with, then life had suddenly granted her this possible reprieve—the man sitting there on the ground, the man who had shown her there could actually be romance in the world. But then, just as suddenly, that gift had been taken away. Yet there might be other gifts, other revelations waiting out there in the world for her to receive them. She knelt down in front of him and kissed him on the forehead; then she turned around and snuggled back into the curve of his body, resting her head on his chest. She took his arms and crossed them in front of her, cupped his hands around her breasts. He would hold her that way for a while, then he would begin to tease her breasts with the tips of his fingers and kiss her on the side of her neck, and soon they would be naked, his hardness against her softness, and he would play with her until she was wild to take him inside her, an act of completion, of being made whole. She was determined to believe that somehow, despite everything, her own age of miracles might someday come around at last.

CHAPTER 27

O'KEEFE RODE A few yards behind her as she guided Pegasus at a walk out of the small canyon, down the side of the corral, and past the big boulders toward the barn. Lenny charged out of the back door of the house as if he had been waiting there, watching for them. He carried the shotgun at the ready. She halted Pegasus in the middle of the open ground between the house and the corral. She had never been afraid of Lenny before, but she sensed she should be very afraid of him now. His jaws clenched tight, his face crimson, his eyes bugging like a madman's. When O'Keefe rode up beside her, Lenny brought the shotgun up to his shoulder and aimed it at O'Keefe.

"Been enjoying yourself, O'Keefe?" Lenny said. "Well, that's all over now. Get down off that horse."

"Quit it, Lenny," Tag said. "You know you won't fire that gun, so stop playing games."

"It isn't me that's gonna get fed to the buzzards out there, O'Keefe," Lenny said. "It's you."

"Stay right where you are, Pete," Tag said.

"Get away from him, Tag," Lenny said.

Instead she spurred her horse and put herself between the two of them.

"Get away from him, Tag, or I'll shoot you too."

"Is that what it's come to, Lenny?"

Lenny began to move sideways, maneuvering for a clear shot at O'Keefe. Tag moved her horse sideways too. O'Keefe, the pawn in their game, inched his hand toward the pistol holstered against his side. When he heard the first shot, he didn't realize it was the pop of a rifle, not the blast of a shotgun. Lenny screamed and collapsed in the dirt. Then the firefight broke out, like a Viet Cong ambush all over again. Tag spurred Pegasus toward the barn. His own horse reared and bucked him off. Stunned by the fall, he lay there, watching Lenny crawl on his belly toward the house. Shots hit the dirt around Lenny as he crawled. O'Keefe jumped up and sprinted for the barn. Rounds exploded all around him. As he dived for the side of the barn, a bullet slapped into his right foot and spun him around sideways in the air. He flopped on his belly and rolled himself over and over until out of the line of fire. When he looked down at his foot, he saw that the heel of his boot had disappeared. Tag, panting and dazed, hunched next to him against the side of the barn, which shielded them from the firing. Neither of them could see the four men moving down the hill toward the front of the house.

LENNY HAD MANAGED to drag himself to the back porch. He grabbed the doorknob, pulled himself upright, and balanced on his left foot, his right leg hanging forlorn and useless, the flesh of his thigh a hunk of raw meat where the bullet had twisted out.

"He helped us all right!" Lenny screamed at Tag. "He brought them down on us! The bastard brought them down on us!"

Lenny pulled open the screen door and hopped into the house.

"You're bleeding," Tag said very softly, looking at O'Keefe's foot.

O'Keefe's face twisted in pain, but the pain was more in his mind than in his foot. He thought he might black out. He floundered in a muddy darkness of shame and rage. Then the nausea came. He gagged, almost threw up. He *had* brought them down on her. He had no right to have done that.

"Lenny's right," he said. "I hunted you down for them. I brought them down on you. I had no right . . ."

She seemed to shake off what he said, looked at the house, then back toward the mouth of the small canyon.

"We can get three on Pegasus if we ride him bareback."

His face told her he thought that was crazy.

"All we've got to do is make it to the canyon back there. If we can get to the canyon, they won't be able to follow us. But I have to get to the house first."

"What for?"

"For Lenny. For the pack."

"Forget the damn dope!"

"I'm not gonna forget it!" she said sharply. "Or the money. There's no future for me without it."

"Don't go in there."

"Yes, I am."

"He's sure as hell not worth it."

That didn't seem to faze her either. Her will had always been stronger than his so he unloosened the sling buckle and swung the rifle off his back and into his hands, crawled to the side of the barn, flipped the rifle on automatic, brought the scope to his eye, and pumped steel at the hillside while she ran to the house.

FROM THE KITCHEN Tag could see Lenny on the couch, weeping and clutching the backpack to his chest, seeming not to understand or care that he was directly across from the front window, exposed to fire from outside the house.

"Come on, Lenny. Let's go."

"We're not gonna make it, are we?" he sobbed. "After all this, we're not gonna make it."

"We are gonna make it. We're gonna ride out of here right now. Come on. Get away from that window."

"I can't ride a horse like this!"

"Yes, you can!" she screamed back at him. "Now get away from there!"

The first bullet shattered the window, the second pierced Lenny's throat and exited through his ear. His hands jerked up to his neck, he coughed, reached for his ear, and fell over onto his side on the couch. Shards of flying glass slashed Tag across the right cheekbone and above the right eye. She crawled across the floor to the couch. "Lenny," was all she could think to say to him when she saw that he was dead.

As she crawled back across the room toward the kitchen, dragging the pack, someone was kicking the front door off its hinges. When she jumped up and started to run, the back door crashed open. O'Keefe filled the doorframe. She wondered why he was aimed his rifle directly at her. She did not see the man who had appeared behind her, where the front door had once been.

"Get down!" O'Keefe yelled, and she dived for his legs. The spent cartridges clattered around her as his rifle obliterated the man in the door frame. When he stopped shooting, the silence seemed to promise a truce.

"We've got to get back to the barn," she said, jumping up, the pack still in her hand.

"Come on," said O'Keefe. "And leave that damn pack!"

She did not leave it. He heard her clumping heavily after him out of the house and toward the barn. His heel cried out in pain each time he stepped down on it. He turned around in time to see the man with the rifle coming around the far side of the house and bringing the rifle up to his shoulder O'Keefe managed to fire a burst from the M-16 before he pitched backward, knocked flat on his back.

Tag watched the man twist on the ground like a mechanical toy winding down. After a few seconds he lay still. She ran to O'Keefe, lying there in the dust, blood all over the side of his head, his eyes closed in what looked like perpetual sleep. As with Lenny, she could think of nothing to say except his name, and she sat down and cradled his head in her arms.

In a few seconds he opened his eyes.

"You're alive," she said in relief and surprise. She kissed him on the forehead. "Let's ride," she said. "Can you ride?"

He nodded his head, and they crawled together into the barn.

While she tightened the cinch on her horse's saddle, O'Keefe reloaded the rifle and slung it behind his back again. He was unable to stand with his weight on his right leg while he put his left in the stirrup, so he tried to mount the horse from the other side, right foot in the stirrup, but he could not tolerate the pain it took to try to lift himself into the saddle. Finally, he grabbed the saddle horn and pulled himself up on the horse without using the stirrups while she steadied him and pushed from behind.

She mounted in front of him. "Hold on to me as tight as you can, no matter what happens," she said and spurred the horse into a gallop out of the barn. "Duck!" she warned him just in time as they cleared the barn door.

For a few seconds he thought it just might be easy. The men did not start shooting until Pegasus had galloped across the clearing and was pounding down the path along the side of the corral toward the canyon. A few yards before they reached the mouth of the canyon, the bullet hit him. She had told him to hold on tight, but he did not try to, afraid he would pull her off with him. All he could remember of the fall was a flash of white shirt as she galloped away from him. He flew through the air, hit on his left side, bounced once or twice, and ended up on his belly, eating dirt and seeing stars.

The shooting had stopped, so he crawled for the canyon, but it started again as soon as he made a move. The bullet had punctured his upper back below his right shoulder. He could tell from the stabbing pain in his chest that the bullet had come out the front of his right breast directly across from his heart. As he stretched his body in the crawl, his right lung felt like it was tearing apart. He hoped it was not a sucking wound. He remembered the look on the corpsmen's faces when they saw that a man had a sucking wound. *The same look every time.* Another bullet nicked him, slicing off a small chunk of his right thigh below his rump.

Tag, the expert rider, could easily have made it into the canyon, out of their line of fire, on up the trail, across the bowl and into the mountains, and from there on to Mexico and, maybe, freedom. But she looked toward the distant mountains as if saying farewell, then turned Pegasus around. She jumped down off the horse and knelt beside O'Keefe, who had crawled behind a boulder that partly shielded them.

"Unbuckle the sling," he whispered, hardly able to speak at all. "Take the rifle off and put it in my hands."

She did as he told her, and she had blood on her hands when she finished. He did not bother to tell her there was a dressing in his first-aid kit. It was no bigger than a feminine napkin. Placing it on the wound would only make the wound seem even more gaping.

"Now slip my pack off."

When she dragged the right strap of the pack across his right breast, he cried out in agony.

"Now open it," he said.

He reached into the open pack and pulled out several magazines, rounds for the M-16, and stacked them side by side on the ground next to him.

He said, "Where are they? See if you can tell where they are."

She peered around the rock, then ducked back.

"One of them is coming up the trail," she said. "Can you shoot?"

"I can do better than that," he said, gasping in pain as he reached for one of the grenades hooked onto his cartridge belt. "But I'm afraid if I try to heave it over the rocks, I won't make it."

He handed her the grenade.

"See that little pin? Pull it out. It won't blow up as long as you keep hold of the thing and press the spoon, that silver clip there. Press it against the side of the grenade as hard as you can."

Her jaw clenched as she pressed on the spoon with all her strength.

"Now pull the pin, but keep pressing on the spoon. You toss it like this," he said, gesturing, and was surprised that he could move his right arm at all.

She looked quickly around the rock and ducked back again.

"How far away?"

"Twenty yards and moving slow."

"Wait until you can hear his feet crunching the dirt."

She listened and, in a few seconds, tossed the grenade. They heard the man yell "Hey!" as if he'd discovered a treasure, then an explosion.

"Let's go," she said. "Let's ride."

He looked so very weary when he shook his head.

"Pete, we're almost there. Don't quit now."

"I'm done. I'd bleed to death before we got across the mountains. Go on."

"You're losing too much blood. If you pass out . . ."

There was no need to say more. Each had seen the same vision, a rifleman standing over O'Keefe, rifle barrel pointed down, pumping rounds into O'Keefe's head.

"I'm going for help," she said. "I can ride around to the main road. I can get there in an hour. You think you can hold on here for a couple of hours?"

"You said there was nothing for you here. You were right. Go on."

"I will. After I get you some help. I can call the police from the pay phone at the filling station up the road. Then I'll go on."

"Forget the pay phone. Just go." Just a gesture on his part, he knew. She would do what she wanted. He had never been able to bend her will to his. That was the wild creature in her, the thing in her that had kept her spirit alive through all those empty years since her father had stolen into her room that night long ago.

"I'll cover you," he said, and pushed himself up to a sitting position, leaned back against the rock, and brought the rifle to his shoulder. Despite pain so fierce he thought he might faint, he forced the rifle to his shoulder and aimed. He squeezed off a round toward the back of the canyon to see if he could tolerate the recoil. He could. Barely. He tried to keep her from seeing his pain. She embraced him and held him to her. When she released him, her white shirt was smeared with his blood.

"Promise me you'll come."

"I promise," he said, a promise he did not intend to keep, but she did not need to know that if it would help her move on.

She jumped up and ran for Pegasus, who stood a few yards away, waiting for her, tense but with no thought of running away and abandoning her. O'Keefe refused to watch her run away from him again, so he rolled over onto his belly and pointed the rifle down the trail back toward the ranch house. He could not see anyone, yet a rifle fired from somewhere. *Above. From the rocks above us somewhere.* A bullet pinged crazily off the canyon wall behind him.

Karl had worked his way up into the rocks above them and brought the rifle to his shoulder in time to see Tag run for the horse. His first shot missed. He had made the amateur's mistake, aiming too high. His next shot hit the top of her left shoulder, a grazing wound that still packed enough punch to make her stumble forward and fall to her knees, but she scrambled up and ran toward Pegasus, burdened by the backpack that she would not relinquish.

Karl now aimed at her horse. As she reached up for the saddle horn, Pegasus groaned—a monstrous, guttural groan of expiration—lurched, stumbled, and fell down. She saw that he would never rise again, the artery in his neck severed by the bullet, his blood spurting out on the ground.

It was then that she seemed to surrender. Suddenly. Entirely. She dropped the backpack and turned around to face the man in the rocks above her. She stood there, and waited, as if offering herself in sacrifice to a god known only to her.

O'Keefe brought the man in the rocks into the lens of his scope. By no means an expert shot, he worried that he would miss, but the loss of blood had numbed him and relaxed him, so that, for the first time in his life, his arms did not quiver at all, and the sight on the end of his rifle remained perfectly still when he took aim and fired. But he had hesitated too long, and Karl managed a final shot before O'Keefe's bullet hit him.

When O'Keefe looked around behind him, he saw two colors, palomino and white, sprawled on the ground. The palomino whinnied miserably, kicked its forelegs feebly, trying vainly to struggle back on its feet. The white shirt and the girl in it did not move at all. He crawled over to her. There might be more of them coming, but he did not care now.

She lay flat on her back where the bullet had put her when it had punctured her heart. Her heart was still pumping, but that stream had an outlet now, and her life, red and gushing, flowed out of her and onto her shirt and the thirsty ground. It seemed like she could still recognize him when he brought her up into his arms.

"I didn't have the right," he said, "I didn't have the right . . ."

She seemed to want to tell him something, but she was fast drifting away from the world. He clutched her to him until he knew she was dead and then forced himself to look into her eyes. Empty eyes. She had finally escaped them. Her father, the gunmen, O'Keefe himself. The wondrously embodied spirit they had madly, vainly tried to capture and cage would elude them forever now. "No right." he said again, only to himself this time, then clawed with his hand at the pain that rended his lung seam to seam. The world turned gray. He swooned and keeled over, still clutching the dead girl in his arms.

Then it came to him that he was dying too, that he was going to die there with her. *Good. I don't deserve to live. They'll find our skeletons locked together like this, like the Hunchback and Esmeralda.* For so long he had so much feared the idea of death—eternal extinguishment, perpetual oblivion—ever since he had lost faith in the soul immortal and then fought in a war that had seemed to rob death of either dignity or meaning. But now, as he lay there in the blood and the dust and the sun, death came to him, lapping at him gently like a wave at low tide, and he wondered if this was how each leaf felt as it fell. But even now he was human still. Even now he did not stop wishing, or hoping either. He wished most of all that he had not helped to kill this girl in his arms. He wished too that he could have done better for the people he loved, at least told them goodbye, at least left them a note. And he hoped, in spite of all the evidence he hoped, that his body would die but his spirit would soar off to somewhere eternal. And, lastly, he hoped he would die before nightfall so he would not have to die in the cold.

CHAPTER 28

GEORGE WAS NO worrier, but on the flight home he could not stop worrying about O'Keefe. Moreover, he could not stop worrying about him the next day and the day after that, especially when he talked to Sara and found out that O'Keefe had not called in, thus breaking the sacred, unbreakable vow made by everyone who worked there, even O'Keefe. You called in every day no matter what. If you did not call in, you would be assumed to be in trouble, and someone would set about tracking you down. And this wasn't O'Keefe's typical case in any way, shape, or form. There was murder in this case, and O'Keefe thought the underworld was involved too. So the rule ought to be enforced now more than ever. Jarvis was apparently too lazy or stupid or timid to enforce it himself. O'Keefe, asshole that he could be sometimes, had as good as told George to get lost back there in the desert, but O'Keefe was his friend, and friends did not have to be perfect for you to take a risk for them. The risk would be that he would blunder into O'Keefe's private, little adventure that seemed so dear to his heart and screw it up somehow. *Tough shit.* He made a reservation that night for the morning plane to Tucson.

THE OLD TRUCK remained in the same place he had seen it before. When he saw the dead man on the porch, he drew his pistol from his shoulder holster and stepped slowly toward the house. Through the shattered front window he saw someone dead on the couch. He recognized the corpse from the photos O'Keefe had given him. Lenny Parker. At the back of the house he found a body sprawled in the dirt. It was not O'Keefe.

A brown horse stood at the front of the corral as if waiting for someone to come and let him back into his prison. Birds made a racket in the mesquite trees. Something moved in the barn. He whipped the pistol up to chest level and aimed it at the barn door. A road runner, sauntering out of the barn like a sleepy suburbanite looking for his morning paper.

Spent cartridges at the side of the barn. M-16 cartridges. O'Keefe had an M-16. George understood now why O'Keefe had wanted to drive out here. He couldn't get the M-16 on the plane.

George moved slowly across the clearing, past the big boulders, and onto the trail that ran along the far side of the corral. Up the path, toward the mouth of a small canyon, another body, a body that reminded him of one of those small animals hit by a car while running across the highway at night, mangled and smashed, torn flesh turning gray in the sun. The body was missing one leg and one arm. It was not O'Keefe.

He saw the palomino first, then the body lying in front of it. No, there were two bodies in front of it. The woman and O'Keefe, dried blood scabbing on the side of his head, the sun burning his upturned face. The woman was dead, but O'Keefe seemed to be breathing. Blood seeped slowly from a wound in his chest.

George ran back to the car and brought it around to where O'Keefe lay. He picked up O'Keefe and laid him in the front seat. He had to tuck up O'Keefe's legs, knees pointing at the roof, in order to close the car door. He thought he had heard O'Keefe groan faintly when he laid him down. *Good. If you could feel pain, you were still in the land of the living, your birthright intact.*

He ran around the front of the car to the driver's side and jumped in. He put O'Keefe's head on his thigh. He jammed down the accelerator and bounced down the dirt road and onto the highway. *Hold on, Pete. There's a town down this road not very far that will surely have a hospital in it. Dumb shit. Hold on. Dumb shit. You had to go it alone. Dumb shit.*

George could not remember the last time he'd cried, but, halfway to town, he started crying, and he did not stop crying until he pulled up to the emergency-room door.

THEY KEPT O'KEEFE alive at the tiny, rural hospital until the helicopter transferred him to the medical center in Tucson. He stayed conscious enough to understand that they were loading him into a helicopter, but he thought he was back in Vietnam, and he kept trying to tell them that something was wrong. It was not he they were supposed to be loading into the helicopter. It was the others, the dead and the wounded. He was the door gunner, his job to protect them on the way back to the base camp, until they installed them in beds or rubber bags tagged with their names and service numbers.

THE HEEL OF his foot healed the fastest. He could soon walk without a cane and with only a slight limp. They said they could rebuild the heel so there would be no limp at all. The bullet that had ripped off a chunk of his thigh had not hit muscle or bone, a manageable wound. A plastic surgeon reassembled his ear. The right side of his chest was a mass of scar tissue, and they told him he definitely could not smoke anymore.

Sara brought Kelly out to see him in the hospital. Sara cried when she first saw him. Kelly wanted to see his new scars.

"You told me you never carried a gun," Kelly said. He said nothing; he did not know what to say.

"No more lies, Dad. Never again, okay?"

He nodded in agreement. A fair request.

Kelly brought a note from her mother that he read after Sara and Kelly left for the airport.

Pete,

Those days after George found you, when we all thought you were going to die, I realized that life was just too short for hatred and recrimination. It still seems a shame to me that we couldn't have made it, but I've accepted it now. Take care, Pete. I don't want Kelly to have to grow up without a father like you did. You might have been a lousy husband, but you're a better father than you think or than I've been willing to give you credit for. Just take care of her. Our job is to keep her <u>out</u> of danger.

When Kelly, restless and bored, left the room to go browse in the hospital gift shop, Sara said. "Pete, you look like a man who's lost his dream. I'm sorry it ended that way for you, I really am."

"All I want to know is whether I can tear up that resignation letter of yours."

"No. You can't tear it up. But you can hold it. It won't be effective until you decide you want to destroy yourself again."

"Sara, there's a lot of things I want to change. I'm thinking about selling the business to Jarvis. Maybe he'll pay me at least enough to take care of the debt. Then I want to start over. With just you and me and George. Maybe then we can afford to pick and choose what we work on instead of taking every piece-of-shit job that walks in the door."

Then came the corrosion of doubt.

"But I don't know if we can make any money that way."

"Well, we'll never know until we try," she said.

"And if we do that, Sara, you're gonna have to be a lot more than a secretary, because we're not even gonna care about answering the damn phone anyway. You'll have to work right along with me and George. You'll have to be one of the boys."

She said, "I thought you'd never ask."

He laughed.

"I mean it," she said. "Never."

CHAPTER 29

SHE HAD WANTED to spend her eternity in Arizona, in a grave in the desert facing the mountains, but they had buried her in an old-fashioned cemetery in the family plot. The gravestone called her "Constance," but it was Tag underneath it, and the only difference between her and him was that he had been lucky enough to have a friend and she had not. Whatever else he had been to her, he had not been her friend.

He stood there, one red rose in his hand, tears on his face. A marvel such as she surely could not be gone from the world, her brave candle snuffed out by heedless obsession. But she was. She was gone, forever beyond his wishing, forever beyond his hoping, forever beyond his foolish grasp.

Tag, if I could touch you, I'd tell you . . . But she was beyond touching or telling, and beyond forgiving him too. Since he could not ask for forgiveness, he would have to live it somehow. When they had told him he would survive, life had seemed like a sentence far worse than death, and he had wished he had died out there in the desert with her. But death was too easy an expiation. Now he would have to spend his whole life trying to give something back.

But no amend could be made to that girl in the ground. Except maybe he could carry her spirit in his heart. That was it.

It was so little, but it was the best he could do now. He dropped the rose on the brown winter grass that grew over her grave.

When he turned around, Ernest Anderson was standing behind him. The two men stood looking at each other, two men standing amid the gravestones as if only the guilty still lived. Then Anderson raised his right hand like an executioner who had forgotten his axe.

"You!" Anderson said, advancing on him. "You were supposed to protect her! You filth! All you did was take advantage of her!"

No, O'Keefe thought, *he had done somewhat better than that. Not much better but somewhat better than that.*

Anderson tried to strike him, but O'Keefe caught his arm with his left hand, grabbed the front of his coat, and whirled him around so he would have to face his daughter's grave.

"How does this fit into the Plan, you old warlock? Tell me how this fits into the Plan."

He threw Anderson down on top of the grave and walked away. Behind him he heard Anderson bawling and calling to Tag. O'Keefe climbed into the van and rolled himself away. He drove through the late-afternoon twilight toward his apartment where Sara and George and Kelly and Harrigan were gathering to celebrate his homecoming. He turned on the defroster to dissolve the thin film of frost that had formed on the windshield. The bare, ravaged trees, stripped of their leaves, stood like forlorn guardsmen watching him pass. News flashes on the car radio: A group of British scientists had, for the first time, confirmed the Greenhouse Effect—that carbon dioxide and other pollutants were trapping and sealing in the heat from the earth's surface, causing an extraordinary warming of the globe. And the White House admitted that profits from U.S. arm sales to Iran had been diverted to the Nicaraguan contras. National Security Adviser John Poindexter had resigned. His aide, Colonel Oliver North, had been fired. Immediately following these announcements, the station played that week's #1 pop single, Bruce Hornsby's *The Way It Is.* As he pulled into his driveway, he heard a horn sound behind him. Harrigan. In a new, black Jaguar.

"Now there's some shining armor for you, buddy," Harrigan said, pointing to the Jaguar. They hugged awkwardly, half afraid someone might be watching two men embrace. "George claims he's a gourmet chef so get ready to barf," Harrigan said as they walked up the sidewalk.

"That article was really something," O'Keefe said. Harrigan had fed the mink-farm story to a friendly reporter at the local newspaper. The article had portrayed O'Keefe as some kind of hero, a lone knight errant fighting organized crime single-handedly. There would be no chance now that they would indict him or try to revoke his license.

"What a pack of lies," O'Keefe said. "You're incredible, Mike."

"Not lies exactly. 'Spin,' they're calling it now." Harrigan always brushed off compliments. He couldn't handle them. But his modesty was a little false. He knew he was better than any compliment you could give him.

"Those political contributions I've been making for years and wondering why came in handy too. About time."

A fire blazed in the fireplace. A banner hanging above the mantel said, "Welcome Home, Dad." He heard laughter from the kitchen where Kelly and Sara and George were preparing the dinner.

"Smells good," Harrigan said. "Here, give me your coat." Harrigan took the coats into the exercise room, leaving O'Keefe alone and unannounced in the living room. *Hail the conquering hero,* he thought. *More like the prodigal son.* It embarrassed him that they were making this fuss over him, but he had determined that he would not let his own mournfulness, his own sense of loss and diminishment, spoil their day.

Kelly came out of the kitchen. "Dad!" she said, startled. "Dad's here!" she yelled back to the others.

He hesitated, but she did not hold back. She ran to him and locked her arms around his waist and squeezed him hard. Sara and then George appeared in the doorway. Harrigan had come back into the living room. They all smiled, but none of them seemed to know what to say. Kelly pulled back from the embrace, and Sara came to him then, huge brown eyes shining with tears. She hugged him for the briefest of moments, and when she broke away, he was a little dazed, swirling in a haze of her fragrance, the black silk of her blouse, the white of the skin on her cheek.

George stood in the doorway, an oven mitt covering his right hand, a small towel draped over his shoulder, and a goofy grin on his face. *And George, all you did for me was save my life.* George, who had not been willing to let him go it alone like he had wanted. O'Keefe stifled his tears. But George must have sensed danger coming, he would avoid tears and manly embraces at all costs. He said, "Welcome home, Boss," then turned on his heel and disappeared into the kitchen.

George really had cooked the dinner. A cold celery soup. Coq au vin—plump chicken pieces roasted brown in a dark sauce with mushrooms and onions and tiny potatoes. A choice of red wine or white. White-chocolate mousse for dessert. And when the atmosphere at the table threatened to become too serious, George served up a generous portion of mirth to lighten the mood.

After they ate, they lingered for a while, talking by the fire. O'Keefe watched the others drink the Sangria that George had made from fine red wine and fresh fruit that he claimed had been flown into the city special delivery by a local chef he knew. And O'Keefe was tempted to have at least a small drink of that gorgeous brew, beckoning him from the crystal pitcher, but he just sipped at his coffee and let the feeling pass, listening to Bach's Brandenburg Concertos playing on the stereo. The stately music, dignified and self-assured, promised a new life if one could only embody its truths—complexity mastered, worship offered, praise given, the insoluble mystery embraced.

Harrigan kept unusually quiet. He seemed uncomfortable and out of place. O'Keefe thought his old friend looked like an exile who had been gone from home so long he was not sure he wanted to return, as if he would refuse any amnesty that might be offered him. Soon Harrigan stood up, mumbled apologies, and said he had to leave. O'Keefe walked with Harrigan out to his car, an indistinct and vaguely sinister shape in the darkness.

"What about our friend Mr. Canada?" O'Keefe said. "Mr. Jagoda, that is."

"Well, they know who he is now because they know who those dead gunmen worked for. But they can't tie him to the mink farm or to your little shoot-em-up out there either. I can't believe he'd try anything against you with all that publicity shining on the both of you. But . . ."

"But what?"

"Just be careful."

Harrigan suddenly reached out for O'Keefe and hugged him hard.

"Jesus, Pete," he said, "I almost lost you, didn't I? What would I do without you?"

"I want you to tell me something, Mike. I want you to tell me when you're gonna let yourself be okay."

Harrigan said nothing. He had obviously not even considered the question before.

"You know, that Saturday in your office, you said that, when we were kids, we thought life was going to be some wonderful quest, but it didn't turn out that way at all. Well, I know the secret now. You want in on it?"

Harrigan looked like he didn't really want to, and O'Keefe knew that was because his friend was not ready to give it all up. "Here it is. Don't look for the answer. There isn't one."

O'KEEFE WATCHED THE sleek black car glide down the street and out of sight, then he stood alone in the dark and the cold, watching the puffs of his breath disappear into the black void of the night. *It'll be okay, Mike. Like the song says, "Next time we'll get it right."*

The others were waiting for him inside, but he felt like taking a walk, felt like wrapping himself in his loneliness in his old solitary way. Up above the full moon looked lonely too. He could see a few stars. Was Perseus, the Champion, out there? Pegasus, the Flying Horse? Andromeda, the Chained Princess? *Tag.* His heart went out, a sensation almost physical, groping for something across the void, a communion of some kind.

The front porch light switched on behind him.

"Dad?"

Her voice was full of apprehension.

He hesitated, lingered in the dark, looking at the night sky.

"Dad?" Kelly said again, sounding really afraid this time. He looked up again at the bright, beckoning stars, then turned away from the sky and walked toward the sound of the little girl's voice.

ABOUT THE AUTHOR

DAN FLANIGAN IS a novelist, poet, and playwright, as well as a practicing lawyer. In addition to developing a screenplay version of Mink Eyes, he has published a book of verse and prose poetry, *Tenebrae: A Memoir of Love and Death,* and *Dewdrops,* a collection of his shorter fiction. He has also written the full-length plays—*Secrets* (based on the life of Eleanor Marx) and *Moondog's Progress* (based on the life of Alan Freed).

For more information, please visit
www.DanFlaniganBooks.com